MEMOIRS OF FANNY HILL

MEMOIRS OF
FANNY HILL

— BY —

JOHN CLELAND

A GENUINE REPRINT OF
THE RARE EDITION OF 1749

PRIVATELY PRINTED

THE KAMASHASTRA SOCIETY

Valhalla Books
New York

INTRODUCTION

THIS entertaining book is the production of John Cleland, who was born in 1707. His father, Colonel Cleland, was the original of "Will Honeycomb," a character of Addison and Steele. Colonel Cleland's dissipation left his son penniless; but he had, happily, provided him with a good education, which proved of great advantage in the way of getting a fair government position in the Indies. A quarrel, however, with his superior brought him back to London, where he soon was in a condition bordering on starvation, and it did not take much longer to find him in a prison for debt. He had, during this stay in London, made some reputation in writing for the public prints; so as soon as he was in prison he received an offer from a publisher to write a book that would readily sell and put him out of debt. The result was the "Memoirs of Fanny Hill." On publication of the book Cleland was summoned before the Privy Council, and on promising not to repeat his offence was dismissed, and Earl Granville generously provided that he was allowed a pension of one hundred pounds a year by the government.

The first edition of the book appeared between 1745-50, and the one from which this
edition is reprinted appeared in 1749, under the
title, "Memoirs of a Woman of Pleasure." A
great many editions have appeared since, all of
which were published in a cheap form for the
sake of profit. A great many of them have been
so altered and the text "modernized" in such a
way that they should have borne some other
title. As this edition has been printed for
private circulation only, it has been the work of
the editor to see that the text of the best edition,
that of 1749, has been strictly followed, except
in orthography, and that the book has been
printed in a manner that all books worth preserving from the "tooth of time" should be.

MEMOIRS OF FANNY HILL

LETTER THE FIRST

MADAME:

I sit down to give you an undeniable
proof of my considering your desires as in-
dispensable orders. Ungracious then as the
task may be, I shall recall to view those scandalous stages of my life out of which I emerged,
at length, to the enjoyment of every blessing in
the power of love, health, and fortune to bestow, whilst yet in the flower of youth, and not
too late to employ the leisure afforded me by
great ease and affluence, to cultivate an understanding naturally not a despicable one, and
which even amidst the whirl of loose pleasures
I had been tossed in, exerted more observation
on the characters and manners of the world
than what is common to those of my unhappy
profession, who, looking on all thought or reflections as their capital enemy, keep it at as
great a distance as they can, or destroy it without mercy. Hating, as I mortally do, all long
unnecessary prefaces, I shall give you good
quarter in this, and use no further apology,
than to prepare you for seeing the loose part
of my life, written with the same liberty that I
led it. Truth, stark naked truth, is the word!
and I will not so much as take the pains to
bestow the strip of a gauze wrapper on it, but
paint situations such as they actually rose to

me in nature, careless of violating those laws
of decency that were never made for such unreserved intimacies as ours; and you have too
much sense, too much knowledge of the
originals, to snuff prudishly and out of character at the pictures of them. The greatest men,
those of the first and most leading taste, will
not scruple adorning their private closets with
nudities, though, in compliance with vulgar
prejudices they may not think them decent
decorations of the stair-case or saloon. This,
and enough, promised, I go some into my
personal history.

My maiden name was Frances Hill. I was
born at a small village near Liverpool, in Lancashire, of parents extremely poor, and I piously
believe, extremely honest. My father, who had
received a maim on his limbs, that disabled him
from following the more labourious branches of
country drudgery, got, by making of nets, a
scanty subsistance, which was not much en-
larged by my mother's keeping a little day-
school for the girls in her neighbourhood. They
had had several children; but none lived to any
age except myself, who had received from
nature a constitution perfectly healthy. My
education, till past fourteen, was no better than
very vulgar, reading, or rather spelling, an
illegible scrawl, and a little ordinary plain work,
composed the whole system of it; and then all
my foundation in virtue was no other than a
total ignorance of vice, and the shy timidity
general to our sex, in the tender age of life,

when objects alarm or frighten more by their
novelty than anything else. But then, this is a
fear too often cured at the expense of innocence,
when Miss, by degrees, begins no longer to look
on a man as a creature of prey that will eat her.
My poor mother had divided her time so entirely between her scholars and her little domestic cares, that she had spared very little to
my instruction, having from her own innocence
of all ill, no hint or thought of guarding me
against any.

I was now entering on my fifteenth year,
when the worst of ills befell in the loss of my
fond, tender parents, who were both carried off
by the smallpox, within a few days of each
other; my father dying first, and thereby
hastening the death of my mother; so that I
was now left an unhappy friendless orphan,
for my father's coming to settle there was
accidental, he being originally a Kentishman.
That cruel distemper which had proven so fatal
to them, had indeed seized me, but with such
mild and favourable symptoms, that I was
presently out of danger, and what then I did
not know the value of, was entirely unmarked.
I skip over here an account of the natural grief
and affliction which I felt on this melancholy
occasion. A little time, and the giddiness of
that age, dissipated too soon my reflections on
that irreparable loss; but nothing contributed
more to reconcile me to it than the notions that
were immediately put into my head, of going to
London and looking out for a service, in which

I was promised all assistance and advice from
one Esther Davis, a young woman that had
been down to see her friends, and who after
the stay of a few days, was to return to her
place. As I had now nobody left alive in the
village, who had concern enough about what
should become of me, to start any objections to
this scheme, and the woman who took care of
me to pursue it, I soon came to a resolution of
making this launch into the wide world, by
repairing to London, in order to seek my
fortune, a phrase which, bye-the-bye, has ruined
more adventurers of both sexes, from the
country, than ever it made or advanced.

Nor did Esther Davis a little comfort and
inspirit me to venture with her by piquing my
childish curiosity with the fine sights that were
to be seen in London; the Tombs, the Lions, the
King, the Royal Family, the fine plays and
operas, and, in short, all the diversions which
fell within her sphere of life to come at; the
detail of all which perfectly turned the little
head of me. Nor can I remember, without laughing, the innocent admiration, not without a
spice of envy, with which we poor girls, whose
church-going clothes did not rise above dowlas
shifts and stiff gowns, beheld Esther's scoured
satin gowns, caps bordered with an inch of
lace, tawdry ribbons, and shoes laced with
silver, all which we imagined grew in London,
and entered for a great deal into my determination of trying to come in for my share
of them.

The idea however of having the company of a towns-woman with her, was the trivial, and all the motives that engaged Esther to take charge of me during my journey to town, where she told me, after her manner and style, "as how several maids out of the country had made themselves and all their kin forever: that by preserving their virtue, some had taken so with their masters, that they had married them, and kept them coaches, and lived vastly grand and happy; and some, may-hap, came to be duchesses; luck was all, and why not I as well as another?"; with other almanacs to this purpose, which set me a tip-toe to begin this promising journey, and to leave a place which, though my native one, contained no relations that I had reason to regret, and was grown insupportable to me, from the change of the tenderest usage into a cold air of charity, with which I was entertained, even at the only friend's house that I had the least expectation of care and protection from. She was, however, so just to me, as to manage the turning into money the little matters that remained to me after the debts and burial charges were allowed for, and, at my departure, put my whole fortune into my hands, which consisted of a very portable box, and eight guineas with seventeen shillings in silver, stowed in a spring pouch, which was a greater treasure than ever I had yet seen together, and which I could not conceive there was a possibility of running out; and indeed, I was so entirely taken up with the joy of seeing myself mistress of such an immense sum, that I gave very little attention to a world of good advice which was given me with it.

Places then being taken for Esther and I in the Chester wagon, I pass over a very immaterial scene of leave taking, at which I dropped a few tears betwixt grief and joy; and, for the same reasons of insignificance, skip over all that happened to me on the road, such as the waggoner's looking liquorish on me, the schemes laid for me by some of the passengers, which were defeated by the vigilance of my guardian, Esther; who, to do her justice, took a motherly care of me, at the same time that she taxed me for her protection by making me bear her travelling charges, which I defrayed with the utmost cheerfulness, and thought myself much obliged to her into the bargain. She took indeed great care that we were not over rated, or imposed on, as well as of managing as frugally as possibly; expensiveness was not her vice.

It was pretty late in a summer evening when we reached the town, in our slow conveyance, though drawn by six at length. As we passed through the greatest streets that led to our inn, the noise of the coaches, the hurry, the crowds of foot passengers, in short, the new scenery of the shops and houses, at once pleased and amazed me. But guess at my mortification and surprise when we came to the inn, and our things were landed and delivered to us, when my fellow traveller and protectoress, Esther

Davis, who had used me with the utmost
tenderness during the journey, and prepared
me by no preceding signs for the stunning blow
I was to receive, when I say, my only dependence and friend in this place, all of a sudden
assumed a strange cool air toward me, as if
she dreaded my becoming a burden to her.
Instead, then, of proffering me the continuance
of her assistance and good offices, which I relied
upon, and never more wanted, she thought herself, it seems, abundantly acquitted of her
engagements to me, by having brought me safe
to my journey's end, and seeing nothing in her
procedure towards me but what was natural
and in order, began to embrace me by taking
leave, whilst I was so confounded, so struck,
that I had not spirit or sense enough so much
as to mention my hopes or expectations from
her experience, and knowledge of the place she
had brought me to.

Whilst I stood thus stupid and mute, which
she doubtless attributed to nothing more than a
concern at parting, this idea procured me perhaps a slight alleviation of it, in the following
harangue: "That now we were got safe to
London, and that she was obliged to go to her
place, she advised me by all means to get into
one as soon as possible; that I need not fear
getting one; there were more places than parish
churches; that if she heard of anything stirring,
she would find me out and let me know; that,
in the mean time, I should take a private
lodging, and acquaint her where to send to me;

that she wished me good luck, and hoped I
should always have the grace to keep myself
honest, and not bring disgrace on my parentage." With this, she took her leave of me, and
left me, as it were, on my own hands, full as
lightly as I had been put into hers. Left thus
alone, absolutely destitute and friendless, I
began to feel most bitterly the severity of this
separation, the scene of which had passed in a
little room in the inn; and no sooner was her
back turned, but the affliction I felt at my help-
less, strange circumstances, burst out into a
flood of tears, which infinitely relieved the
oppression of my heart; though I still remained
stupefied and most perfectly perplexed how to
dispose of myself.

One of the drawers coming in, added yet
more to my uncertainty, by asking me, in a
short way, if I "called for anything?" to which
I replied innocently: "No." But I wished him
to tell me where I might get a lodging for that
night. He said he would go and speak to his
mistress, who accordingly came, and told me
dryly, without entering into the least distress
she saw me in, that I might have a bed for a
shilling, and that, as she supposed I had some
friends in town (there I fetched a deep sigh in
vain), I might provide for myself in the
morning.

It is incredible on what trifling consolations
the human mind will seize in its greatest
afflictions. The assurance of nothing more
than a bed to lie on that night, calmed my

agonies; and being ashamed to acquaint the
mistress of the inn that I had no friends to
apply to in town, I proposed to myself to proceed the very next morning, to an intelligence
office, to which I was furnished with written
directions on the back of a ballad of Esther's
giving me. There I counted on getting information of any place that such a country girl
as I might be fit for, and where I could get into
any sort of being, before my little stock should
be consumed; and as to a character, Esther had
often repeated to me, that I might depend on
her managing me one; nor, however affected I
was at her leaving me thus, did I entirely cease
to rely on her, as I began to think, good
naturedly, that her procedure was all in course,
and that it was only my ignorance in life that
had made me take it in the light I at first did.

Accordingly, the next morning I dressed myself as clean and as neat as my rustic wardrobe
would permit me, and having left my box, with
special recommendation, to the landlady, I
ventured out by myself, and without any more
difficulty than can be supposed of a young
country girl, barely fifteen, and to whom every
sign or shop was a gazing trap, I got to the
wished for intelligence office. It was kept by
an elderly woman, who sat at the receipt of
custom, with a book before her in great form
and order, and several scrolls made out, of
directions for places. I made up then to this
important personage, without lifting up my
eyes or observing any of the people round me,

who were attending there on the same errand as myself, and dropping her courtesies, nine deep, just made shift to stammer out my business to her. Madame heard me out, with all the gravity and brow of a petty minister of state, and seeing at one glance over my figure, what I was, made me no answer, but to ask me the preliminary shilling, on receipt of which she told me places for women were exceedingly scarce, especially as I seemed too slight built for hard work; but that she would look over her book and see what was to be done for me, desiring me to stay a little, till she had dispatched some other customers.

On this I drew back a little, most heartily mortified at a declaration which carried with it a killing uncertainty, that my circumstances could not well endure. Presently, assuming more courage, and seeking some diversion from my uneasy thoughts, I ventured to lift up my head a little and sent my eyes on a course round the room, where they met full tilt with those of a lady (for such my extreme innocence pronounced her) sitting in a corner of the room, dressed in a velvet mantle, in the midst of the summer, with her bonnet off, squab fat, red faced, and at least fifty. She looked as if she would devour me with her eyes, staring at me from head to foot, without the least regard to the confusion and blushes her eyeing me so fixedly put me to, and which were to her, no doubt, the strongest recommendations and marks of my being fit for her purpose. After

a little time, in which my air, person and whole
figure had undergone a strict examination,
which I had, on my part, tried to render
favourable to me, by primming, drawing up my
neck, and setting my best looks, she advanced
and spoke to me with the greatest demureness:

"Sweetheart, do you want a place?"

"Yes, and please you," (with a courtesy down
to the ground).

Upon this she acquainted me she was actually
come to the office herself, to look out for a
servant; that she believed I might do, with a
little of her instructions; that she could take
my very looks for a sufficient character; that
London was a very wicked, vile place; that she
hoped I would be tractable, and keep out of
bad company; in short, she said all to me that
an old experienced practitioner in town could
think of, and which was much more than was
necessary to take in an artless, unexperienced
country maid, who was even afraid of becoming
a wanderer about the streets, and therefore
gladly jumped at the first offer of a shelter,
especially from so grave and matron-like a lady,
for such my flattering fancy assured me this
new mistress of mine was; I being actually
hired under the nose of the good woman that
kept the office, whose shrewd smiles and shrugs
I could not help observing, and innocently
interpreted them as marks of being pleased at
my getting into a place so soon; but, as I
afterwards came to know, these beldams understood one another very well, and this was a

market where Mrs. Brown, my mistress, frequently attended, on the watch for any fresh
goods that might offer there, for the use of her
customers, and her own profit.

Madame was, however, so well pleased with
her bargain, that fearing, I presume, lest better
advice, or some accident might occasion my
slipping through her fingers, she would officiously take me in a coach to my inn, where,
calling herself for my box, it was, I being
present, delivered without the least scruple or
explanation as to where I was going. This
being over, she bid the coachman drive to a shop
in St. Paul's Churchyard, where she bought a
pair of gloves, which she gave me, and thence
renewed her directions to the coachman to drive
to her house in —— street, who accordingly
landed us at the door, after I had been cheered
up and entertained by the way with the most
plausible flams, without one syllable from which
I could conclude anything but that I was, by
the greatest good luck, fallen into the hands of
the kindest mistress, not to say friend, that the
varsal world would afford; and accordingly I
entered her doors with most complete confidence
and exultation, promising myself that, as soon
as I should be a little settled, I would acquaint
Esther Davis with my rare good fortune.

You may be sure the good opinion of my
place was not lessened by the appearance of a
very handsome back parlour, into which I was
led and which seemed to me magnificently furnished, who had never seen better rooms than

the ordinary ones in inns upon the road. There were two gilt pier glasses, and a buffet, in which a few pieces of plate, set out to the most show, dazzled and altogether persuaded me that I must be got into a very reputable family. Here my mistress first began her part, with telling me that I must have good spirits, and learn to be free with her; that she had not taken me to be a common servant, to do domestic drudgery, but to be a kind of companion to her; and that if I would be a good girl, she would do more than twenty mothers for me; to all which I answered only by the profoundest and the awkwardest courtesies, and a few monosyllables, such as yes, no, to be sure. Presently my mistress touched the bell, and in came a strapping maid servant, who had let us in. "Here, Martha," said Mrs. Brown. "I have just hired this young woman to look after my linen; so step up and show her her bedchamber and I charge you to use her with as much respect as you would myself, for I have taken a prodigious liking to her, and I do not know what I shall do for her."

Martha, who was an arch jade, and being used to this decoy, had her cue perfect, made me a kind of courtesy and led me, to a neat room two pair of stairs backwards, in which there was a handsome bed where Martha told me I was to lie with a young gentlewoman, a cousin of my mistress, who she was sure, would be vastly good to me. Then she ran out into such affected enconiums on her good mistress! her sweet mistress! and how happy I was to light upon her! and that I could not have bespoke a better; with other the like gross stuff, such as would itself have started suspicions in any but such an unpractised simpleton, who was perfectly new to life, and who took every word she said in the very sense she laid out for me to take it; but she readily saw what a penetration she had to deal with, and measured me very rightly in her manner of whistling to me, so as to make me be pleased with my care, and blind to the wires.

In the midst of these false explanations of the nature of my future service, we were rung for down again, and I was reintroduced into the same parlour, where there was a table laid with three covers; and my mistress had now got with her one of her favourite girls, a notable manager of her house, and whose business it was to prepare and break such young fillies as I was to the mounting block; and she was accordingly, in that view, allotted me for a bed fellow, and, to give her the more authority, she had the title of cousin conferred on her by the venerable president of this college. Here I underwent a second survey, which ended in the full approbation of Miss Phoebe Ayres, the name of my tutoress elect, to whose care and instruction I was affectionately recommended.

Dinner was now set on the table, and in pursuance of treating me as a companion, Mrs. Brown, with a tone to cut off all dispute, soon overruled my most humble and most confused protestations against sitting down with her suggested to me could not be right, or in the order of things. At table, the conversation was chiefly kept up by the two madams, and carried on in double meaning expressions, interrupted every now and then by kind assurance to me, all tending to confirm and fix my satisfaction with my present condition; augment it they could not, so very a novice was I then. It was here agreed that I should keep myself up and out of sight for a few days, till such clothes could be procured for me as were fit for the character I was to appear in, of my mistress' companion, observing withal, that on the first impressions of my figure much might depend, and, as they rightly judged, the prospect of exchanging my country clothes for London finery, made the clause of confinement digest perfectly well with me. But the truth was, Mrs. Brown did not care that I should be seen or talked to by any, either of her customers, or her does, as they called the girls provided for them, till she had secured a good market for my maidenhead, which I had at least all the appearance of having brought into her ladyship's service.

To slip over minutes of no importance to the main of my story, I pass the interval to bed time, in which I was more and more pleased with the views that opened to me, of an easy service under these good people; and after supper, being shewed up to bed, Miss Phoebe,

who observed a kind of reluctance in me to
strip and go to bed, in my shift, before her, now
the maid was withdrawn, came up to me, and
beginning with unpinning my handkerchief and
gown, soon encouraged me to go on with undressing myself; and still blushing at now
seeing myself naked to my shift, I hurried to
get under the bed clothes out of sight. Phoebe
laughed, and was not long before she placed
herself by my side. She was about five and
twenty, by her most suspicious account, in
which, according to all appearances, she must
have sunk at least ten good years, allowance,
too, being made for the havoc which a long
course of hackneyship and hot waters must
have already brought on, upon the spur, that
stale stage in which those of her profession
are reduced to think of showing company, instead of seeing it.

No sooner then was this precious substitute
of my mistress lain down, but she, who was
never out of her way when any occasion of
lewdness presented itself, turned to me, embraced and kissed me with great eagerness. This
was new, this was odd; but imputing it to
nothing but pure kindness, which, for aught I
knew, it might be the London way to express
in that manner, I was determined not to be
behind hand with her, and returned her the
kiss and embrace, with all the fervor that perfect innocence knew. Encouraged by this, her
hands became extremely free, and wandered
over my whole body, with touches, squeezes,

pressures, that rather warmed and surprised me with their novelty, than they either shocked or alarmed me. The flattering praises she intermingled with these invasions, contributed also not a little to bribe passiveness; and, knowing no ill, I feared none, especially from one who had prevented all doubts of her womanhood, by conducting my hands to a pair of breasts that hung loosely down, in a size and volume that full sufficiently distinguished her sex, to me at least, who had never made any other comparison.

I lay then all tame and passive as she could wish, whilst her freedom raised no other emotion but those of a strange, and, till then, unfelt pleasure. Every part of me was open and exposed to the licentious courses of her hands, which, like a lambent fire, ran over my whole body, and thawed all coldness as they went. My breasts, if it is not too bold a figure to call so, two hard, firm, rising hillocks, that just began to show themselves, or signify anything to the touch, employed and amused her hands awhile, till, slipping down lower, over a smooth track, she could just feel the soft, silky down, that had but a few months before put forth and garnished the mount pleasant of those parts, and promised to spread a grateful shelter over the sweet seat of the most exquisite sensation, and which had been, till that instant, the seat of the most insensible innocence. Her fingers played and strove to twine in the young tendrils of that moss, which nature has contrived at once for use and ornament. But, not contented with these outer posts, she now attempts the main spot, and began to twitch, to insinuate, and at length to force an introduction of a finger into the quick itself, in such a manner, that had she not proceeded by insensible gradations, that inflamed me beyond the power of modesty to oppose its resistance to their progress, I should have jumped out of bed and cried for help against such strange assaults.

Instead of which, her lascivious touches had lighted up a new fire that wantoned through all my veins, but fixed with violence in that center appointed them by nature, where the first strange hands were now busied in feeling, squeezing, compressing the lips, then opening them again, with a finger between, till an oh! expressed her hurting me, where the narrowness of the unbroken passage refused it entrance to any depth. In the meantime, the extension of my limbs, languid stretching, sighs, short heavings, all conspired to assure that experienced wanton, that I was more pleased than offended at her proceedings, which she seasoned with repeated kisses and exclamations, such as "Oh! what a charming creature thou art! What a happy man will be he that first makes a woman of you! Oh! that I were a man for your sake!" with the like broken expressions, interrupted by kisses as fierce and lascivious as ever I received from the other sex. For my part, I was transported, confused, and out of myself; feelings so new were too much for me. My heated and alarmed senses were in a tumult that robbed me of all liberty of thought; tears of pleasure gushed from my eyes, and somewhat assuaged the fire that raged all over me.

Phoebe herself, the hackneyed, thoroughbred Phoebe, to whom all modes and devices of pleasure were known and familiar, found, it seems, in this exercise of her art to break young girls, the gratification of one of those arbitrary tastes, for which there is no accounting. Not that she hated men, or did not even prefer them to her own sex; but when she met with such occasions as this was, a satiety of enjoyments in the common road, perhaps, too, a great secret bias, inclined her to make the most of pleasure, wherever she could find it, without distinction of sexes. In this view, now well assured that she had, by her touches, sufficiently inflamed me for her purpose, she rolled down the bed clothes gently, and I saw myself stretched naked, my shift being turned up to my neck, whilst I had no power or sense to oppose it. Even my glowing blushes expressed more desire than modesty, whilst the candle, left (to be sure not undesignedly) burning, threw a full light on my whole body.

"No," says Phoebe, "you must not, my sweet girl, think to hide all these treasures from me. My sight must be feasted as well as my touch. I must devour with my eyes this springing bosom. Suffer me to kiss it. I have not seen enough. Let me kiss it once more. What firm,

smooth, white flesh is here! How delicately
shaped! Then this delicate down! Oh! let me
view the small, dear, tender cleft! This is too
much, I cannot bear it! I must. I must."
Here she took my hand, and in a transport
carried it where you will easily guess. But what
a difference in the state of the same thing! A
spreading thicket of bushy curls marked the
full grown, complete woman. Then the cavity
to which she guided my hand easily received
it; and as soon as she felt it within her, she
moved herself to and fro, with so rapid a friction, that I presently withdrew it, wet and
clammy, when instantly Phoebe grew more
composed, after two or three sighs, and heart-
fetched ohs! and giving me a kiss that seemed
to exhale her soul through her lips, she replaced the bed clothes over us. What pleasure
she had found I cannot say; but this I know,
that the first sparks of kindling nature, the
first ideas of pollution, were caught by me that
night; and that the acquaintance and communi-
cation with the bad of our sex, is often as fatal
to innocence as all the seductions of the other.
But to go on. When Phoebe was restored to
that calm, which I was far from the enjoyment
of myself, she artfully sounded me on all the
points necessary to govern the designs of my
virtuous mistress on me, and by my answers,
drawn from pure, undissembled nature, she had
no reason but to promise herself all imaginable
success, so far as it depended on my ignorance,
easiness, and warmth of constitution.

After a sufficient length of dialogue, my
bedfellow left me to my rest, and I fell asleep,
through pure weariness, from the violent
emotions I had been led into, when nature,
which had been too warmly stirred and ferment-
ed to subdue without allaying by some means
or other, relieved me by one of those luscious
dreams, the transports of which are scarce inferior to those of waking real action.

In the morning I awoke about ten, perfectly
gay and refreshed; Phoebe was up before me,
and asked me in the kindest manner how I did,
how I had rested, and if I was ready for breakfast? carefully at the same time, avoiding to
increase the confusion she saw I was in, at
looking her in the face, by any hint of the
night's bed scene. I told her if she pleased I
would get up, and begin any work she would
be pleased to set me about. She smiled,
presently the maid brought in the tea equipage,
and I had just huddled my clothes on, when in
waddled my mistress. I expected no less than
to be told of, if not chid for, my late rising,
when I was most agreeably disappointed by
her compliments on my pure and fresh looks.
I was "a bud of beauty" (this was her style),
"and how vastly all the fine men would admire
me;" to all which my answers did not, I can
assure you, wrong my breeding; they were as
simple and silly as they could wish, and, no
doubt flattered them infinitely more than had
they proved me enlightened by education and
a knowledge of the world.

We breakfasted, and the tea things were
scarce removed, when in were brought two
bundles of linen and wearing apparel; in short,
all the necessaries for rigging me out, as they
termed it, completely. Imagine to yourself,
madam, how my little coquette heart fluttered
with joy at the sight of a white lutestring,
flowered with silver, scoured indeed, but passed
on me for spick and span new, a Brussels lace
cap, braided shoes, and the rest in proportion,
all second hand finery, and procured instantly
for the occasion, by the diligence and industry
of the good Mrs. Brown, who had already had
a chapman for me in the house, before whom
my charms were to pass in review; for he had
not only, in course, insisted on a previous sight
of the premises, but also an immediate surren-
dering to him, in case of agreeing for me;
concluding very wisely, that such a place as I
was in, was of the hottest to trust the keeping
of such a perishable commodity in, as a maidenhead. The care of dressing, and tricking me
out for the market, was then left to Phoebe,
who acquitted herself, if not well, at least perfectly to the satisfaction of everything but my
impatience of seeing myself dressed. When it
was over, and I viewed myself in the glass, I
was no doubt, too natural, too artless, to hide
my childish joy at the change, a change, in the
real truth, for much the worse, since I must
have much better become the neat easy simplicity of my rustic dress, than the awkward,
untoward, tawdry finery, that I could not con-

ceal my strangeness to. Phoebe's compliments,
however, in which her own share in dressing
me was not forgot, did not a little confirm me
in the now first notions I had ever entertained
concerning my person, which, be it said without
vanity, was then tolerable to justify a taste for
me, of which it may not be out of place to
sketch you an unflattered picture.

I was tall, yet not too tall of my age, which,
as I before remarked, was barely turned fifteen;
my shape perfectly straight, thin waisted, and
light and free, without owing anything to
stays; my hair was a glossy auburn, and as soft
as silk, flowing down my neck in natural
buckles, and did not a little set off the whiteness of a smooth skin; my face was rather too
ruddy, though its features were delicate, and
the shape was a roundish oval, except where a
pit in my chin had far from a disagreeable
effect; my eyes were as black as can be imagined, and rather languishing than sparkling,
except on certain occasions, when I have been
told they struck fire fast enough; my teeth,
which I ever carefully preserved, were small,
even and white; my bosom was finely raised, and
one might then discern rather the promise, than
the actual growth, of the round, firm breast,
that in a little time made that promise good.
In short, all the points of beauty that are most
universally in request, I had, or at least my
vanity forbids me to appeal from the decision
of our sovereign judges the men, who all, that
I ever knew at least, gave it thus highly in my

favour; and I met with, even in my own sex, some that were above denying me that justice, while others praised me yet more unsuspectedly, by endeavouring to detract from me, in points of person and figure that I obviously excelled in. This is, I own, too much, too strong of self-praise; but I should be ungrateful to nature, and to a form to which I owe such singular blessings of pleasure and fortune, were I to suppress, through an affection of modesty, the mention of such valuable gifts.

Well then, dressed as I was, and little did it then enter into my head that all this gay attire was no more than decking the victim out for sacrifice, whilst I innocently attributed all to mere friendship and kindness in the sweet, good Mrs. Brown, who, I was forgetting to mention, had, under pretence of keeping my money safe, got from me, without the least hesitation, the driblet, so I now call it, which remained to me after the expenses on my journey. After some little time most agreeably spent before the glass, in scarce self-admiration, since my new dress had by much the greatest share in it, I was sent for down to the parlour, where the old lady saluted me, and wished me joy of my new clothes, which she was not ashamed to say, fitted me, as if I had worn nothing but the finest all my life-time; but what was it she could not see me silly enough to swallow? At the same time, she presented me another cousin of her own creation, an elderly gentleman, who got up at my entry

into the room, and on my dropping a courtesy
to him, saluted me, and seemed a little affronted
that I had only presented my cheek to him; a
mistake, which, if one, he immediately correct-
ed, by glueing his lips to mine, with an ardour
which his figure had not at all disposed me to
thank him for; his figure, I say, than which
nothing could be more shocking or detestable,
for ugly, and disagreeable, were terms too
gentle to convey a just idea of it.

Imagine to yourself, a man rather past three-
score, short and ill-made, with a yellow cadaver-
ous hue, great goggling eyes, that stared as if
he was strangled; an out-mouth for two more
properly tusks than teeth, livid lips, and a
breath like a jake's; then he had a peculiar
ghastliness in his grin, that made him perfectly
frightful, if not dangerous to women with
child; yet, made as he was thus in mock of man,
he was so blind to his own staring deformities,
as to think himself born for pleasing, and that
no woman could see him with impunity, in consequence of which idea, he had lavished great
sums on such wretches as could gain upon themselves to pretend love to his person, whilst to
those who had no art or patience to dissemble
the horror it inspired, he behaved even brutally.
Impotence, more than necessity, made him seek
in vanity the provocative that was wanting to
raise him to the pitch of enjoyment, which he
too often saw himself baulked of by the failure
of his powers; and this always threw him into
a fit of rage, which he wreaked, as far as he

durst, on the innocent objects of his fit of momentary desire. This then was the monster to which my conscientious benefactress, who had long been his purveyor this way, had doomed me, and sent for me down purposely for his examination. Accordingly she made me stand up before him, turned me round, unpinned my handkerchief, remarked to him the rise and fall, the turn and whiteness of a bosom just beginning to fill; then made me walk, and took even a handle from the rusticity of my charms, in short, she omitted no point of jockeyship, to which he only answered by gracious nods and approbation, whilst he looked goats and monkeys at me, for I sometimes stole a corner glance at him, and encountering his fiery eager stare, looked another way from pure horror and affright, which he, doubtless in character, attributed to nothing more than maiden modesty, or at least the affectation of it.

However, I was soon dismissed, and recon-ducted to my room by Phoebe, who stuck close to me, by way of not leaving me alone, and at leisure, to make such reflections as might naturally rise to anyone, not an idiot, on such a scene as I had just gone through; but to my shame be it confessed, that such was my invinci-ble stupidity, or rather portentous innocence, that I did not yet open my eyes on Mrs. Brown's designs, and saw nothing in this titular cousin of hers, but a shocking hideous person, which did not at all concern me, unless that my grati-tude for my benefactress made me extend my

respect to all her cousinhood. Phoebe, however, began to sift the state and pulses of my
heart towards this monster, asking me how I
should approve of such a fine gentleman for a
husband? (fine gentleman, I suppose she called
him, from his being daubed with lase). I
answered her very naturally, that I had no
thoughts of a husband, but that if I was to
choose one, it should be among my own degree;
sure, so much had my aversion to that wretch's
hideous figure indisposed me to all fine gentlemen, and confounded my ideas, as if those of
that rank had been necessarily cast in the same
mould that he was. But Phoebe was not to be
beat off so, but went on with her endeavours to
melt and soften me for the purposes of my reception into that hospitable house; and whilst
she talked of the sex in general, she had no
reason to despair of a compliance, which more
than one reason showed her would be easily
enough obtained of me; but then she had too
much experience not to discover that my particular fixed aversion to that frightful cousin,
would be a block not so readily to be removed,
as suited with the consummation of their
bargain and sale of me. Mother Brown had in
the mean time agreed the terms of this liquorish
old goat, which I afterwards understood were
to be fifty guineas peremptory, for the liberty
of attempting me, and one hundred more at
the complete gratification of his desires, in the
triumph over my virginity; and, as for me, I
was to be left entirely at the discretion of his

liking and generosity. This unrighteous con-
tract being thus settled, he was so eager to be
put in possession, that he insisted on being
introduced to drink tea with me that afternoon,
when we were to be left alone; nor would he
hearken to the procuress's remonstrances, that
I was not sufficiently prepared, and ripened for
such an attack, that I was too green and un-
tamed, having been scarce twenty-four hours
in the house; it is the character of lust to be
impatient, and his vanity arming him against
any supposition of other than the common resistance of a maid on those occasions, made him
reject all proposals of a delay, and my dreadful
trial was thus fixed, unknown to me, for that
very evening.

At dinner, Mrs. Brown and Phoebe did
nothing but run riot in praise of this wonderful
cousin, and how happy that woman would be
that he would favour with his addresses, in
short my two gossips exhausted all their rhetoric
to persuade me to accept them; "That the
gentleman was violently smitten with me at
first sight; that he would make my fortune if
I would be a good girl and not stand in my own
light; that I should trust his honour; that I
would be made forever, and have a chariot to go
abroad in;" with all such stuff as was fit to
turn the head of such a silly ignorant girl as
I then was; but luckily here my aversion had
taken already such deep root in me, my heart
was so strongly defended from him by my
senses, that wanting the art to mask my senti-

ments, I gave them no hopes to their employer's succeeding, at least very easily, with me. The glass too marched pretty quick, with a view, I suppose, to make a friend of the warmth of my constitution, in the minutes of the imminent attack. Thus they kept me pretty long at the table, and about six in the evening, after I was retired to my apartment, and the tea board was set, enters my mistress, followed close by that satyr, who came in grinning in a way peculiar to him, and by his odious presence, confirmed me in all the sentiments of detestation which his first appearance had given birth to. He sat down fronting me, and all the tea time kept ogling me in a manner that gave me the utmost pain and confusion, all the marks of which he still explained to be my bashfulness, and not being used to see company. Tea over, the commode old lady pleaded urgent business, which indeed was true, to go out, and earnestly desired me to entertain her cousin kindly till she came back, both for my own sake and hers; and then with a "Pray, sir, be very good, be very tender of the sweet child," she went out of the room, leaving me staring, with my mouth wide open, and unprepared, by the suddeness of her departure, to oppose it.

We were now alone, and on that idea a sudden fit of trembling seized me. I was so afraid, without a precise notion why, and what I had to fear, that I sat on the settee, by the fireside, motionless, and petrified, without life or spirit, not knowing how to look or how to

stir. But long I was not suffered to remain in
this state of stupefaction; the monster squatted
down by me on the settee, flings his arms about
my neck, and drawing me pretty forcibly towards him, obliged me to receive, in spite of
my struggles to disengage from him, his
pestilential kisses, which quite overcame me.
Finding me then next to senseless, and unresisting, he tears off my neck handkerchief, and
laid all open there to his eyes and hands; still
I endured all without flinching, till emboldened
by my sufferance and silence, for I had not the
power to speak or cry out, he attempted to lay
me down on the settee, and I felt his hand on
the lower part of my naked thighs, which were
crossed and which he endeavoured to unlock.
Oh then, I was roused out of my passive en-
durance, and springing from him with an
activity he was not prepared for, threw myself
at his feet, and begged him, in the most moving
tone, not to be rude, and that he would not
hurt me. "Hurt you, my dear?" says the brute,
"I intend you no harm, has not the old lady
told you that I love you, that I shall do handsomely by you?" "She has indeed, sir," said I,
"but I cannot love you, indeed I cannot! pray
let me alone, yes, I will love you dearly if you
will let me alone, and go away." But I was
talking to the wind; for whether my tears, my
attitude, or the disorder of my dress proved
fresh incentives, or whether he was now under
the dominion of desires he could not bridle, but
snorting and foaming with lust and rage, he

renews his attack, seizes me, and again attempts to extend and fix me on the settee; in which he succeeded so far as to lay me along, and even to toss my petticoats over my head, and lay my thighs bare, which I obstinately kept closed, nor could he, though he attempted with his knee to force them open, effect it so as to stand fair for being master of the main avenue; he was unbuttoned, both waistcoat and breeches, yet I only felt the weight of his body upon me, whilst I lay struggling with indignation, and dying with terrors; but he stopped all of a sudden, and got off, panting, blowing, cursing, and rehearsing upon me, "old and ugly!" for so I had very naturally called him in the heat of my defense. The brute had, it seems, as I afterwards understood, brought on, by his eagerness and struggle, the ultimate period of his hot fit of lust, which his power was too short-lived to carry him through the full execution of, of which my thighs and linen received the effusion.

When it was over, he bid me, with a tone of displeasure, get up, "that he would not do me honour to think of me any more, that the old bitch might look out for another cully; that he would not be fooled so by e'er a country mock modesty in England; that he supposed I had left my maidenhead with some bobnail in the country, and was come to dispose of my skimmiik in town," with a volley of the like abuse, which I listened to with more pleasure than ever fond woman did to protestations of

love from her darling minion; for, incapable as
I was of receiving any addition to my perfect
hatred and aversion to him, I looked on this
railing, as my security against his renewing
his most odious caresses. Yet, plain as Mrs.
Brown's views were now come out, I had not
the heart, or spirit to open my eyes on them,
still I could not part with my dependence on
that beldam, so much did I think myself hers,
soul and body; or rather, I sought to deceive
myself with the continuation of my good
opinion of her, and chose to wait the worst at
her hands, sooner than being turned out to
starve in the streets, without a penny of money
or a friend to apply to; these fears were my
folly.

While this confusion of ideas was passing in
my head and I sat pensive by the fire, with my
eyes brimming with tears, my neck still bare,
and my cap fallen off in the struggle, so that
my hair was in the disorder you may guess;
the villain's lust began, I suppose, to be again
in flow, at the sight of all that bloom of youth
which presented itself to his view, a bloom yet
unenjoyed, and in course not yet indifferent to
him. After some pause, he asked me, with a
tone of voice mightily softened, whether I
would make it up with him before the old lady
returned, and all would be well; he would restore me his affections, at the same time offering to kiss me and feel my breasts. But now
my extreme aversion, my fears, my indignation,
all acting upon me, gave me a spirit not natural

to me, so that breaking loose from him, I ran
to the bell, and rang it, before he was aware,
with such violence and effect, as brought up
the maid to know what was the matter, or
whether the gentleman wanted anything; and
before he could proceed to greater extremities,
she bounced into the room, and seeing me
stretched on the floor, my hair all disheveled,
my nose gushing out blood, which did not a
little tragedize the scene, and my odious pros-
ecutor still intent on pushing his brutal point,
unmoved by all my cries and distress, she was
herself confounded and did not know what to
do. As much, however, as Martha might be
prepared and hardened to transactions of this
sort, all womanhood must have been out of her
heart, could she have seen this unmoved. Besides she thought that, matters had gone greater
lengths than they really had, and that the
courtesy of the house had been actually con-
summated on me, and flung me into the condition I was in. In this notion she instantly
took my part, and advised the gentleman to go
down and leave me to recover myself, and "that
all would soon be over with me; that when Mrs.
Brown and Phoebe, who were gone out, were
returned, they would take order for everything
to his satisfaction; that nothing would be lost
by a little patience with the poor tender thing;
that for her part she was frightened, she could
not tell what to say to such doings; but that
she would stay by me till my mistress came
home." As the wench said all this in a

resolute tone, and the monster himself began to
perceive that things would not mend by his staying, he took his hat and went out of the room
murmuring, and pitting his brows like an old
ape, so that I was delivered from the horrors
of his detestable presence.

As soon as he was gone, Martha very tenderly offered me her assistance in anything, and
would have got some hartshorn drops, and put
me to bed, which last I, at first positively refused, in the fear that the monster might return and take me at that disadvantage. However, with much persuasion, and assurances
that I should not be molested that night, she
prevailed on me to lie down; and indeed I was
so weakened by my struggles, so dejected by
my fearful apprehensions, so terror-struck, that
I had not power to sit up, or hardly to give
answers to the questions with which the curious
Martha perplexed me. Such too, and so cruel
was my fate, that I dreaded the sight of Mrs.
Brown, as if I had been the criminal, and she
the person injured; a mistake which you will
not think so strange, on distinguishing that
neither virtue or principles had the least share
in the defense I had made, but only the particular aversion I had conceived against this
first brutal and frightful invader of my tender
innocence. I passed then the time till Mrs.
Brown came home under all the agitations of
fear and despair that may easily be guessed.

About eleven at night my two ladies came
home, and having received rather a favorable

report from Martha, who had run down to let
them in, for Mr. Crofts, that was the name of
my brute, was gone out of the house, after
waiting till he had tired his patience for Mrs.
Brown's return, they came thundering up stairs,
and seeing me pale, my face bloody, and all the
marks of the most thorough dejection, they
employed themselves more to comfort and reinspirit me, than in making me the reproaches
I was weak enough to fear, I who had so many
juster and stronger to retort upon them. Mrs.
Brown withdrawn, Phoebe came presently to
bed to me, and what with the answers she drew
from me, what with her own method of palpably
satisfying herself, she soon discovered that I
had been more frightened than hurt; upon
which, I suppose, being herself seized with sleep,
and reserving her lectures and instructions till
the next morning, she left me, properly speaking, to my unrest; for, after tossing and turning the greatest part of the night, and tor-
menting myself with the falsest notions and
apprehensions of things, I fell through mere
fatigue into a kind of delirious doze, out of
which I waked late in the morning in a violent
fever, a circumstance which was extremely
critical to reprieve me, at least for a time, from
the attacks of a wretch, infinitely more terrible
to me than death itself.

The interested care that was taken of me
during my illness, in order to restore me to a
condition of making good the bawd's engagements, or of enduring further trials, had how-

ever such an effect on my grateful disposition,
that I even thought myself obliged to my un-
doers for their attention to promote my recovery; and, above all, for the keeping out of
sight that brutal ravisher, the author of my
disorder, on their finding I was too strongly
moved at the bare mention of his name. Youth
is soon raised, and a few days were sufficient
to conquer the fury of my fever, but, what
contributed most to my reconciliation with life,
was the timely news, that Mr. Cofts, who was
a merchant of considerable dealings, was
arrested at the King's suit, for near forty
thousand pounds, on account of his driving a
certain contraband trade, and that his affairs
were so desperate, that even were it in his
inclination, it would not be in his power to
renew his designs upon me, for he was instantly
thrown into a prison, which it was not likely
he would get out of in haste.

Mrs. Brown, who had touched his fifty
guineas, advanced to so little a purpose, and
lost all hopes of the remaining hundred, began
to look upon my treatment of him with a more
favourable eye; and as they had observed my
temper to be tractable and conformable to their
views, all the girls that composed her flock were
suffered to visit me, and had their cue to dispose me, by their conversation, to a perfect
resignation of myself to Mrs. Brown's direction. Accordingly they were let in upon me,
and all that frolic and thoughtless gaiety in
which those giddy creatures consume their

leisure, made me envy a condition of which I
only saw the fair side; insomuch, that the being
one of them became even my ambition, a disposition which they all carefully cultivated; and
I wanted now nothing but to restore my health,
that I might be able to undergo the ceremony
of the initiation. Conversation, example, in
short all, contributed, in that house, to corrupt
my native purity, which had taken no root in
education; whilst now the inflammable principle
of pleasure, so easily fired at my age, made
strange work within me, and all the modesty
I was brought up in the habit, not the instruction of, began to melt away like the dew
before the sun's heat; not to mention that I
made a vice of necessity, from the constant
fears I had of being turned out to starve.

I was soon pretty well recovered, and at
certain hours allowed to range all over the
house, but cautiously kept from seeing any
company till the arrival of Lord B., from Bath,
to whom Mrs. Brown, in respect to his experienced generosity on such occasions, proposed to offer the perusal of that trinket of
mine, which bears too great an imaginary value;
and his lordship being expected in town in less
than a fortnight, Mrs. Brown judged I would
be entirely renewed in beauty and freshness by
that time, and afford her the chance of a better
bargain than she had driven with Mr. Crofts.
In the meantime, I was so thoroughly, as they
call it, brought over, so tame to their whistle,
that, had my cage door been set open, I had no

idea that I ought to fly any where, sooner than
stay where I was; nor had I the least sense of
regretting my condition, but waited very quietly
whatever Mrs. Brown should order concerning
me, w'io on her side, by herself and her agents,
took more than the necessary precautions to
lull and lay asleep all just reflections over the
shoulder; a life of joy painted in the gayest
colours; caresses, promises, indulgent treatment; nothing, in short, was wanting to do-
mesticate me entirely and to prevent my going
out anywhere to get better advice.   Alas!   I
dreamed of no such thing.

Hitherto I had been indebted only to the
girls of the house for the corruption of my
innocence; their luscious talk, in which modesty
was far from respected, their description of
their engagements with men, had given me a
tolerable insight into the nature and mysteries
of their profession, at the same time that they
highly provoked an itch of florid warm spirited
blood through every vein; but above all, my bed
fellow Phoebe, whose pupil I more immediately
was, exerted her talents in giving me the first
tinctures of pleasure, whilst nature, now
warmed and wantoned with discoveries so interesting, piqued a curiosity which Phoebe artfully whetted, and leading me from question to
question of her own suggestion, explained to
me all the mysteries of Venus. But I could not
long remain in such a house as that, without
being an eye witness of more than I could conceive from her descriptions.

One day, about twelve at noon, being thoroughly recovered of my fever, I happened to be in Mrs. Brown's dark closet, where I had not been half an hour, resting upon the maid's bed, before I heard a rustling in the bed chamber, separated from the closet only by two sash doors, before the glasses of which were drawn two yellow damask curtains, but not so close as to exclude the full view of the room from any person in the closet. I instantly crept softly, and posted myself so, that seeing everything minutely, I could not myself be seen; and who should come in but the venerable mother abbess herself handed in by a tall, browny young horse grenadier, moulded in the Hercules style, in fine, the choice of the most experienced dame, in those affairs, in all London. Oh, how still and hush did I keep at my stand, lest any noise should baulk my curiosity, or bring madam into the closet. But I had not much reason to fear either, for she was so entirely taken up with her present great concern, that she had no sense of attention to spare to anything else.

Droll was it to see that clumsy fat figure of hers, flop down on the foot of the bed, opposite to the closet door, so that I had a full front view of all her charms. Her paramour sat down on her; he seemed to be a man of very few words, and a great stomach; for proceeding instantly to essentials, he gave her some hearty smacks, and thrusting his hands into her breasts, disengaged them from her stays, in scorn of whose confinement they broke loose, and swaggered down, navel low at least. A more enormous pair did my eyes never behold, nor of a worse colour, flagging soft, and most lovingly continuous, yet such as they were, this neck beef-eater seemed to paw them with a most unenviable gust, seeking in vain to confine or cover one of them with a hand scarce less than a shoulder of mutton. After toying with them thus some time, as if they had been worth it, he laid her down pretty briskly, and canting up her petticoats, made barely a mask of them to her broad red face, that blushed with nothing but brandy. As he stood on one side, unbuttoning his waist coat and breeches, her fat brawny thighs hung down, and the whole greasy landscape lay open to my view; a wide open mouthed gap, overshaded with a grizzly bush, seemed held out like a beggar's wallet for its provision.

But I soon had my eyes called off by a more striking object that entirely engrossed them. Her sturdy stallion had now unbuttoned, and produced naked, stiff and erect, that wonderful machine, which I had never seen before, and which, for the interest my own seat of pleasure began to take furiously in it, I stared at with all the eyes I had; however, my senses were too much flurried, too much centered in that now burning spot of mine, to observe anything more than in general the make and turn of that instrument, from which the instinct of nature, yet more than all I had heard of it, now strongly informed me, I was to expect that supreme pleasure which she had placed in the meeting of those parts so admirably fitted for each other. Long, however, the young spark did not remain before giving it two or three shakes, by way of brandishing it; he threw himself upon her, and his back being now towards me, I could only take his being engulphed for granted, by the directions he moved in, and the impossibility of missing so staring a mark; and now the bed shook, the curtains rattled so, that I could scarce hear the sighs and murmurs, the heaves and pantings that accompanied the action, from the beginning to the end; the sound and sight of which thrilled to the very soul of me, and made every vein in my body circulate liquid fires; the emotion grew so violent that it almost intercepted my respiration. Prepared then, and disposed as I was by the discourse of my companions, and Phoebe's minute detail of everything, no wonder that such a sight gave the last dying blow to my native innocence.

Whilst they were in the heat of the action, guided by nature only, I stole my hand up my petticoats, and with fingers all on fire, seized, and yet more inflamed that center of all my senses; my heart palpitated, as if it would force its way through my bosom; I breathed with pain; I twisted my thighs, squeezed, and compressed the lips of that virgin slit, and following mechanically the example of Phoebe's manual operation on it, as far as I could find admission, brought on at last the critical ecstacy: the melting flow, into which nature, spent with excess of pleasure, dissolves and dies away. After which my sense recovered coolness enough to observe the rest of the transaction between this happy pair.

The young fellow had just dismounted, when the old lady immediately sprung up with all the vigor of youth, derived, no doubt from her late refreshment, and making him sit down, began in her turn to kiss him, to pat and pinch his cheeks, and play with his hair, all which he received with an air of indifference and coolness, that showed him to me much altered from what he was when he first went onto the breach. My pious governess, however, not being above calling in auxiliaries, unlocks a little case of cordials that stood near the bed, and made him pledge her in a very plentiful dram, after which, and a little amorous parley, madam set herself down upon the same place, at the bed's foot, and the young fellow standing sidewise by her side, she with the greatest effrontery imaginable, unbuttons his breeches, and removing his shirt, draws out his affair, so shrunk and diminished, that I could not but remember the difference, now crestfallen and just faintly lifting its head, but our experienced matron very soon, by chafing it with her hands, brought it to swell to that size and erection I had before seen it up to. I admired then, upon a fresh account, and with a nicer survey, the texture of that capital part of man; the flaming red head as it stood uncapt, the whiteness of the shaft, and the shrub growth of curling hair that embrowned the roots of it, the roundish bag that dangled down from it, all exacted my eager attention, and renewed my flame. But, as the main affair was now at the point the industrious dame had laboured to bring it to, she was not in the humour to put off the payment of her pains, so laying herself down, she drew him gently upon her, and thus they finished, in the same manner as before, the old last act. This over, they both went out lovingly together, the old lady having first made him a present, as near as I could observe, of three or four pieces; he being not only her particular favourite on account of his performances, but a retainer to the house, from whose sight she had taken care hitherto to secret me, lest he might not have had patience to wait for my lord's arrival, but insisted on being his taster, which the old lady was under too much subjection to him to dare dispute with him, for every girl of the house fell to him in course, and the old lady only now and then got her turn, in consideration of the maintenance he had, and which he could scarce be accused of not earning from her.

As soon as I heard them go down stairs, I stole softly up to my own room, out of which I had luckily not been missed; there I began to breathe more freely and to give way to those warm emotions which the sight of such an encounter had raised in me. I laid me down on the bed, stretched myself out, longing and ardently wishing and requiring any means to divert or allay the rekindled rage and tumult of

my desires which pointed strongly to their pole,
man. I felt about the bed as if I sought something that I grasped in my waking dream, and
not finding it, I could have cried for vexation;
for every part of me was glowing with stim-
ulated fires. At length I resorted to the only
present remedy, that of vain attempts of degita-
tion, where the smallness of the theatre did
not yet afford room enough for action, and
where the pain my fingers gave me in striving
for admission, though they procured me a slight
satisfaction for the present, started an apprehension, and I could not be easy till I had
communicated with Phoebe and received her
explanation of it.

The opportunity, however, did not offer till
next morning, for Phoebe did not come to bed
till long after I was gone to sleep. As soon
then as we were both awake, it was but in
course to bring our lay-a-bed chat to hand, on
the subject of my uneasiness, to which a recital
of the love scene I had thus by chance been
spectatress of, served for a preface. Phoebe
could not hear it to the end without more than
one interruption by peals of laughter, and my
ingenious way of relating matters did not a little
heighten the joke to her. But, on her sounding
me how the sight had affected me, without
mincing or hiding the pleasurable emotions it
had inspired me with, I told her at the same
time that one idea had perplexed me, and that
very considerably. "Ay," said she, "what was
that?" "Why," replied I, "having very cautious-

ly and attentively compared the size of that enormous machine, which did not appear, at least to my fearful imagination, less than my wrist, and at least three of my handfuls long, to that small, tender part of me which was framed to receive it, I could not conceive its being possible to allow it entrance without dying, perhaps in the greatest pain, since she well knew that even a finger thrust in there hurt me beyond bearing. As to my mistress's and yours, I can very plainly distinguish the different dimensions of them from mine, palpable to the touch, and visible to the eye, so that, in short, great as the promised pleasure may be, I am afraid of the pain of the experiment."

Phoebe at this redoubled her laugh, and whilst I expected a very serious solution of my doubts and apprehensions in this matter, only told me that she had never heard of a mortal wound being given in those parts by that terrible weapon, and that some she knew younger and as delicately made as myself, had outlived the operation. That she believed at the worst I would take a great deal of killing; that it was true there was a great diversity of sizes in those parts owing to nature, child-bearing, frequent over-stretching with unmerciful machines, but with a certain age and habit of body even the most experienced in those affairs could not well distinguish between the maid and the woman, supposing too, an absence of all artifice and things in their natural condition. Now

that chance had thrown in my way one sight
of that sort, Phoebe promised to procure me
another that should feast my eyes more delicately and go a great way in the cure of my
fears from that imaginary disproportion.

She then asked me if I knew Polly Phillips.
"Undoubtedly," says I, "the fair girl which was
so tender of me when I was sick, and has been,
as you told me, but two months in the house?"
"The same," says Phoebe. "You must know
then, she is kept by a young Genoese merchant,
whose uncle, who is immensely rich and whose
darling he is, sent over here with an English
merchant, his friend, on a pretext of settling
some accounts, but in reality to humour his
inclinations for travelling and seeing the world.
He met casually with this Polly once in
Company, and taking a liking to her, makes it
worth her while to keep entirely to him. He
comes to her twice or thrice a week, and she
receives him in the light closet up one pair of
stairs, where he enjoys her to a taste, I suppose
peculiar to the heat or perhaps the caprices of
his country. I say no more, but to-morrow
being his day, you shall see what passes between
them from a place only known to yourself and
myself."

You may be sure in the play I was now taking
I had no objection to the proposal, and was
rather a tip-toe for its accomplishment. At
five in the evening next day, Phoebe punctual
to her promise, came for me as I sat alone in
my own room and beckoned me to follow her.

We went down the back stairs very softly and opening the door of a dark closet where there was some old furniture kept and cases of liquor, she drew me in after her, and fastened the door upon us. We had no light except what came through a long crevice in the partition between our and the light closet, where the scene of action lay, so that sitting on some low cases we could with the greatest ease as well as clearness (our selves unseen) see all objects by only applying our eyes close to the crevice where the moulding of a panel had warped or started a little on the other side.

The young gentleman was the first person I saw, with his back directly towards me looking at a print. Polly was not yet come; in less than a minute though, the door opened and she came in. At the noise the door made he turned about and came to meet her with an air of the greatest tenderness and satisfaction. After saluting her, he led her to a couch that fronted us, where they both sat down and the young Genoese helped her to a glass of wine, with some Naples biscuit on a salver. Presently, when they had exchanged a few kisses and questions in broken English on one side, he began to unbutton, and in fine, strip unto his shirt. As if this had been the signal agreed on for pulling off all their clothes, a scheme which the heat of the season perfectly favoured, Polly began to draw her pins and as she had no stays to unlace, she was in a trice, with her gallant's assistance, undressed to all but her shift. When he saw

this, his breeches were immediately loosened,
waist and knee bands, and slipped over his
ankles, clean off; his shirt collar was unbuttoned
too; then, first giving Polly an encouraging
kiss, he stole, as it were, the shift off the girl,
who being, I suppose, broke and familiarized
to this humour, blushed indeed, but less than I
did at the apparition of her, now standing stark
naked just as she came out of the hands of pure
nature, with her hair loose and afloat down her
dazzling white neck and shoulders, whilst the
deepened carnations of her cheeks went off
gradually into the hue of glazed snow, for such
were the blended tints and polish of her skin.

This girl could not be above eighteen; her
face regular and sweet featured, her shape exquisite; nor could I help envying two ripe en-
chanting breasts, finely plumed out in flesh, but
withal so round, so firm that they sustained
themselves in scorn of any stay; then their
nipples pointing different ways, marked their
pleasing separation. Beneath them lay the
delicious tract of her belly, which terminated
in a parting or rift scarce discernible that
modesty seemed to retire downwards to seek
shelter between two plump, fleshy thighs; the
curling hair that overspread its delightful front
clothed it with the richest sable fur in the universe; in short she was evidently a subject for
painters to court her sitting to them for a
female beauty pattern in all the true pride and
pomp of nakedness. The young Italian, still in
his shirt, stood gazing and transported at the

sight of beauties that might have fired a dying hermit; his eager eyes devoured her, as she shifted attitudes at his direction, neither were his hands excluded their share of the high feast, but wandered on the hunt of pleasure over every part and inch of her body, so qualified to afford the most exquisite sense of it. In the meantime one could not help observing the swell of his shirt front which bolstered out and pointed out the condition of things behind the curtain; but he soon removed it by slipping his shirt over his head and now, as to nakedness, they had nothing to reproach one another.

The young gentleman, by Phoebe's guess, was about two and twenty, tall and well limbed. His body was finely formed and of a most vigorous make, square shouldered and broad chested; his face was not remarkable in any way, but for a nose inclining to the Roman, eyes large, black, and sparkling, and a ruddiness in his cheeks that was the more a grace, for his complexion was of the brownest, not of that dusky dun colour which with life dazzles perhaps less than fairness and yet pleases more when it excludes the idea of freshness, but of that clear, olive gloss which when glowing at all, pleases. His hair being too short to tie, fell no lower than his neck in short easy curls, and he had a few sprigs about his paps that garnished his chest in a style of strength and manliness. His grand monument which seemed to rise out of a thicket of curling hair which spread from the root all over the thighs and belly up to his navel, stood stiff and upright, but of a size to frighten me out of sympathy for the small tender part which was the object of its fury and which now lay exposed to my fairest view; for he had immediately on stripping off his shirt gently pushed her down on the couch, which stood conveniently to break her willing fall. Her thighs were spread out to their utmost extension and disclosed between them the mark of her sex, the red-centered cleft of flesh, lips vermillioning inwards, expressed a small rubid line in sweet miniature such as Guido's touch or colouring could never attain the life or delicacy of. Phoebe, at this, gave me a gentle jog to prepare me for a whispered question: "Whether I thought my little maidenhead was much less?" But my attention was too much engrossed, too much enwrapped with all I saw to be able to give her answer.

By this time the young gentleman had changed his posture from lying breadth to length-wise on the couch, but her thighs were still spread, and the mark lay fair for him, who now kneeling between them, displayed to us a side view of that fierce, erect machine of his, which threatened no less than splitting the tender victim who lay smiling at the uplifted stroke, nor seemed to decline it. He looked upon his weapon himself with some pleasure, and guiding it with his hand to the inviting slit, drew aside the lips and lodged it, after some thrusts which Polly even seemed to assist,

about half way in her, but there it stuck, I suppose from its growing thickness; he draws it
out and wetting it with spittal, re-enters and
sheathed it with ease up to the hilt, at which
Polly gave a deep sigh, which was quite in
another tone than of pain; he thrusts, she
heaves, at first gently and in a regular cadence,
but presently the transport began to be too
violent to observe any order or measure; their
motions were too rapid, their kisses too fierce
and fervent for nature to support such fury
long; both seemed to me out of themselves.
Their eyes darted fires. "Oh! oh! I can't bear
it, it is too much, I die, I am coming!" were
Polly's expressions of ecstacy. His joys were
more silent, but some broken murmurs, sighs
heart-fetched, and at length a dispatching
thrust as if he would have forced himself up
her body, and then the motionless languor of
all his limbs all showed that the die-away
moment was come upon him, which she showed
signs of joining with by the wild throwing
about of her hands, closing her eyes and giving
a deep sob in which she seemed to expire in an
agony of bliss. When he had finished his
stroke and got off of her, she lay still without
the least motion, breathless, as it were from
pleasure. He replaced her again breadth-wise
on the couch, unable to stand up, with her thighs
open, between which I could observe a kind of
white liquid, like froth, hanging about the lips
of that recently opened wound, which now
glowed with a deeper red. Presently she got

up and throwing her arms around him seemed
far from undelighted with the trial he had put
her to, to judge at least by the fondness with
which she eyed, and hung upon him.

For my part, I will not pretend to describe
what I felt all over me during this scene; but
from that instant, adieu all fears of what man
can do to me, they were now changed into such
ardent desires, such ungovernable longings,
that I could have pulled the first of that sex
that should present himself by the sleeve and
offered him my bauble, which I now imagined
the loss of would be a gain I could not too
soon procure myself. Phoebe, who had more
experience and to whom such sights were not
so new, could not, however, be unmoved at so
warm a scene, and drawing me away quietly
from the peeping hole, for fear of being overheard, guided me as near the door as possible,
all passive and obedient to her least signals.
Here was no room either to sit or lie, but
making me stand with my back towards the
door, she lifted my petticoats, and with her busy
fingers fell to explore that part of me, where
now the heat and irritations were so violent
that I was perfectly sick and ready to die with
desire, that the bare touch of her finger in that
critical place, had the effect of a fire to a train,
and her hand instantly made her sensible to
what a pitch I was wound up to, and melted by
the sight she had thus procured me. Satisfied
then with her success in allaying a heat that
would have made me impatient of seeing the

continuation of the transactions between our amorous couple, she brought me again to the crevice so favourable to our curiosity.

We had certainly been but a few instants away from it and yet on our return we saw everything in good forwardness for recommencing the tender hostilities. The young foreigner was sitting down, fronting us, on the couch, with Polly upon one knee, who had her arms round his neck, whilst the extreme whiteness of her skin was not undelightfully contrasted by the smooth glossy brown of her lover's. But who could count the fierce, unnumbered kisses given and taken, in which I could often discover their exchanging velvet thrust, when both their mouths were double tongued, and seemed to favour the mutual insertion with the greatest gust and delight! In the mean time his red headed champion, that had so lately fled the pit, quelled and abashed, was now recovered to the top of his condition, perked and crested up between Polly's thighs, who was not wanting on her part to coax and keep it in good humour, stroking it with her head down and receiving its velvet tip between her lips; whether she did this out of any particular pleasure, or whether it was to render it more glib and easy of entrance I could not tell; but it had such an effect that the young gentleman seemed by his eyes, that sparkled with more excited lustre and his inflamed countenance, to receive increase of pleasure. He got up and taking Polly in his arms, embraced her, and said something too softly for me to hear, leading her withall to the foot of the couch and taking delight in slapping her thighs and posteriors with that stiff sinew of his, which hit them with a spring that he gave it with his hand and made them resound, but hurt her about as much as he meant it to hurt her, for she seemed to have as frolicking a taste as himself. But guess my surprise when I saw the lazy young rogue lie down on his back and gently pull down Polly upon him, who giving away to his humour, straddled, and with her hands conducted her blind favourite to the right place and following her impulse, ran directly upon the flaming point of this weapon of pleasure, which she staked herself upon, up-pierced and infixed to the extremest hair breadth of it; thus she sat on him for a few instants enjoying and relishing her situation, whilst he toyed with her provoking breasts. Sometimes she would stoop to meet his kisses, but presently the sting of pleasure spurred them to fiercer action; then began the storm of heaves, which from the undermost combatant, were thrusts, at the same time he crossed his hands over her and drew her home to him with a sweet violence. The inverted strokes of anvil over hammer soon brought on the critical period in which all the signs of a close conspiring ecstacy informed us of the point they were at.

For me, I could bear to see no more; I was so overcome, so inflamed at the second part of the same play, that, mad to an intolerable degree.

I hugged, I clasped Phoebe, as if she had the
wherewithal to relieve me. Pleased however
with, and pitying the taking she could feel me
in, she drew towards the door, and opening it
as softly as she could, we both got off undiscovered, and she reconducted me to my room,
where, unable to keep my legs in the agitation
I was in, I instantly threw myself down on the
bed, where I lay transported though ashamed
at what I felt. Phoebe lay down by me and
asked me archly, "if, now that I had seen the
enemy, and fully considered him, I was still
afraid of him, or did I think I could come to
a close engagement with him?" To all which,
not a word on my side; I sighed and could
scarce breathe. She takes hold of my hand and
having rolled up her own petticoats, forced it
half strivingly towards those parts, where,
now grown more knowing, I missed the main
object of my wishes, and finding not even a
shadow of what I wanted, where everything
was so flat, or so hollow, in the vexation I was
in at it, I should have withdrawn my hand, but
for fear of disobliging her. Abandoning it then
entirely to her management, she made use of
it as she thought proper, to procure herself
rather the shadow than the substance of any
pleasure. For my part, I now pined for more
solid food, and promised tacitly to myself that
I would not be put off much longer with this
foolery of woman to woman, if Mrs. Brown did
not soon provide me with the essential specific.
In short, I had all the air of not being able to

wait the arrival of my lord B., though he was
now expected in a very few days, nor did I
wait for him, for love itself took charge of the
disposal of me, in spite of interest, or gross
lust.

It was now two days after the closet scene,
that I got up about six in the morning; and
leaving my bedfellow fast asleep, stole down,
with no other thought than of taking a little
fresh air in a small garden, which our back
parlour opened into, and from which my confinement debarred me, at the times company
came to the house; but now sleep and silence
reigned all over it. I opened the parlour door
and well surprised was I at seeing, by the side
of a fire half out, a young gentleman in the old
lady's elbow chair, with his legs laid upon
another, fast asleep, and left there by his
thoughtless companions, who had drank him
down and then went off with every one his
mistress, whilst he stayed behind by the courtesy of the old matron, who would not disturb
or turn him out in that condition at one in the
morning, and beds, it is more than probable,
there were none to spare. On the table, still
remained the punch bowl and glasses, strewed
about in their usual disorder after a drunken
revel. But when I drew nearer to view the
sleeping estray, heavens, what a sight! No,
no term of years, no turn of fortune, could ever
erase the lightning-like impression his form
made on me. Yes, dearest object of my earliest
passion, I command forever the remembrance

of thy first appearance to my ravished eyes; it calls thee up at present, and I see thee now!

Figure to yourself, madam, a fair stripling between eighteen and nineteen, with his head reclined on one of the sides of the chair, his hair in disordered curls, irregularly shading a face, on which all the roseate bloom of youth and all the manly graces conspired to fix my eyes and heart; even the languor and paleness of his face, in which the momentary triumph of the lily over the rose was owing to the excesses of the night, gave an inexpressible sweetness to the finest feature imaginable; his eyes, closed in sleep, displayed the meeting edges of their lids beautifully bordered with long eyelashes, over which no pencil could have described two more regular arches than those that graced his forehead, which was high, perfectly white and smooth; then a pair of vermillion lips, pouting and swelling to the touch, as if a bee had freshly stung them, seemed to challenge me to get the gloves of this lovely sleeper had not modesty and respect, which in both sexes are inseparable from a true passion, checked my impulses. But on seeing his shirt collar unbuttoned, and bosom whiter than a drift of snow, the pleasure of considering it could not bribe me to lengthen it, at the hazard of a health that made me timid, taught me to be tender too; with a trembling hand I took hold of one of his, and waking him as gently as possible, he started, and looking at first a little wildly, said, with a voice that sent its harmoni-

ous sound to my heart, "Pray, child, what
o'clock is it?" I told him and added that he
might catch cold if he slept longer with his
breast open in the cool of the morning air.
On this he thanked me with a sweetness perfectly agreeing with that of his features and
eyes, the last now broad open, and eagerly
surveying me, carried the sprightly fires they
sparkled with directly to my heart.

It seemed that having drank too freely before
he came upon the rake with his young companions, he had put himself out of a condition
to go through all the weapons with them, and
crown the night with getting a mistress, so that
seeing me in a loose undress, he did not doubt
that I was one of the misses of the house, sent
in to repair his loss of time, but though he
seized that notion, and a very obvious one it
was, without hesitation, yet, whether my figure
made a more than ordinary impression on him,
or whether it was his natural politeness, he
addressed me in a manner far from rude,
though still on the foot of one of the house
pliers come to amuse him, and giving me the
first kiss that I ever relished from man in
my life, asked me if I could favour him with
my company, assuring me that he would make
it worth my while; but had not even new born
love, that true refiner of lust, opposed so sudden
a surrender, the fear of being surprised by the
house was a sufficient bar to my compliance.
I told him then, in a tone sent me by love itself,
that for reasons I had not time to explain to

him, I could not stay with him, and might not even ever see him again, with a sigh at these last words, which broke from the bottom of my heart. My conqueror, who as he afterwards told me, had been struck with my appearance and liked me as much as he could think of liking any one in my supposed way of life, asked me briskly at once, if I would be kept by him, and that he would take a lodging for me directly, and relieve me from all engagements he presumed I might be under to the house. Rash, sudden, undigested, and even dangerous as this offer might be from a perfect stranger, and that stranger a giddy boy, the prodigious love I was struck with for him, had put a charm into his voice there was no resisting, and blinded me to every objection; I could, at that instant have died for him; think if I could resist an invitation to live with him! Thus my heart, beating strong to the proposal, dictated my answer, after scarce a minute's pause, that I would accept his offer, and make my escape in what way he pleased and that I would be entirely at his disposal, let it be good or bad. I have often since wondered that so great an easiness did not disgust him or make me too cheap in his eyes, but my fate had so appointed it, that in his fears of the hazard of the town, he had been some time looking out for a girl to take into keeping, and my person happening to hit his fancy, it was by one of those miracles reserved to love, that we struck the bargain in the instant, which we sealed by an exchange of kisses, that the hopes of a more uninterrupted enjoyment engaged him to content himself with.

Never, however, did dear youth carry in his head more wherewith to justify the turning of a girl's head, and making her set all consequences at defiance, for the sake of following a gallant. For, besides all the perfections of manly beauty which were assembled in his form, he had an air of neatness and gentility, a certain smartness in the carriage and port of his head that more distinguished him; his eyes were sprightly and full of meaning, his looks had in them something at once sweet and commanding; his complexion out bloomed the lovely coloured rose, whilst its inimitable tender vivid glow clearly saved it from the reproach of wanting life, of raw and dough-like, which is commonly made to those so extremely fair as he was. Our little plan was that I should get out about seven the next morning, which I could readily promise, as I knew where to get the key of the street door, and he would wait at the end of the street with a coach to convey me safe off, after which, he would send and clear any debt incurred by my stay at Mrs. Brown's, who, he only judged, in gross, might not care to part with one, he thought, so fit to draw custom to the house. I then just hinted to him not to mention in the house his having seen such a person as me, for reasons I would explain to him more at leisure. And then, for fear of miscarrying, by being seen together, I tore myself from him with a bleeding heart, and stole up softly to my room, where I found Phoebe still fast asleep, and hurrying off my few clothes, lay down by her, with a mixture of joy and anxiety, that may be easier conceived than expressed.

The risks of Mrs. Brown discovering my purpose, of disappointment, misery, ruin, all vanished before this new kindled flame. The seeing, the touching, the being if but for a night with this idol of my fond virgin heart, appeared to me a happiness above the purchase of my liberty or life. He might use me ill, let him, he was the master; happy, too happy, even to receive death at so dear a hand. To this purpose were the reflections of the whole day, of which every minute seemed to me a little eternity. How often did I visit the clock, nay, was tempted to advance the tedious hand, as if that would have advanced the time with it! Had those of the house made the least observations of me, they must have remarked something extraordinary from the discomposure I could not help betraying, especially when at dinner mention was made of the charmingest youth having been there and stayed to breakfast. "Oh, he was such a beauty! I should have died for him! they would pull caps for him!" and the like fooleries, which, however, was throwing oil on a fire I was sorely put to it to smother the blaze of.

The functions of my mind, the whole day, produced one good effect, which was, that, through mere fatigue I slept tolerably well till five in the morning, when I got up, and having

dressed myself, waited, under the double
tortures of fear and impatience, for the appointed hour. It came at last, the dear, critical,
dangerous hour came; and now, supported only
by the courage love lent me, I ventured, a tip-
toe, down stairs, leaving my box behind, for
fear of being surprised with it in going out. I
got to the street door, the key whereof was
always laid on the chair by our bed side, in
trust with Phoebe, who having not the least
suspicion of my entertaining any design to go
from them, nor, indeed, had I but the day before, made no reserve or concealment of it from
me. I opened the door with great ease; love,
that emboldened, protected me too; and now,
got safe into the street, I saw my new guardian
angel waiting at a coach door, ready open. How
I got to him I know not; I suppose I flew; but I
was in the coach in a trice, and he by the side
of me, with his arms clasped round me, and
giving me the kiss of welcome. The coachman
had his orders and drove to them. My eyes
were instantly filled with tears, but tears of the
most delicious delight, for to find myself in the
arms of that beauteous youth, was a rapture
that my little heart swam in; past or future
were equally out of the question with me; the
present was as much as my powers of life were
sufficient to bear the transport of without fainting. Nor were the most tender embraces, the
most soothing expressions wanting on his side,
to assure me of his love, and of never giving
me cause to repent the bold step I had taken in

throwing myself thus entirely upon his honour
and generosity. But, alas, this was no merit
in me, for I was drove to it by a passion too
impetuous for me to resist, and I did what I did
because I could not help it.

In an instant, for time was now annihilated
with me, we were landed at a public house in
Chelsea, hospitably commodious for the reception of duet parties of pleasure, where a
breakfast of chocolate was prepared for us.
An old jolly stager, who kept it, and understood life perfectly well, breakfasted with us,
and leering archly at me, gave us both joy, and
said, "we were well paired, i' faith! that a
great many gentlemen and ladies used his
house, but he had never seen a handsomer
couple; he was sure I was a fresh piece; I looked
so country, so innocent, well, my spouse was a
lucky man!" all which, common landlord's cant,
not only pleased and soothed me, but helped to
divert my confusion at being with my new
sovereign, whom, now the minute approached,
I began to fear to be alone with; a timidity
which true love had a greater share in than
maiden bashfulness. I wished, I doated, I could
have died for him; and yet, I know not how,
or why, I dreaded that point which had been
the object of my fiercest wishes; my pulses beat
fears, amidst a flush of the warmest desires.
This struggle of the passions, however, this
conflict between modesty and love sick longings,
made me burst into tears, which he took, as he
had done before, only for the remains of con-

cern and emotion at the suddenness of my change of condition, in committing myself to his care, and, in consequence of that idea, did and said all that he thought would most comfort and reinspirit me.

After breakfast, Charles, the dear familiar name I must take the liberty henceforward to distinguish my Adonis by, with a smile full of meaning, took me gently by the hand, and said: "Come, my dear, I will show you a room that commands a fine prospect over some gardens;" and without waiting for an answer, in which he relieved me extremely, he led me up in a chamber, airy and lightsome, where all seeing of prospects was out of the question, except that of a bed, which had all the air of recommending the room to him. Charles had just slipped the bolt of the door, and running, caught me in his arms, and lifting me from the ground, with his lips glued to mine, bore me, trembling, panting, dying, with soft fears and tender wishes, to the bed; where his impatience would not suffer him to undress me, more than just un-pinning my handkerchief and gown and un-lacing my stays. My bosom was now bare, and rising in the warmest throbs, presented to his sight and feeling the firm hard swell of a pair of young breasts, such as may be imagined of a girl not sixteen, fresh out of the country, and never before handled; but even their pride, whiteness, fashion, pleasing resistance to the touch, could not bribe his restless hands from roving, but, giving them the loose, my petticoats and shift were soon taken up, and their stronger center of attraction laid open to their tender invasion. My fears, however, made me mechanically close my thighs; but the very touch of his hand inserted between them, unclosed them and opened a way for the main attack. In the mean time, I lay fairly exposed to the examination of his eyes and hands, quiet and unresisting, which confirmed him in the opinion he proceeded so cavalierly upon, that I was no novice in these matters, since he had taken me out of a common bawdy house, nor had I said one thing to inform him of my virginity, and if I had, he would sooner have believed that I took him for a cully that would swallow such an improbability, than that I was still mistress of that darling treasure, that hidden mine so eagerly sought after by the men, and which they never dig for but to destroy.

Being now too high wound up to bear a delay, he unbuttoned, and drawing out his engine of love assaults, drove it currently, as at a ready made breach. Then, for the first time did I feel that stiff horn-hard gristle, battering against the tender part; but imagine to yourself his surprise, when he found, after several vigorous pushes, which hurt me extremely, that he made not the least impression. I complained, but tenderly complained: "I could not bear it, indeed he hurt me!" Still he thought no more, than that being so young, the largeness of his machine, for few men could dispute with him, made all the difficulty, and that possibly I had not been enjoyed by any so advantageously made in that part as himself; for still, that my virgin flower was yet uncropped, never entered into his head, and he would have thought it idling with time and words to have questioned me upon it. He tries again, still no admittance, still no penetration, but he had hurt me yet more, whilst my extreme love made me bear extreme pain, almost without a groan. At length, after repeated fruitless trials, he lay down panting by me, kissed my falling tears, and asked me tenderly "what was the meaning of so much complaining, and if I had not borne it better from others than I did from him?" I answered, with a simplicity framed to persuade, that he was the first man that ever served me so. Truth is powerful, and it is not always that we do not believe what we eagerly wish. Charles, already disposed by the evidence of his senses to think my pretenses to virginity not entirely apocryphal, smothers me with kisses, begs me in the name of love to have a little patience and that he will be as tender of hurting me as he would of himself. Alas, it was enough I knew his pleasure to submit joyfully to him, whatever pain I foresaw it would cost me!

He now resumes his attempts in more form; first he put one of the pillows under me to give the blank of his aim a more favourable elevation, and another one under my head, in ease of it; then spreading my thighs, and placing himself standing between them, made them rest upon his hips; applying then, the point of his machine to the slit, into which he sought entrance, it was so small, he could scarce assure himself of its being rightly pointed. He looks, he feels, and satisfies himself, then driving on with fury, its prodigious stiffness, thus impacted, wedge-like, breaks the union of these parts, and gained him just the insertion of the tip of it, lip deep; which being sensible of, he improved his advantage, and following well his stroke, in a straight line, forcibly deepens his penetration, but put me to such intolerable pain, from the separation of the sides of that soft passage by a hard thick body I could have screamed out, but as I was unwilling to alarm the house, I held my breath, and crammed my petticoat, which was turned over my face, into my mouth and bit it through in the agony. At length, the tender texture of that tract giving way to such fierce tearing and rending, he pierced something further into me, and now, outrageous and no longer his own master, but borne headlong away by the fury and over mettle of that member, now exerting itself with a kind of native rage, he breaks in, carries all before him, and one violent, merciless lunge, sent it, imbrued and reeking with virgin blood, up to the very hilt in me. Then, then all my resolution deserted me; I screamed out, and fainted away with the sharpness of the pain, and, as he told me afterwards, on his drawing out when emission was over with him, my thighs were instantly all in a stream of blood, that flowed from the wounded passage.

When I recovered my senses, I found myself
undressed and a-bed, in the arms of the sweet
relenting murderer of my virginity, who hung
mourning tenderly over me, and holding in his
hand a cordial, which coming from the still dear
author of so much pain, I could not refuse; my
eyes, however, moistened with tears, and
languishingly turned upon him, seemed to reproach him with his cruelty, and asked him, if
such were the rewards of love. But Charles,
to whom I was now infinitely endeared by his
complete triumph over a maidenhead, where he
so little expected to find one, in tenderness to
that pain which he had put me to, in procuring
himself the height of pleasure, smothered his
exultation and employed himself with so much
sweetness, so much warmth, to soothe, to caress,
and comfort me in my soft complainings, which
breathed, indeed, more love than resentment,
that I presently drowned all sense of pain in the
pleasure of seeing him, of thinking that I belonged to him, he who was now the absolute
disposer of my happiness, and, in one word, my
fate. The sore was, however, too tender, the
wound too bleeding fresh, for Charles' good
nature to put my patience presently to another
trial, but as I could not stir, or walk across the
room, he ordered the dinner to be brought to
the bedside, where it could not be otherwise
than my getting down the wing of a fowl and
two or three glasses of wine, since it was my
adored youth who both served and urged them

on me, with that sweet irresistible authority
with which love had invested him over me.

After dinner and everything but the wine
was taken away, Charles very impudently asks
a leave, he might read the grant in my eyes, to
come to bed to me, and accordingly falls to undressing, which I could not see the progress of
without strange emotions of fear and pleasure.
He is now in bed with me the first time, and
in broad day; but when thrusting up his own
shirt and my shift, he laid his naked glowing
body to mine, oh, insupportable delight! oh,
superhuman rapture! what pain could stand
before a pleasure so transporting? I felt no
more the smart of my wounds below, but curling round him like the tendril of a vine, as if
I feared any part of him should be untouched
or unpressed by me, I returned his strenuous
embraces and kisses with a fervour and gust
only known to true love, and which mere lust
could never rise to. Yes, even at this time,
when all the tyranny of the passions is fully
over, and when my veins roll no longer but a
cold tranquil stream the remembrance of those
passages that most affected me in my youth,
still cheers and refreshes me; let me proceed.
My beauteous youth was now glued to me in
all the folds and twists that we could make our
bodies meet in; when, no longer able to rein in
the fierceness of refreshed desires, he gives his
steed the head and gently inserting his thighs
between mine, stopping my mouth with kisses
of human fire, makes a fresh eruption, and re-

newing his thrusts, pierces, tears, and forces
his way up the torn tender folds, that yielded
him admission with a smart little less severe
than when the breach was first made. I stifled,
however, my cries and bore him with the passive
fortitude of an heroine; soon his thrusts, more
and more furious, cheeks flushed with a deeper
scarlet, his eyes turned up in the fervent fit,
some dying sighs, and an agonizing shudder
announced the approaches of that ecstatic
pleasure I was yet in too much pain to come in
for my share of.

Nor was it till after a few enjoyments had
numbed and blunted the sense of the smart,
and given to me to feel the titillating inspersion
of balsamic sweets, drew from me the delicious
return, and brought down all my passion, that
I arrived at excess of pleasure through excess
of pain. But, when successive engagements
had broke and inured me, I began to enter into
the true unalloyed relish of that pleasure of
pleasures, when the warm gush darts through
all the ravished inwards; what floods of bliss!
what melting transports! what agonies of delight! too fierce, too mighty for nature to
sustain! well has she therefore, no doubt, provided the relief of a delicious momentary dissolution, the approaches of which are inti-
mated by a dear delirium, a sweet thrill, on the
point of emitting those liquid sweets, in which
enjoyment itself is drowned, when one gives
the languishing stretch out, and dies at the
discharge. How often, when the rage and

tumult of my senses had subsided, after the
melting flow, have I in a tender meditation,
asked myself coolly the question, if it was in
nature for any of its creatures to be so happy
as I was? Or, what were all fears of the consequences, put in the scale of one night's enjoyment, of anything so transcendently the
taste of my eyes and heart, as that delicious,
fond, matchless youth?

Thus we spent the whole afternoon till
supper time in a continued circle of love delights, kissing, turtle-billing, toying, and all the
rest of the feast. At length, supper was served
in, before which Charles had, for I know not
what reason, slipped his clothes on, and sitting
down by the bed side, we made table cloth of
the bed and sheets, whilst he suffered nobody
to attend or serve but himself. He ate with a
very good appetite and seemed charmed to see
me eat. For my part, I was so transported with
the comparison of the delights I now swam in
with the insipidity of all my past scenes of life
that I thought them sufficiently cheap at even
the price of my ruin, or the risk of their not
lasting. The present possession was all my
little head could find room for. We lay together
that night, when, after playing repeated prizes
of pleasure, nature, overspent and satisfied,
gave us up to the arms of sleep; those of my
dear youth encircled me, the consciousness of
which made even that sleep more delicious.

Late in the morning I waked first, and observing my lover slept profoundly, softly dis-

engaged myself from his arms, scarcely daring
to breathe for fear of shortening his repose;
my cap, my hair, my shift, were all in disorder,
from the rufflings I had undergone, and I took
this opportunity to adjust and set them as well
as I could, whilst, every now and then, looking
at the sleeping youth, with inconceivable fondness and delight, and reflections on all the pain
he had put me to, tacitly owned that the pleasure
had overpaid me for my sufferings. It was then
broad day. I was sitting up in bed, the clothes
of which were all tossed, or rolled off by the
unquietness of our motions or from the sultry
heat of the weather, nor could I refuse myself
a pleasure that solicited me so irresistibly, as
this fair occasion of feasting my sight with all
those treasures of youthful beauty I had enjoyed and which lay now entirely naked, his
shirt being trussed up in a perfect wisp, which
the warmth of the season and room made me
easy about the consequence of. I hung over
him enamoured indeed, and devoured all his
naked charms with only two eyes, when I could
have wished them at least an hundred, for the
fuller enjoyment of the gaze.

Oh, could I paint his figure as I see it now,
still present to my transported imagination! a
whole length of an all-perfect manly beauty in
full view. Think of a face without a fault,
glowing with all the opening bloom and verdant
freshness of an age, in which beauty is of either
sex, and which the first down over his upper
lip scarce began to distinguish. The parting

of the double ruby pout of his lips seemed to
exhale an air sweeter and purer than what it
drew in; ah, what violence did it not cost me
to refrain the so tempted kiss! Then a neck
exquisitely turned, graced behind and on the
sides with his hair, playing freely in natural
ringlets, connected his head to a body of the
most perfect form, and of the most vigorous
contexture, in which all the strength of manhood was concealed and softened to appearance
by the delicacy of his complexion, the smooth-
ness of his skin and the plumpness of his flesh.
The platform of his snow white bosom, which
was laid out in manly fashion, presented on the
vermillion summit of each pap, the idea of a
rose about to blow. Nor did his shirt hinder
me from observing that symmetry of his limbs,
that exactness of shape, in the fall of it towards
the loins, where the waist ends and the rounding
swell of the hips commences; where the skin,
sleek, smooth, and dazzling white; burnishes on
the stretch-over firm, plump, ripe flesh, that
crimped and ran into dimples at the least
pressure, or that the touch could not rest upon,
but slid over as on the surface of the most
polished ivory. His thighs, finely fashioned
and with a florid glossy roundness, gradually
tapering away to the knees, seemed pillars
worthy to support that beauteous frame, at the
bottom of which I could not, without some remains of terror, some tender emotions too, fix
my eyes on that terrible machine, which had not
long before with such fury broke into, torn

and almost ruined those soft, tender parts of
mine, that had not done smarting with the
effects of its rage; but behold it now, crest
fallen, reclining its half capped vermillion head
over one of his thighs, quiet, pliant, and to all
appearance incapable of the mischiefs and
cruelty it had committed. Then the beautiful
growth of the hair, in short and soft curls
round its roots, its whiteness, branched veins,
the supple softness of the shaft, as it lay fore-
shortened, rolled and shrunk up into a squab
thickness, languid and borne up from between
his thighs, by its globular appendage, that
wondrous treasure bag of nature's sweets,
which lay revealed round, and pursed up in the
only wrinkles that are known to please, per-
fected the prospect and altogether formed the
most interesting moving picture in nature, and
surely infinitely superior to those nudities
furnished by the painters, statuaries, or any
art, which are purchased at immense prices,
whilst the sight of them in actual life is scarce
sovereignly tasted by any but the few whom
nature has endowed with a fire of imagination,
warmly pointed by a truth of judgment to the
spring head, the originals of beauty, of nature's
unequaled composition, above all the imitations
of art or the reach of wealth to pay their price.

But everything must have an end. A motion
made by this angelic youth in the listlessness of
going-off sleep, replaced his shirt and the bed
clothes in a posture that shut up that treasury
from longer view. I lay down then, and carry-

ing my hands to that part of me in which the
objects just seen had begun to raise a mutiny,
that prevailed over the smart of them, my
fingers now opened themselves an easy passage;
but long I had not time to consider the wide
difference there, between the maid and the now
finished woman, before Charles waked and
turning towards me kindly enquired how I had
rested, and, scarce giving me time to answer,
imprinted on my lips one of his burning kisses,
which darted a flame to my heart, that from
thence radiated to every part of me; and
presently, as if he had proudly meant revenge
for the survey I had smuggled of all his naked
beauties, he spurns off the bed clothes and
trussing up my shift as high as it would go,
took his turn to feast his eyes on all the gifts
nature had bestowed on my person, his busy
hands also ranged intemperately over every
part of me. The delicious austerity and hardness of my yet unripe budding breasts, the
whiteness and firmness of my flesh, and the
freshness and regularity of my features, the
harmony of my limbs, all seemed to confirm
him in his satisfaction with his bargain; but
when curious to explore the havoc he had made
in the center of his overfierce attack, he not only
directed his hands there, but with a pillow put
under, placed me favourably for his wanton
purpose of inspection. Then, who can express
the fire his eyes glistened and his hands glowed
with, whilst sighs of pleasure and tender broken
exclamations were all the praises he could utter.

By this time his machine, stiffly risen at me, gave me to see it in its highest state and bravery. He feels it himself, seems pleased at its condition, and smiling loves and graces seizes one of my hands and carries it with a gentle compulsion to this pride of nature and its richest masterpiece. I, struggling faintly, could not help feeling what I could not grasp, a column of the whitest ivory, beautifully streaked with blue veins, and carrying, fully uncapped, a head of the liveliest vermillion; no horn could be harder or stiffer, yet no velvet more smooth or delicious to the touch. Presently he guided my hand lower, to that part in which nature and pleasure keep their stores in concert, so aptly fastened and hung onto the root of their first instrument and minister that might not improperly be styled their purse bearer too; there he made me feel distinctly through their cover the contents, a pair of roundish balls that seemed to play within, and elude all pressure, but the tenderest from without.

But now, this visit of my soft warm hand, in those so sensitive parts had put every thing into such ungovernable fury, that disdaining all further preluding and taking advantage of my commodious posture, he made the storm fall where I scarce patiently expected, and where he was sure to lay it; presently, then, I felt the stiff intersection between the yielding, divided lips of the wound now open for life, where the narrowness no longer put me to intolerable pain and afforded my lover no more

difficulty than what heightened his pleas in the
strict embrace of that tender, warm sheath,
round the instrument it was so delicately adjusted to, and which now cased home, so gorged
me with pleasure that it perfectly suffocated
me and took away my breath; then the killing
thrusts, the unnumbered kisses every one of
which was a joy inexpressible, and that joy lost
in a crowd of yet greater blisses! But this
was a disorder too violent in nature to last long;
the vessels so stirred and intensely heated, soon
boiled over, and for that time put out the fire;
meanwhile all this dalliance and sport had so
far consumed the morning, that it became a
kind of necessity to lay breakfast and dinner
into one.

In our calmer intervals Charles gave the
following account of himself, every title of
which was true. He was the only son of a
father, who, having a small post in the revenue,
rather overlived his income, and had given this
young gentleman a very slender education; no
profession had he bred him up to, but designed
to provide for him in the army, by purchasing
him an ensign's commission, that is to say,
provided he could raise the money, or procure
it by interest, either of which clauses was rather
to be wished than hoped for by him. On not
better a plan, however, had this improvident
father suffered this youth, a youth of great
promise, to run up to the age of manhood, or
near it at least, in next to idleness; and had,
besides, taken no sort of pains to give him even

the common premonitions against the vices of
the town, and the dangers of all sorts which
wait the unexperienced and unwary in it. He
lived at home, and at discretion with his father,
who himself kept a mistress, and for the rest,
provided Charles did not ask him for money,
he was indolently kind to him; he might lie out
when he pleased, an excuse would serve, and
even his reprimands were so slight, that they
carried with them rather an air of connivance
at the fault, than any serious control or constraint.   But, to supply his calls for money,
Charles, whose mother was dead, had, by her
side, a grandmother who doted upon him. She
had a considerable annuity to live on and very
regularly parted with every shilling she could
spare to this darling of hers, to the no little
heart-burn of his father who was vexed, not
that she by this means fed his son's extrava-
gance, but that she preferred Charles to himself and we shall soon see what a fatal turn
such a mercenary jealousy could operate in the
breast of a father.

Charles was, however, by the means of his
grandmother's lavish fondness, very sufficiently
enabled to keep a mistress so easily contented as
my love and good fortune made me, for such I
must ever call that which threw me in his way,
in the manner above related, just as he was on
the lookout for one. As to temper, the even
sweetness of it made him seem born for domestic happiness; tender, naturally polite, and
gentle-mannered; it could never be his fault, if

jars or animosities ruffled a calm he was so
qualified every way to maintain or restore.
Without those great and shining qualities that
constitute a genius, or are fit to make a noise in
the world, he had all those humble ones that
compose the softer social merit; plain common
sense, set off with every grace of modesty and
good nature, made him, if not admired, what is
much happier, universally beloved and esteemed.
But, as nothing but the beauties of his person
had at first attracted my regard and fixed my
passion, neither was I then a judge of that in-
ternal merit, which I afterwards had full occasion to discover, and which, perhaps, in that
season of giddiness and levity, would have
touched my heart very little, had it been lodged
in a person less the delight of my eyes and idol
of my senses. But to return to our situation.

After dinner, which we ate a-bed in the most
voluptuous disorder, Charles got up, and taking
a passionate leave of me for a few hours, he
went to town, where concerting matters with a
sharp, young lawyer, they went together to my
late venerable mistress's, from whence I had
but the day before made my elopement, and
with whom he was determined to settle accounts
in a manner that should cut off all after
reckonings from that quarter. Accordingly
they went, but by the way, the Templar, his
friend, on thinking over Charles' information,
saw reason to give their visit another turn, and,
instead of offering satisfaction, to demand it.
On being let in, the girls of the house flocked

round Charles, whom they knew, and from the
earliness of my escape, and their perfect ignorance of his ever having so much as seen me,
not having the least suspicion of his being
accessory to my flight, they were, in their way,
making up to him, and as for his companion,
they took him probably for a fresh cully. But
the Templar soon checked their forwardness, by
enquiring for the old lady, with whom he said,
with a grave judge-like countenance, that he
had some business to settle. Madam was immediately sent for down, and the ladies being
desired to clear the room, the lawyer asked her
severly if she did not know, or had not decoyed,
under pretense of hiring as a servant, a young
girl, just come out of the country, called
Frances or Fanny Hill, describing me withal
as particularly as he could from Charles description. It is peculiar to vice to tremble at
the enquiries of justice; and Mrs. Brown, whose
conscience was not entirely clear upon my account, as knowing as she was of the town, as
hackneyed as she was in bluffing through all
the dangers of her vocation, could not help
being alarmed at the question, especially when
he went on to talk of a justice of peace, New-
gate, the Old Bailey, indictments for keeping
a disorderly house, pillory, carting, and the
whole process of that nature. She, who, it is
likely, imagined I had lodged an information
against her house, looked extremely blank and
began to make a thousand protestations and
excuses. However, to abridge, they brought

away triumphantly my box of things, which, had she not been under an awe, she might have disputed with them, and not only that, but a clearance and discharge of any demands on the house, at the expense of no more than a bowl of arrack punch, the treat of which, together with the choice of the house conveniences, was offered and not accepted. Charles all the time acted the chance companion of the lawyer, who had brought him there, as he knew the house, and appeared in no wise interested in the issue; but he had the collateral pleasure of hearing all that I had told him verified, so far as the bawd's fears would give her leave to enter into my history, which, if one may guess by the composition she so readily came into, were not small. Phoebe, my kind tutoress Phoebe, was all that time gone out, perhaps in search of me, or their cooked up story had not, it is probably, passed so smoothly.

This negotiation had, however, taken up some time, which would have appeared much longer to me, left, as I was in a strange house, if the landlady, a motherly sort of woman, to whom Charles had liberally recommended me, had not come up and borne me company. We drank tea, and her chat helped to pass away the time very agreeably, since he was our theme; but as the evening deepened, and the hour set for his return was elapsed, I could not dispel the gloom of impatience and tender fears which gathered upon me, and which our timid sex are apt to feel in proportion to their love. Long,

however, I did not suffer; the sight of him
overpaid me, and the soft reproach I had prepared for him, expired before it had reached
my lips. I was still a-bed, yet unable to use my
legs otherwise than awkwardly, and Charles
flew to me, catches me in his arms, raised and
extending mine to meet his dear embrace, and
gave me an account, interrupted by many sweet
parentheses of kisses, of the success of his
measures. I could not help laughing at the
fright the old woman had been put into, which
my ignorance and indeed my want of innocence
had far from prepared me for bespeaking. She
had, it seems, apprehended that I flew for shelter
to some relation I had relocated in town, on my
dislike of their ways and proceedings towards
me, and that this application came from thence,
for, as Charles had rightly judged, not one
neighbour had at that still hour seen the circumstance of my escape into the coach, or at
least, noticed him; neither had any in the house,
the least hint or clue of suspicion of my having
spoke to him, much less of my having clapt up
such a sudden bargain with a perfect stranger;
thus the greatest improbability is not always
what we should most distrust. We supped
with all the gaiety of two young giddy creatures at the top of their pleasures, and as I had
given up to Charles the whole charge of my
future happiness, I thought of nothing beyond
the exquisite pleasure of possessing him. He
came to bed in due time, and this second night,
the pain being pretty well over, I tasted, in full

draughts, all the transports of perfect enjoyment; I swam, I bathed in bliss, till both fell fast asleep through the natural consequences of satisfied desires, and appeased flames; nor did we wake but to renew raptures.

Thus, making the most of love, and life, did we stay in this lodging in Chelsea about ten days, in which time Charles took care to give his excursions from home a favourable gloss, and to keep his footing with his fond indulgent grandparent, from whom he drew constant and sufficient supplies for the charge I was to him, and which was very trifling in comparison with his former less regular course of pleasure. Charles removed me then to a private ready furnished lodging in D. street, St. James', where he paid half a guinea a week for two rooms and a closet on the second floor, which he had been some time looking out for, and was more convenient for the frequency of his visits than where he had at first placed me, in a house, which I cannot say but that I left with regret, as it was infinitely endeared to me by the first possession of my Charles, and the circumstances of losing there, that jewel, which can never be twice lost. The landlord, however, had no reason to complain of anything, but of a procedure in Charles too liberal not to make him regret the loss of us. Arrived at our new lodgings, I remember I thought them extremely fine, though ordinary enough, even at that price; but, had it been a dungeon that Charles brought me to, his presence would have

made it a little Versailles. The landlady, Mrs.
Jones, waited on us to our apartment, and, with
great volubility of tongue, explained to us all its
conveniences: "that her own maid should wait
on us; that the best of quality had lodged at her
house; that her first floor was let to a foreign
secretary of an embassy and his lady; that I
looked like a very good natured lady." At the
word lady I blushed out of flattered vanity;
this was too strong for a girl of my condition,
for though Charles had the precaution of dressing me in a less tawdry, flaunting style than
were the clothes I escaped to him in, and of
passing me for his wife, that he had secretly
married, and kept private (the old story) on
account of his friends, I dare swear this appeared extremely apocryphal to a woman who
knew the town so well as she did, but that was
the least of her concern; it was impossible to
be less scruple-ridden than she was, and the
advantage of letting her rooms being her sole
object, the truth itself would have far from
scandalized her or broke her bargain.

A sketch of her picture and personal history
will dispose you to account for the part she is to
act in my concern. She was about forty-six
years old, tall, meagre, red haired, with one of
those trivial ordinary faces you meet with
everywhere and go about unheeded and un-
mentioned. In her youth she had been kept
by a gentleman, who, dying, left her forty
pounds a year during her life, in consideration
of a daughter he had by her, which daughter

at the age of seventeen she sold, for not a very considerable sum neither, to a gentleman who was going an envoy abroad, and took his purchase with him where he used her with the utmost tenderness, and, it is thought, was secretly married to her, but had constantly made a point of her not keeping up the least correspondence with a mother base enough to make a market of her own flesh and blood. However, as she had no nature, nor, indeed, any passion but that of money, this gave her no further uneasiness except that she thereby lost a handle of squeezing presents or other after advantages out of the bargain. Indifferent then, by nature of constitution, to every other pleasure but that of increasing the lump, by any means whatever, she began as a kind of private procuress, for which she was not amiss fitted by her grave, decent appearance, and sometimes did a job in the match making way; in short, there was nothing that appeared to her under the shape of gain, that she would not have undertaken. She knew most of the ways of the town, having not only herself been upon, but kept up constant intelligences in promoting a harmony between the two sexes, in private pawn-broking and other profitable secrets. She rented the house she lived in and made the most of it by letting it out in lodgings; though she was worth at least near three or four thousand pounds, she would not allow herself even the necessities of life, and pinned her subsistence entirely on what she could squeeze out of her lodgers. When she saw such a young pair come under her roof, her immediate notions, doubtless, were how she should make the most money of us, by every means that money might be made, and which, she rightly judged our situation and inexperience would soon beget her occasions of.

In this hopeful sanctuary, and under the clutches of this harpy, did we pitch our residence. It will not be mighty material to you, or very pleasant to me to enter into a detail of all the petty cut-throat ways and means with which she used to fleece us, all which Charles indolently chose to bear with rather than take the trouble of removing, the difference of expense being scarce attended to by a young gentleman who had no ideas of stint, or even economy, and a raw country girl who knew nothing of the matter. Here, however, under the wings of my sovereignly beloved, did the most delicious hours of my life flow on; my Charles I had, and, in him, everything my fond heart could wish or desire. He carried me to plays, operas, masquerades, and every diversion of the town, all which pleased me, indeed, but pleased me infinitely the more for his being with me and explaining everything to me, and enjoying perhaps the natural impressions of surprise and admiration which such sights, at the first, never fail to excite in a country girl, new to the delights of them; but to me, they sensibly proved the power and domination of the sole passion of my heart over me, a passion in which soul and body were concentrated and left me no room for any other relish of life but love. As to the men I saw at those places, they suffered so much in the comparison my eyes made of them with my all perfect Adonis, that I had not the infidelity even of one wandering thought to reproach myself with upon his account. He was the universe to me and all that was not him was nothing to me.

My love, in fine, was so excessive, that it arrived at annihilating every suggestion or kindling spark of jealousy, for one idea only, tending that way, gave me such exquisite torment, that my self-love and dread of worse than death, made me forever renounce and defy it; nor had I, indeed, occasion, for were I to enter here on the recital of several instances wherein Charles sacrificed to me women of much greater importance than I dare hint, which considering his form, was no such wonder, I might, indeed, give you full proof of his unshaken constancy to me, but would not you accuse me of warming up a feast which my vanity ought long ago to have been satisfied with?

In our cessations from active pleasure, Charles framed himself one in instructing me, as far as his own lights reached, in a great many points of life, that I was in cansequence of no education, perfectly ignorant of, nor did I suffer one word to fall in vain from the mouth of my lovely teacher; I hung on every syllable he uttered, and received, as oracles all he said,

whilst kisses were all the interruption I could
not refuse myself the pleasure of admitting,
from lips that breathed more than Arabian
sweetness. I was in a little time enabled by the
progress I had made to prove the deep regard
I had paid to all he had said to me, repeating
it to him almost word for word, and to show
that I was not entirely the parrot, but that I
reflected upon and entered into it, I joined my
own comments and asked him questions of explanation. My country accent and the rusticity
of my gait, manners and deportment began
now sensibly to wear off, so quick was my observation and so efficacious my desire of growing every day worthier of his heart.

As to money, though he brought me constantly all he received, it was with difficulty he even
got me to give it room in my bureau, and what
clothes I had, he could prevail on me to accept
of no other return than that of pleasing him
by the greater neatness in my dress, beyond
which I had no ambition. I could have made a
pleasure of the greatest toil and worked my
fingers to the bone with joy to have supported
him, guess, then, if I could harbour any idea
of being burthensome to him; and this dis-
interested turn in me was so unaffected, so
much the dictate of my heart, that Charles
could not but feel it, and if he did not love me
as much as I did him, which was the constant
and only matter of sweet contention between
us, he managed so at least as to give me the
satisfaction of believing it impossible for man

to be more tender, more true, more faithful than he was.

Our landlady, Mrs. Jones, came frequently up to our apartment, from whence I never stirred on any pretext without Charles, nor was it long before she wormed out, without much art, the secret of our having cheated the church of a ceremony, and, in course, of the terms we lived together upon, a circumstance which far from displeased her, considering the designs she had upon me and which, alas, she will have too soon room to carry into execution! But in the mean time her own experience of life let her see that any attempt, however indirect or disguised, to divert or break, at least presently, so strong a cement of hearts as ours was, could only end in losing two lodgers, of whom she had made very competent advantages, if either of us came to smoke her commission, for a commission she had from one of her customers, either to debauch or get me away from my keeper at any rate. But the barbarity of my fate soon saved her the task of disuniting us. I had now been eleven months with this part of my life, which had passed in one continued rapid stream of delight; but nothing so violent was ever made to last. I was about three months gone with child by him, a circumstance which would have added to his tenderness, had he ever left me room to believe it could receive an addition, when the mortal, the unexpected blow of separation fell upon us. I shall gallop past over the particulars,

which I shudder yet to think of and cannot to
this instant reconcile myself how, or by what
means I could out-live it.

Two livelong days had I lingered through
without hearing from him, I who breathed,
who existed but in him, and had never yet seen
twenty-four hours pass without seeing or hearing from him. The third day my impatience
was so strong, my alarms had been so severe,
that I perfectly sickened with them, and being
unable to support the shock longer, I sunk upon
the bed, and ringing for Mrs. Jones, who had
far from comforted me under my anxieties, she
came up, and I had scarce breath and spirit
enough to find words to beg of her if she would
save my life to fall upon some means of finding
out instantly what was become of its only prop
and comfort. She pitied me in a way that
rather sharpened my affliction than suspended it
and went out upon this commission. For she
had but to go to Charles' house, who lived but
an easy distance, in one of the streets that run
into Covent Garden. There she went into a
public house and from thence sent for a maid
servant, whose name I had given her as the
best one to inform her. The maid readily
came, and as readily, when Mrs. Jones inquired
of her what had become of Mr. Charles, or
whether he was gone out of town, acquainted
her with the disposal of her master's son,
which the very day after was no secret to the
servant. Such sure measures had he taken,
for the most cruel punishment of his child for

having more interest with his grandmother than he had, though he made use of a pretence, plausible enough to get rid of him in this secretly abrupt manner, for fear her fondness should have interposed a bar to his leaving England and proceeding on a voyage he had conceived for him; which pretext was, that it was indispensably necessary to secure a considerable inheritance that was left to him by a rich merchant, his own brother, at one of the factories in the South Seas, of which he had lately received advice, together with a copy of the will. In consequence of which resolution to send away his son, he had unknown to him, made the necessary preparations for fitting him out, struck a bargain with the captain of a ship whose punctual execution of his orders he had secured by his interest with his principal owners, and, in short, planned his scheme so secretly and effectually, that whilst his son thought he was going down the river, which would only take a few hours, he was held on board ship, kept from writing and watched more carefully than a state criminal. Thus was the idol of my soul torn from me and forced on a long voyage without taking leave of one friend or receiving one line of comfort, except a dry explanation and instructions from his father how to proceed when he should arrive at his destined port, enclosing withal, some letters of recommendation to a factor there; all these particulars I did not learn minutely till some time after. The maid at the same time added that she was sure this usage of her sweet young master would be the death of his grandmother, and indeed it proved true, for the old lady, hearing it, did not survive the news a whole month, and as her fortune consisted in an annuity, out of which she had laid up no reserves, she left nothing worth mentioning to her so fatally envièd darling, but absolutely refused to see his father before she died.

When Mrs. Jones returned, and I observed her looks, they seemed so unconcerned and even pleased that I flattered myself she was going to set my tortured heart at ease by bringing me good news, but this indeed was a cruel delusion of hope; the barbarian with all the coolness imaginable, stabbed me to the heart, by telling me easily that he was sent away on at least a four years' voyage, here she stretched maliciously, and said that I need not expect to see him again; this with such pregnant circumstances I could not help but give credit to, and they were indeed, too true.

She had hardly finished her report before I fainted away, and after several successive fits, all the while wild and senseless, I miscarried of the dear pledge of my Charles' love; but the wretched never die and women are hard-lived to a proverb. The cruel and interested care taken to make me recover, saved an odious life, which, instead of the happiness and joys it had overflowed in, all of a sudden presented no view before me of anything but the depth of misery, horror, and the sharpest affliction.

Thus I lay six weeks in the struggle of youth
and constitution against the friendly efforts of
death, which I constantly invoked to my relief
and deliverance, but which proved too weak for
my wish. I recovered at length, but into a
state of stupefaction and despair that threatened
me with the loss of my senses, and a mad house.
Time, however, that great comforter usually,
began to assuage the violence of my suffering
and to numb my feeling of them. My health
returned to me, though I still retained an air
of grief, dejection and languor, which took off
the ruddiness of my country complexion and
rendered it rather more delicate and affecting.

The landlady had all this while officiously
provided and seen that I wanted for nothing,
and as soon as she saw me revived into a condition of answering her purpose, one day, after
we had dined together, she congratulated me on
my recovery, the merit of which she took
entirely to herself, and with this led up to an
introduction of a most terrible and scurvy
epilogue: "You are now," says she, "Miss
Fanny, tolerably well, and you are very welcome to stay in these lodgings as long as you
please; you see I have asked you for nothing
this long time, but truly I have a call to make
up a sum of money which must be answered."
And with that presents me with a bill of arrears
for rent, diet, apothecaries' charges, nurse, etc.,
a sum total of twenty-three pounds, seventeen
and six-pence, towards discharging which I
had nothing in the world, which she well knew,

more than seven guineas, left by chance of my dear Charles' common stock with me. At the same time she desired me to tell her what course I would take for payment. I burst out into a flood of tears, and told her my condition; that I would sell what few clothes I had, and that for the rest, I would pay her as soon as possible. But my distress, being favourable to her views, only stiffened her the more. She told me very coolly that, "she was indeed sorry for my misfortunes, but that she must do herself justice, though it would go to the very heart of her to send such a tender young creature to prison." At the word prison every drop of blood chilled and my fright acted so strongly upon me, that, turning as pale and faint as a criminal at the first sight of his place of execution, I nearly swooned away. My landlady, who wanted only to terrify me to a certain point and not to throw me into a state of mind inconsistent with her designs, began to soothe me again and told me in a tone composed to more gentleness and pity, that "it would be my own fault if she were forced to proceed to such extremities, but that she believed there was a friend to be found in the world who would make up matters to both our satisfactions and that she would bring him to drink tea with us that very afternoon, when she hoped we would come to a right understanding in our affairs." To all this I sat mute, confounded, terrified, with not a word of answer.

Mrs. Jones, however, judging rightly that it

was time to strike while the impressions were
so strong upon me, left me to myself and to
all the terrors of an imagination, wounded to
death by the idea of going to prison, and,
from a principle of self-preservation, snatching at every glimpse of redemption from it. In
this situation I sat near half an hour, swallowed
up in grief and despair, when my landlady came
in and observing a death-like dejection in my
countenance, still in pursuance of her plan, put
on a false pity and bidding me be of good heart.
Things, she said, would not be so bad as I
imagined, if I would be but my own friend,
and ended by telling me she had brought a very
honourable gentleman to drink tea with me,
who would give me the best advice how to get
rid of all my troubles, upon which, without
waiting for a reply, she goes out and returns
with this very honourable gentleman, whose
very honourable procuress she had been on this
as well as other occasions. This gentleman, on
his entering the room made me a very civil
bow, which I had scarce strength or presence
of mind enough to return a courtesy to, when
the landlady, taking upon herself to do all the
honours of the first interview, for I had never
that I remember seen the gentleman before,
set a chair for him and another for herself.
All this while not a word on either side; a
stupid stare was all the face I could put on this
strange visit.

The tea was made and the landlady, unwilling
I suppose to lose any time, observing my silence

and shyness before this entire stranger:
"Come, Miss Fanny," says she, in a course
familiar style and tone of authority, "hold up
your head, child, and do not let sorrow spoil
that pretty face of yours. What, sorrows are
only for a time; come, be free, here is a worthy
gentleman who has heard of your misfortunes
and is willing to serve you; you must be better
acquainted with him, do not you now stand
upon that punctilio, and this and that, but make
your market while you may." At this so
delicate and eloquent harangue, the gentleman,
who saw I looked frightened and amazed, and,
indeed incapable of answering, took her up for
breakfast things in so abrupt a manner, as
rather to shock than incline me to an acceptance
of the good he intended me; then, addressing
himself to me, told me "he was perfectly acquainted with my whole story and every circumstance of my distress, which he owned was a
cruel plunge for one of my youth and beauty
to fall into; that he had long taken a liking to
my person, for which he appealed to Mrs. Jones,
there present; but finding me so deeply engaged
to another he had lost all hopes of succeeding
till he had heard the sudden reverse of fortune
that had happened to me, on which he had given
particular orders to my landlady to see that I
should want for nothing; and that, had he not
been forced abroad to the Hague on affairs he
could not refuse he would himself have attended
me during my sickness; that on his return,
which was but the day before, he had on learn-

ing of my recovery, desired my landlady's good offices to introduce him to me, and was as angry as I was shocked at the manner in which she had conducted herself towards obtaining him that happiness; but, that to show me how much he disdained her procedure, and how far he was from taking any ungenerous advantage of my situation or from extracting any security for my gratitude, he would before my face, that instant, discharge my debt entirely to my land-lady and give me her receipt in full; after which I should be at liberty either to reject or grant his suit, as he was much above putting any force upon my inclinations."

While he was exposing his sentiments to me I ventured just to look up to him, and observed his figure, which was that of a very good look-ing gentleman, well made, of about forty, dressed in a suit of plain clothes, with a large diamond ring on one of his fingers, the lustre of which played in my eyes as he waved his hand in talking, and raised my notions of his importance. In short, he might pass for what is commonly called a comely black man, with an air of distinction natural to his birth and con-dition. To all his speeches, however, I answered only in tears that flowed plentifully to my relief, and choking up my voice, excused me from speaking, very luckily, for I should not have known what to say. The sight, how-ever, moved him as he afterwards told me, irresistibly, and by way of giving me some reason to be less powerfully afflicted he drew

out his purse and calling for pen and ink, which
the landlady was prepared for, paid her every
farthing of her demand, independent of a
liberal gratification which was to follow unknown to me, and taking a receipt in full,
very tenderly forced me to secure it by guiding
my hand, which he had thrust it into, so as to
make me passively put it into my pocket. Still
I continued in a state of stupidity or melancholy despair, as my spirits could not yet recover from the violent shocks they had received;
and the obliging landlady had actually left the
room, before I had observed it, and then I
observed it without alarm for I was lifeless
and indifferent to everything.

The gentleman, however, no novice in affairs
of this sort, drew near me, and, under the pretence of comforting me, first with his handkerchief dried my tears as they ran down my
cheeks; presently he ventured to kiss me, on my
part, neither resisting nor complying, I sat
stock still, and now looking on myself as bought
by the payment that had been transacted before
me, I did not care what became of my wretched
body, and wanting life, spirit or courage to offer
the least struggle, even that of the modesty of
my sex, I suffered tamely whatever the gentleman pleased, who proceeding insensibly from
freedom to freedom, insinuating his hand between my handkerchief and bosom, which he
handled at discretion; finding thus no repulse
and that everything favoured beyond expectation the completion of his desires, he took me in

his arms and bore me without life or motion to
the bed, on which laying me gently down and
having me at what advantage he pleased. I did
not so much as know what he was about until
recovering from a trance of lifeless insensibility,
I found him buried in me, whilst I lay passive
and unconscious of the least sensation of
pleasure; a death-cold corpse could scarce have
had less life in it. As soon as he had thus
pacified a passion which had no respect for the
condition I was in, he got off me, and after
adjusting my clothes, employed himself with
the utmost tenderness to calm the transport of
remorse and madness at myself with which I
was seized, too late, for having suffered on that
bed the embraces of an utter stranger, I tore
my hair, wrung my hands, and beat my breasts
like a mad woman. But when my new master,
for in that light I then viewed him, applied
himself to appease me, as my whole rage
levelled at myself, no part of which I thought
myself permitted to aim at him, I begged him
with more submission than anger to leave me
alone that I might at least enjoy my affliction
in quiet. This he positively refused for fear,
as he pretended, that I should do myself a
mischief.

Violent passions seldom last long and those
of women least of any. A dead still calm
succeeded this storm which ended in a profuse
shower of tears. Had anyone but a few instants before told me that I should have ever
known any man but Charles, I would have spit

in his face, or had I been offered infinitely a
greater sum of money than that I saw paid for
me, I had spurned the proposal in cold blood.
But our virtues and our vices depend too much
on our circumstances; unexpectedly beset as I
was, betrayed by a mind weakened by a long
and severe affliction, and stung with the terrors
of a goal, my defeat will appear the more ex-
cusable, since I certainly was not present at,
or a party in any sense to it. However, as the
first enjoyment is decisive and was now over
the bar, I thought I had no longer a right to
refuse the caresses of one that had got that
advantage over me, no matter how obtained;
conforming myself then to this maxim, I considered myself so much in his power that I endured his kisses and embraces without affecting
struggles or anger, not that they as yet gave
me any pleasure, or prevailed over the aversion
of my soul to give myself up to any sensation
of that sort. I suffered out of a kind of gratitude and as a matter of course what he wished.
He was, however, so regardful as not to attempt
the renewal of those extremities which had
thrown me, just before into such violent
agitation, but now secure of possession, he contented himself with bringing me to temper by
degrees and waiting at the hand of time for
those fruits of generosity and courtship which
he since often reproached himself with having
gathered much too green when yielding to the
invitations of my inability to resist him and
overborne by desires, he had wreaked his

passion on a mere lifeless, spiritless body, dead
to all purposes of joy, since taking none, it
ought to be supposed incapable of giving any.
This is, however, certain, my heart never
thoroughly forgave him the manner in which
I had fallen to him, although in point of interest
I had reason to be pleased that he found in my
person wherewithal to keep him from leaving
me as easily as he had had me.   The evening
was so far advanced that the maid came in to
lay the cloth for supper, when I learned with
joy that my landlady, whose sight was like
poison to me, was not to be with us. Presently
a neat and delicious supper was brought in and
a bottle of Burgundy with the other necessaries
were set on a dumb waiter. The maid leaving
the room, the gentleman insisted with a tender
warmth, that I should sit up in the elbow chair
by the fire and see him eat if I could not be
prevailed on to eat myself. I obeyed with a
heart full of affliction at the comparison it made
between those delicious tete-a-tetes with my
very dear youth, and this forced situation, this
new awkward scene, imposed and obtruded on
me by cruel necessity. At supper, after many
arguments used to comfort and reconcile me to
my fate, he told me that his name was H—.,
brother of the Earl of L—., and that having
by the suggestions of my landlady been led to
see me, he had found me perfectly to his taste
and given her a commission to procure me at
any rate, adding that now he had succeeded, I
should have no cause to repent my knowledge

of him.

I had now got down at least half a partridge
and three or four glasses of wine which he
compelled me to drink by way of restoring
natur:, but whether there was anything extraordinary put into the wine, or whether there
wanted no more to revive the natural warmth
of my nature and give fire to the old train, I
began no longer to look with that constraint,
not to say disgust, on Mr. H. which I had
hitherto done, but, withal, there was not the
least grain of love mixed with this softening
of my sentiments; any other man would have
been just the same to me as Mr. H. who stood
in the same circumstances and had done for me
and with me what he had done. There are not,
on earth at least, eternal griefs; mine were if
not at an end, at least suspended, my heart,
which had been so long overloaded with anguish
and vexation, began to dilate and open to the
least gleam of diversion of amusement. I wept
a little and my tears relieved me; I sighed, and
my sighs seemed to lighten me of a load that
oppressed me; my countenance grew, if not
cheerful, at least more composed and free.

Mr. H. who had watched this change, knew
too well not to seize it; he thrust the table from
between us, and bringing his chair to face me,
he began, after preparing me by all the en-
dearment of assurances and protestations, to
lay hold of my hands, to kiss me, and once
more to make free with my bosom, which
being at full liberty from the disorder of a

loose deshabile, now panted and throbbed, less
with indignation than with fear and bashfulness
at being caressed most familiarly by a stranger.
But he soon gave me greater occasion to ex-
claim by stooping down and slipping his hands
above my garters and striving to regain the
pass, which he had found before so open and
unguarded; but now he could not unlock the
twist of my thighs; I gently complained and
begged him to let me alone as I was not well.
However, he saw there was more form and
ceremony in my resistance than earnestness, he
therefore made his conditions for desisting
from pursuing his point by insisting that I be
put instantly to bed, whilst he gave certain
orders to the landlady and would return in an
hour when he hoped to find me more reconciled
to his passion for me than I seemed at present.
I neither assented nor denied, but my air and
manner of receiving this proposal gave him to
see that I did not think myself enough my own
mistress to refuse it. Accordingly he went out
and left me, when a minute or two after before
I could recover myself into composure for
thinking, the maid came in with her mistress'
service and a small silver porringer of what
she called a bridal posset, and desired me to eat
it as I went to bed, which I did and immediately
felt a warmth run like a hue-and-cry through
every part of my body; I burnt, I glowed, and
desired nothing so much as a man. The maid,
as soon as I was in bed, took the candle away,
and wishing me goodnight went out of the

room and shut the door after her.

She had hardly time to get down stairs before Mr. H. opened my room door softly and came in undressed in his night gown and cap with two lighted wax candles and bolting the door gave me, though I expected him, some sort of alarm. He came a tip-toe to the bed side and saying with a gentle whisper: "Pray, my dear, do not be startled, I will be very tender and kind to you." He then hurried off his night gown and leaped into bed, having given me opening enough whilst he was stripping to observe his brawny structure, strong well made limbs and rough shaggy breast. He lay on the outside where he kept the candles burning, no doubt for the satisfaction of every sense, for as soon as he had kissed me he rolled down the bed clothes and seemed transported with the view of all my person at full length, which he covered with a profusion of kisses, sparing no part of me. Then, being on his knees between my thighs, with his stiff, red topped truncheon rooted in a thicket of curls which covered his belly to the navel he soon made me feel it joining mine. Soon he had driven the nail up to the head and left no partition but the intermediate hair on both sides. I had it all now, I felt it all now, and beginning to drive he soon gave nature such a powerful summons down her favorite quarters that she could no longer refuse repairing thither; all my animal spirits then rushed to that center of attraction and presently warmed and stirred as I was beyond bearing,

I lost all restraint and yielding to the force of the emotion gave those effusions of pleasure which in the strictness of still faithful love I could wished to have kept.

Oh, what an immense difference did I feel between this impression of a pleasure merely animal and struck out of the collision of the sexes, from that sweet fury, that rage of active delight which crowns the enjoyments of a mutual love passion where two hearts, tenderly and truly united, club to exhalt the joy and give it a spirit and soul that bids defiance to that end which mere momentary desires generally terminate in when they die of a surfeit of satisfaction! Mr. H., whom no distinctions of that sort seemed to distract, scarce gave himself or me breathing time from the last encounter, but as if he tasked himself to prove that the appearances of his vigour were not signs hung out in vain, was in a condition for renewing the onset in a few minutes, and preluding it with a storm of kisses, he drove the same course as before with unabated fervour, and thus in repeated engagements, kept me constantly in exercise till dawn of morning, in all of which time he made me fully sensible to the virtues of his firm texture of limbs, his square shoulders, broad chest, compact, hard muscles, and in short a manliness that might not pass for no bad image of our ancient sturdy barons whose race is now so thoroughly refined and frittered away into the more delicate and modern built frame of our pap-nerved sottlings, who are as pale, as pretty, and almost as masculine as their sisters.

Mr. H. content, however, with having the day break upon his triumphs, resigned me to the refreshments of a rest we both wanted, and we soon dropped into a profound sleep. Though he was some time awake before me, yet he did not offer to disturb a repose he had given me so much occasion for; but on my first stirring, which was not till past ten o'clock. I was obliged to endure one more trial of his manhood. About eleven in came Mrs. Jones with two basins of the richest soup which her experience in these matters had moved her to prepare. I pass over the compliments and cant of the procuress with which she saluted us both; but though my blood rose at the sight of her I suppressed my emotions and reflected on what would be the consequences of this new engagement.

Mr. H. who penetrated my uneasiness did not long suffer me to languish under it, and acquainted me that having taken a solid sincere affection to me, he would begin by giving me one leading mark of it in removing me out of a house which must for many reasons be irksome and disagreeable to me, into more convenient lodging, where he would take all imaginable care of me; and desiring me not to have any explanations with my landlady, or be impatient till he returned, he dressed and went out, having left me a purse with two and twenty guineas in it, being all he had about him, as he expressed

it, to keep my pocket till further supplies. As
soon as he was gone I felt the usual consequence
of the first launch into vice, for my love for
Charles never appeared to me in that light. I
was instantly borne away down the stream
without making back to shore. My dreadful
necessities, my gratitude, and above all to tell
the plain truth, the dissipation and diversion I
had to find in this new acquaintance from the
black corroding thoughts my heart had been a
prey to ever since the absence of my dear
Charles, concurred to stun all contrary reflections. If I now thought of my first, my only
charmer, it was still with the tenderness and
regret of him. I could have begged my bread
with him all over the world, but wretch that I
was I had neither the virtue or courage requisite
not to outlive my separation from him. Yet,
had not my heart been thus pre-engaged, Mr.
H. might probably have been the sole master
of it, but the place was full and the force of
conjectures alone had made him the possessor
of my person; the charms of which had been
his sole object and passion, and were of course,
no foundation for a love either very delicate
or durable.

He did not return till six in the evening to
take me away to my new lodgings, and my
moveables being soon packed and conveyed in
a hackney coach, it cost me but little regret to
take leave of a landlady whom I thought I had
so much reason not to be over pleased with;
and as for her part, she made no other difference

to my staying or going but that of the profit created. We soon got to the house selected for me, which was that of a plain tradesman, who on the score of interest, was entirely at Mr. H.'s devotion and let him the first floor very genteely furnished for two guineas a week, of which I was instated mistress with a maid to attend me. He staid with me that evening and we had a supper from a neigbouring tavern, after which, and a gay glass or two, the maid put me to bed. Mr. H. soon followed and notwithstanding the fatigues of the preceding night, I found no quarter nor remission from him; he piqued himself as he told me on doing the honours of my new apartment.

The morning being pretty well advanced we went to breakfast, and the ice now broke, my heart no longer engrossed by love began to take ease and to please itself with such trifles as Mr. H.'s liberal liking led him to make. Silks, laces, earrings, pearl necklace, gold watch, in short, all the trinkets and articles of dress were lavishly heaped upon me, for which if I did not return love, forced a kind of grateful fondness something like love; a distinction which it would be spoiling the pleasure of nine-tenths of the keepers in the town to make, and is, I suppose, the very good reason why so few of them ever do make it. I was now established the kept mistress in form, well lodged with a very sufficient allowance and able to be very well dressed.

Mr. H. continued kind and tender to me, yet

with all this I was far from happy, for, besides
my regrets for my dear youth, which though
often suspended or diverted, still returned to
me in certain melancholy moments with redoubled violence. I wanted more society, more
dissipation. As to Mr. H., he was so much my
superior in every sense, that I felt it too much
to the disadvantage of the gratitude I owed
him. Thus he gained my esteem, though he
could not raise my taste; I was qualified for no
sort of conversation with him; except one sort,
and that is a satisfaction which leaves tiresome
intervals, if not filled by love or amusement.

Mr. H. so experienced, so learned in the
ways of women, numbers of whom had passed
through his hands, doubtless, soon perceived
this uneasiness and, without approving or liking
me the better for it, had complaisance to indulge me. He made suppers at my lodging,
where he brought several companions of his
pleasures with their mistresses, and by this
means I got into a circle of acquaintance that
soon stripped me of all the remains of bashfulness and modesty which might be yet left of my
country education, and were to a just taste,
perhaps, the greatest of my charms. We visited
one another in form and mimicked as near as
we could all the miseries, the follies, and im-
pertinences of the women of quality, in the
round of which they trifle away their time,
without its ever entering their heads that on
earth there can not exist anything more silly,
more flat, more insipid and worthless than,

generally considered, their system of life is; they ought to treat the men as their tyrants, indeed were they to condemn them to it.

Amongst the kept mistresses, and I was now acquainted with a good many, besides some useful matrons who lived by their connections with men, I hardly knew one that did not perfectly detest their keepers, and of course, made little or no scruple of any infidelity they could safely accomplish. I had still no notion of wronging mine, for, besides that no mark of jealousy on his side started me the hint, or gave me the provocation to play him a trick of that sort, and his constant generosity, politeness and tender attention to please me forced a regard to him, that, without affecting my heart, insured him my fidelity; no object had yet presented itself that could overcome the habitual liking I had contracted for him, and I was on the eve of obtaining from his own voluntary generosity a modest provision for life, when an accident happened which broke all the measures he had resolved upon in my favour.

I had now lived near seven months with Mr. H. when one day returning to my lodgings from a visit in the neighbourhood I found the street door open and the maid of the house standing at it talking with some of her acquaintances, so that I came in without knocking, and, as I passed by she told me Mr. H. was above. I stepped up stairs into my own chamber with no other thought than of pulling off my hat, etc., and then to wait upon him in

the dining room as was common enough. Whilst
I was untying my hat strings, I fancied I
heard my maid Hannah's voice and a sort of
tussle, which raised my curiosity. I stole softly
to the door where a knot in the wood had been
slipped out, and afforded a very commanding
peep-hole to the scene then being enacted, the
actors of which had been too earnestly employed to hear my opening my own door from
the landing place of the stairs into my bed
chamber. The first sight that struck me was
Mr. H. pulling and hauling this coarse country
strummel towards a couch that stood in a corner
of the dining room, to which the girl made only
a sort of awkward resistance, crying out so
loud, that I who listened at the door could
scarce hear her say: "Pray, sir, don't; let me
alone; I am not for your turn. You cannot,
sure demean yourself with such a poor body
as I; Lord, sir, my mistress may come home; I
must not indeed; I will cry out." All which did
not hinder her from insensibly suffering herself
to be brought to the foot of the couch, upon
which a push of no great violence served to give
her a very easy fall, and my gentleman having
got his hands up to the stronghold of her virtue,
she, no doubt, thought it was time to give up
the argument, and that all further defense
would be in vain; and he, throwing her petticoats over her face, which was now as red as
scarlet, discovered a pair of stout, plump,
substantial thighs, tolerably white; he mounted
them around his hips and taking his drawn

weapon, stuck it in her cloven spot, where he
seemed to find a less difficult entrance than
perhaps he had hoped to find; for, by the way,
this blouse had left her place in the country
for a bastard; and, indeed, all his motions
showed he was lodged pretty much at large.
After he had done, his "dearee" gets up, drops
her petticoats down, and smooths her apron and
handkerchief. Mr. H. looked a little silly, and
taking out some money gave it to her with an
indifferent enough air, bidding her be a good
girl and say nothing.

Had I loved this man it was not in my nature
to have had patience to see the whole scene
through; I should have broken in and played
the jealous princess with a vengeance. But
that was not the case; my pride alone was hurt,
my heart not, and I could easier win upon myself to see how far he would go, till I had no
uncertainty upon my conscience. The least
delicate of all affairs of this sort being now
over, I retired softly into my closet where I
began to consider what I should do. My first
scheme, naturally, was to rush in and upbraid
them; this, indeed, flattered my present emotions
and vexations, as it would have given immediate
vent to them, but on second thought, not being
so clear as to the consequence to be apprehended
from such a step, I began to doubt whether it
was not better to dissemble my discovery till a
safer season, when Mr. H. should have per-
fected the settlement he had made overtures to
me of, and which I was not to think such a

violent explanation, as I was indeed not equal
to the management of, could possible forward,
and might destroy. On the other hand the
provocation seemed too gross, too flagrant, not
to give me some thoughts of revenge, the very
start of which idea restored me to perfect composure, and delighted as I was with the confused plan of it in my head, I was easily mistress
enough of myself to support the part of ignorance I had prescribed to myself; and as all this
circle of reflections was instantly over, I stole
a tip-toe to the passage door, and opening it
with a noise, passed for having that moment
come home, and after a short pause, as if to
pull off my things, I opened the door into the
dining room where I found the dowdy blowing
the fire and my faithful shepherd walking about
the room and whistling as cool and unconcerned
as if nothing had happened. I think, however,
he had not much to brag of having out dissembled me, for I kept up nobly the character
of our sex for art and went up to him with the
same open air of frankness as I had ever received him. He staid but a little while, made
some excuse for not being able to stay the
evening with me, and went out.

As for the wench, she was now spoiled, at
least for my servant, and scarce eight and forty
hours were gone round before her insolence on
what had passed between Mr. H. and her, gave
me so fair an occasion to turn her away at a
minute's warning, that, not to have done it
would have been the wonder, so that he could

neither disapprove it nor find in it the least
reason to suspect my original motive. What
became of her afterwards, I know not, but
generous as Mr. H. was, he undoubtedly made
her amends, though, I dare say that he kept up
no farther commerce with her, as his stooping
to such a coarse morsel was only a sudden sally
of lust on seeing a wholesome looking, buxom
country wench, and no more strange than
hunger, or even a whimsical appetite's making
a flying meal of neck beef for a change of diet.

Had I considered this escapade of Mr. H. in
no more than that light, and contented myself
with turning away the wench, I should have
acted wisely; but, flushed as I was with
imaginary wrongs, I thought Mr. H. was
getting off too cheaply if I did not push my
revenge farther and repay him as exactly as I
could for the soul of me, in the same coin. Nor
was this worthy act of justice long delayed, for
I had it too much at heart. Mr. H. had about
a fortnight before taken into his service a
tenant's son, just come out of the country; a
very handsome young lad, scarce turned
nineteen, fresh as a rose, well shaped and clean
limbed; in short, a very good excuse for any
woman's liking even though revenge had been
out of the question; any woman I say, who was
prejudiced, and had spirit enough to prefer a
point of pleasure to a point of pride.

Mr. H. had clapped a livery on him, and his
chief employ was to bring and carry letters or
messages between his master and I, and as the

situation of all kept ladies is not the fittest to
inspire respect, even to the meanest of mankind,
and, perhaps less of it from the most ignorant,
I could not help observing that this lad, who
was, I suppose, acquainted with my relation to
his master by his fellow servants, used to eye
me in that bashful confused way, more ex-
pressive, more moving, and readier caught by
our sex than any other declarations whatever;
my figure had, it seems, struck him, and modest
and innocent as he was, he did not himself
know that the pleasure he took in looking at
me was love, or desire; but his eyes, naturally
wantom, and now inflamed with passion, spoke
a great deal more than he dared have imagined
they did. Hitherto, indeed, I had only taken
notice of the comliness of the youth, but without
the least design; my pride alone would have
guarded me from a thought that way had not
Mr. H.'s condescension with my maid, where
there was not half the temptation, in point of
person, set me a dangerous example; but now
I began to look upon this stripling as a delicious
instrument of my retaliation upon Mr. H.   In
order then to pave the way for the accomplishment of my scheme, several times when the
young fellow brought me messages, I managed
to have him admitted to my bedside, or brought
to me at my toilet when I was dressing, and by
carelessly showing or letting him see, as if
without meaning or design, my bosom rather
more bare than it should be, sometimes my hair,
of which I had a very fine head in the natural

flow of it while combing, sometimes a neat leg
that had slipped its garter and which I made
no scruple of tying before him, easily gave him
the impressions favourable to my purpose,
which I could perceive sparkle in his eyes and
glow in his cheeks, then certain slight squeezes
by the hand as I took letters from him, did his
business.

When I saw him thus moved and fired for
my purpose, I inflamed him yet more by asking
him several leading questions, such as: "Had
he a mistress? was she prettier than me? Could
he love such a one as I was?" and the like, to
all which the blushing simpleton answered to
my wish in a strain of perfect undebauched
innocence, but with all the awkwardness and
simplicity of country breeding. When I thought
I had sufficiently ripened him for the laudable
purpose I had in view; one day when I expected
him at a particular hour, I took care to have the
coast clear for the reception I designed for him,
and as I planned it, he came to the dining room
door, tapped on it, and on my bidding him
come in, he did so and shut the door after him.
I desired him then to bolt it on the inside, pretending it would not otherwise keep shut. I
was then lying upon the very couch, the scene
of Mr. H's polite joys, in an undress, which
was all the art of negligence flowing loose, and
in a most tempting disorder; no stays, no hoop,
no incumbrance whatever. On the other hand
he stood at a little distance that gave me a full
view of a fine featured, shapely, healthy,

country lad; breathing the sweets of fresh
blooming youth; his hair, which was a perfect
shining black, played to his face in natural side
curls and was set out with a smart tuck-up
behind; new buckskin breeches, that, clipping
close, showed the shape of a plump, well made
thigh; white stockings, garter-laced livery,
shoulder knot, altogether composed a figure of
pure flesh and blood, and appeared under no
disgrace from the lowness of a dress to which
a certain spruce neatness seemed fitted.

I bid him come towards me and give me his
letter, at the same time throwing down carelessly a book I had in my hand. He coloured
and came within reach of delivering me the
letter, which he held out awkwardly enough
for me to take with his eyes riveted on my
bosom, which was, through the designed disorder of my handkerchief, sufficiently bare and
rather shaded than hid. I, smiling in his face,
took the letter and catching hold of his shirt
sleeve, drew him towards me blushing and almost trembling, for surely his extreme bashfulness and utter inexperience called for at least
all the advances to encourage him. His body
was now conveniently inclined toward me, and
just softly chucking his beardless chin, I asked
him: "If he was afraid of a lady?" and with
that I took his hand and carried it to my breasts,
pressing it tenderly to them. They were now
finely shaped and raised, so that panting with
desire they rose and fell in quick heaves under
his touch; at this the boy's eyes began to lighten

with all the fire of inflamed nature and his
cheeks flushed with a deep scarlet; tongue-tied
with joy, rapture and bashfulness, he could not
speak, but his looks and emotion sufficiently
satisfied me that my fire had caught and that I
had no disappointment to fear.

My lips, which I threw in his way, so that
he could not escape kissing them, fixed, fired
and emboldened him, and glancing toward that
part of his dress which covered the essential
object of my enjoyment, I plainly discovered
the swell and commotion there, and as I was too
far advanced to stop in so fair a way and was
indeed no longer able to contain myself, or
wait the slow progress of his maiden bashfulness, I stole my hand upon his thighs, down
one of which I could both see and feel a stiff
hard body, confined by his breeches, which my
fingers could discover no end to. Curious and
eager to unfold so alarming a mystery, I played
with his buttons, which were bursting ripe
from the active force within, and those of his
waistband and fore-flap flew open at a touch,
when out it started, and now being disengaged
from his clothes, I saw with wonder and surprise, what? not the plaything of a boy, not
the weapon of a man, but a maypole of so enormous a standard, that had proportions been
observed, it must have belonged to a young
giant. I could not without pleasure behold and
feel of such a length, such a breadth of
animated ivory! perfectly well turned and
fashioned, the proud stiffness of which dis-

tended its skin, whose smooth polish and velvet
softness might vie with that of the most delicate
of our sex, and whose exquisite whiteness was
not a little set off by a sprout of black curling
hair around the root, through the sprigs of
which the fair skin showed as on a fair evening you may have remarked the clear light
through the branches of distant trees over-
topping the summit of a hill; then a broad and
bluish-casted incarnate of the head, and blue
serpentines of its veins, altogether composed
the most striking assemblage of figure and
colours in nature. In short it stood an object
of terror and delight. But what was yet more
surprising, the owner of this natural curiosity,
through the want of occasions in the strictness
of his home breeding, and the little time he had
been in town not having afforded him a chance,
was hitherto an absolute stranger, in practice
at least, to the use of that manhood he was so
nobly gifted with, and it now fell to my lot to
initiate his oversize machine so disproportioned
to that tender part of me that it was very likely
to lay it in ruins.

But it was now too late to deliberate, for by
this time the young fellow, over heated, and too
high mettled to be longer curbed in by that
modesty and awe which had hitherto restrained
him, ventured under the strong impulse and
instructive promptings of nature alone, to slip
his hands, trembling with eager impetuous
desires, under my petticoats, and seeing, I
suppose, nothing extremely severe in my looks

to stop or dash him, he feels out and seizes
gently the center spot of his ardors. Oh, then
the fiery touch of his fingers determined me,
and my fears melting away before the glowing
intolerable heat, my thighs opened of themselves and yield all liberty to his hand, and now,
a favourable movement giving my petticoats a
toss, the avenue lay too fair open to be missed.
He is now upon me, I had placed myself with a
jerk under him as commodious and open as
possible to attempts, which were untoward
enough, for his machine meeting with no inlet,
bore and battered stiffly against me in random
pushes, now above, now below, now beside his
mark, till burning with impatience from its
irritating touches, I guided gently with my hand
this furious fescue to where my young novice
was now to be given his first lesson of pleasure.
Thus he nicked at length the warm and insufficient orifice but he was made to find no
breach impracticable, and mine, though so
often entered, was still far from wide enough
to take him in easily.

By my directions, however, the head of his
unwieldy machine was so accurately pointed,
that, feeling him right against my tender opening, a favourable motion from me met his timely
thrust, and the lips of my slit, strenuously dilated, gave way to his impetuous efforts, so that
we could both feel that he had gained a lodging.
Then pursuing his point, he soon, by violent,
and to me, most painfully piercing thrusts,
wedged himself at length so far in as to be

tolerably secure of his entrance; here he stuck, and now felt such a mixture of pleasure and pain, as there is no giving definition of. I dreaded alike his splitting me farther up, or his withdrawing; I could not bear either to keep or part with him. The sense of pain prevailing, however, from his prodigious size and stiffness, acting upon me in those continued rapid thrusts with which he furiously pursued his penetration, made me cry out gently, "Oh, dear me, you hurt me!" This was enough to check the tender boy even in his mid-career, and he immediately drew out the sweet cause of my complaint, whilst his eyes eloquently expressed at once his grief for hurting me and his reluctance at dislodging from quarters, the warmth and closeness of which had given him a gust of pleasure that he was now mad with desire to satisfy, and yet too much a novice not to be afraid of my withholding his relief on account of the pain he put me to.

But I was myself far from being pleased with his having regarded too much my tender exclaims; for now, more fired with the object before me, as it stood with the fiercest erection, unbonneted and displaying its broad vermillion head, I first gave the youth a reencouraging kiss, which he repaid me with a fervour that seemed at once to thank and bribe my further compliance, and then replaced myself in a posture to receive at all risks the renewed invasion which he did not delay an instant, for, being presently remounted, I once more felt the smooth hard gristle, forcing an entrance, which he achieved rather easier than before. Pained, however, as I was with his efforts of gaining a complete admission, the soft straight passage gradually loosened, yielded and stretched to its utmost by this stiff, thick, in-driven engine, sensible at once to the ravishing pleasure of the feel and the pain of the dis-tention, let him in about half way, when all the most nervous activity he now exerted to further his penetration gained him not an inch more, for while he hesitated there, the crisis of pleasure overtook him, and the close com-pression of the warm surrounding fold drew from him the ecstatic gush even before mine was ready to meet it, being kept back by the pain I had endured in the course of the en-gagement from the insufferable size of his weapon, though it was not in half its length.

I expected then, but not wishing it, that he would withdraw, but was pleasingly disappoint-ed, for he was not to be let off so. The healthy youth, hot mettled, and flush with genital juices was now fairly in for making me know my driver. As soon, then, as he had made a short pause, waking, as it were out of the trance of pleasure in which every sense seemed lost for a while; whilst with his eyes shut and short, quick breathings he had yielded down his maiden tribute, he still kept his post, yet unsated with enjoyment and solace in these new delights, till his stiffness, which had scarce perceptibly remitted being thoroughly recovered to him,

without unsheathing he proceeded afresh to
cleave and open for himself an entire entry into
me, which was made easier for him by the
balsamic injection with which he had just
plentifully moistened the whole internals of the
passage. Redoubling then the active energy
of his thrusts and favoured by the fervid efforts
of my motions, the soft oiled walls could no
longer stand so effectual a picklock, but yielded
and opened for him an entrance. And now with
conspiring nature and my endeavours to aid
him, he pierced and penetrated me, at length
winning his way inch by inch, he got entirely in,
and with a final home thrust, sheathed his spear
up to the guard insomuch that from the close
jointure of our bodies, the hair on both sides
interweaved and encircled together, and the
eyes of the transported youth sparkled with
still more joyous fires and all his looks and
motions showed an excess of pleasure which I
now began to share, for I felt him in my very
vitals. I was quite sick with delight and stirred
beyond bearing from the furious agitations
within me which gorged and crammed me even
to a surfeit. Thus I lay gasping and panting
under him till his broken breathing, faltering
accents, lunges more furious and an increased
stiffness, gave me to hail the approaches of the
second period; he came, and the sweet youth,
overpowered with the ecstasy, died away in my
arms, melting in a flood that shot in genial
warmth into the innermost recesses of my body,
warmth into the innermost recesses of my

body, every conduit of which, dedicated to that
pleasure, was on flow to mix with it. Thus we
continued for some instants, lost, breathless,
senseless of everything except those favorite
parts of nature in which everything we could
enjoy of life and sensation was concentrated.

When the mutual trance was a little over and
the young fellow had withdrawn that delicious
stretcher with which he had most plentifully
drowned all thoughts of revenge, the widened
wounded passage refunded a stream of pearly
liquids which flowed down my thighs mixed
with streaks of blood, the marks of the ravage
of that monstrous machine of his, which had
now triumphed over a kind of second maidenhead. I stole, however, my handkerchief to
those parts and wiped them as dry as I could
whilst he was re-adjusting and buttoning up.
I made him now sit down by me, and as he had
gathered courage from such extreme intimacy,
he gave me an after-course of pleasure in a
natural burst of tender gratitude and joy at
the new scenes of bliss I had opened to him;
scenes positively new, as he had never before
had the least acquaintance with that mysterious
mark, the cloven stamp of female distinction,
though nobody was better qualified than he to
penetrate into its deepest recesses, or do it nobler
justice. But when by certain motions, certain
unquietness of his hands that wandered not
without design, I found he languished for
satisfying a curiosity, natural enough, to view
and handle those parts which attract and con-

centrate the warmest force of imagination,
charmed as I was to have any occasion of
obliging and humouring his young desires, I
suffered him to proceed as he pleased without
check or control to the satisfaction of them.
Easily reading in my eyes the full permission
of myself to all his wishes, he scarce pleased
himself more than me, when, having insinuated
his hand under my petticoat and shift, he
presently removed those bars to the sight by
slyly lifting them upwards under favour of a
thousand kisses, which he thought perhaps
necessary to divert my attention from what he
was about. All my drapery being now rolled
up to my waist, I threw myself into a posture
upon the couch and gave to him full view of the
whole region of delight and all the luxurious
landscape round it. The transported youth
devoured everything with his eyes and tried
with his fingers to lay more open to his sight
the secrets of that dark and delicious deep; he
opened the folding lips, the softness of which
yielding entry to any thing of a hard body and
close around it, oppose the sight; feeling further
he met with and wondered at a soft fleshy
excrescence, which, limber and relaxed after
the late enjoyment, now grew under the touch
and examination of his fiery fingers more and
more stiff till the titillating ardours of that so
sensible part made me sigh as if he had hurt
me, on which he withdrew his curious probing
fingers, asking me pardon as it were with a kiss
that increased the flame there.

Novelty ever makes the strongest impressions
and in pleasures especially. No wonder then
that he was swallowed up in raptures of admiration of things interesting by their nature
and now seen and handled for the first time.
On my part, I was richly overpaid for the
pleasure I gave him in that examination of those
objects thus abandoned to him, naked and free
to his loosest wish. His hands convulsively
squeezed, opened, pressed together again the
lips and sides of that deep flesh wound, or gently
twitched the over-grown moss, and proclaimed
the excess, the riot of joys in having his
wantoness thus humoured. He did not long
abuse my patience, for the objects before him
had now put him afire and coming out with his
formidable machine, he let the fury loose, and
pointing it directly at the pouting-lipped mouth,
that bid him defiance, squeezed in the head and
driving with refreshed rage, broke in and
plugged up the whole passage of that soft
pleasure conduit pipe, and put once more all
within me into such an uproar as nothing could
still but a fresh inundation from the very engine
which caused the flames as well as from all the
springs with which nature floods that reservoir
of joy when risen to its flood mark. I was now
so bruised, so battered, so spent with this over-
match, that I could hardly stir, and lay palpitating till the ferment of my senses subsiding
by degrees and the hour striking at which I was
obliged to dispatch my young man, I tenderly
advised him of the necessity there was for

parting, at which I felt as much displeasure as
he, who seemed eagerly disposed to keep the
field and enter on a fresh action. But the
danger was too great, and after some hearty
kisses of leave and recommendations of secrecy
and discretion, I forced myself to send him
away, not without assurances of seeing him
again to the same purpose as soon as possible. I
thrust a guinea into his hands, no more, lest
being too flush with money a suspicion or discovery might arise from thence, having everything to fear from the dangerous indiscretion
of that age in which young fellows would be too
irresistible, too charming, if we had not that
fault to guard against.

Giddy and intoxicated as I was with such
satiating draughts of pleasure, I still lay on the
couch, supinely stretched out, a delicious languor
diffused over all my limbs, hugging myself for
being thus revenged to my heart's content and
in a manner precisely alike and on the identical
spot in which I had received the supposed
injury. No reflections on the consequences
ever once perplexed me, nor did I make myself
one single reproach for having by this step
completely entered myself into a profession
more decried than disused. I should have held
it ingratitude to the pleasure I had received, to
have repented of it and since I was now over
the bar, I thought by plunging over head and
ears into the stream I was hurried away by, to
drown all sense of shame or reflection. Whilst
I was thus making these laudable dispositions

and whispering to myself a kind of tacit vow
of incontinency, enters Mr. H. The consciousness of what I had been doing deepened the
glowing of my cheeks, flushed with the warmth
of the late action, which joined to the piquant
air of my dishabille, drew from Mr. H. a
compliment on my looks which he was proceeding to back the sincerity of with proofs, and
that so brisk an action, as made me tremble
for fear of a discovery from the condition
those parts were left in from their late severe
handling; the orifice dilated and inflamed, the
lips swollen with their uncommon distension,
the ringlets pressed down, crushed and uncurled
with the overflowing moisture that had wet
every thing around it; in short, the different
feel and state of things would hardly have
passed upon one of Mr. H.'s nicety and experience, unaccounted for but by the real cause.
But here the woman saved me; I pretended a
violent disorder of my head and a feverish heat
that indisposed me too much to receive his embraces. He gave into this, and good naturedly
desisted. Soon after an old lady coming in
made a third, very apropos for the confusion
I was in, and Mr. H. after bidding me take
care of myself, left me much at ease and relieved by his absence. In the evening I took a
warm bath of aromatic and sweet herbs, in
which having fully bathed myself, I came out
greatly refreshed.

The next morning waking early after a
night's perfect rest, it was not without some

dread and uneasiness that I thought of what an innovation that tender soft system of mine had sustained from the shock of a machine so sized for its destruction. Struck with this apprehension I scarce dared to carry my hand thither to inform myself of the state and posture of things. But I was soon agreeably cured of my fears. The silky hair that covered the borders, now smoothed and re-pruned, had resumed its wonted curl and trimness, the fleshy pouting lips that had stood the brunt of the engagement were no longer swollen or moisture-drenched; and neither they nor the passage into which they opened and which had suffered so great a dilation, betrayed the least alteration outwardly or inwardly to the most curious research, notwithstanding also the laxity that naturally follows a warm bath. This condition of that useful structure which is in us and the necessity of men for their pleasure, I owed it seems to a healthy body, juicy, plump and furnished around those parts with a fullness of soft springy flesh, which yielding as it does to almost any distension, soon recovers itself so as to retighten that compression of its mantlings and folds which form the sides of the passage it so tenderly embraces, and closely holds any foreign body introduced into it such as my finger was.

Finding then everything in due tone and order, I remembered my fears only to make jest of them to myself. And now, palpably mistress of any size of man, and triumphing in my double achievement of pleasure and revenge, I abandoned myself entirely to the ideas of all the delight I had swam in. I lay stretching out, glowing alive all over and tossing with burning impatience for the renewal of joys that had sinned but in a sweet excess; nor did I lose my longing, for about ten in the morning according to expectation, Will, my new humble sweetheart, came with a message from his master to know how I felt. I had taken care to send my maid on an errand into the city that I was sure would take up time enough, and from the people in the house I had nothing to fear as they were wise enough to mind no more of other people's business than they could well help. All dispositions then made, even to lying in bed to receive him when he entered my bed chamber; I latched the door by means of a lock I controlled by a wire. I could not but observe that my young minion was as much spruced up as could be expected from one in his condition, a desire of pleasing that could not be indifferent to me since it proved that I pleased him, which, I assure you was now a point I was not above having in view. His hair trimly dressed, clean linen, and above all a hale, ruddy, wholesome country look, made him as pretty a piece of woman's meat as you could see, and I should have thought any one much out of taste that could not have made a hearty meal of such a morsel as nature had designed for the highest diet of pleasure.

Why should I suppress the delight I received

from this amiable creature, in noticing each
artless look, each motion of pure undissembled
nature, betrayed by his wanton eyes, or showing transparently the glow of blood through his
fresh, clear skin, whilst even his sturdy rustic
embraces wanted not their peculiar charm? Oh,
but' you say this was a young fellow of too low
rank to deserve so great a display. May be so,
but was my condition, strictly considered, one
jot more exalted, or, had I really been much
above him did not his capacity of giving such
exquisite pleasure sufficiently raise and enoble
him? at least it did to me. I respect and reward
the painter's, the sculptor's and the musician's
art in proportion to the delight I take in them,
and at my age and with my taste for pleasure
the talent of pleasing with which nature has
endowed a handsome person, seemed to me the
greatest of all merits, compared to which the
vulgar prejudices in favour of titles and
honours held a very low rank. Nor perhaps
would the beauties of the body be so much
affected to be held cheaply were they to be
bought. For me, whose natural philosophy all
resided in the favourite center of sense, and
who was ruled by its powerful instinct in taking
pleasure by its right handle, I could scarce have
made a choice more to my purpose. Mr. H.'s
loftier qualifications of birth and fortune put
me under a sort of subjection and constraint
that were far from making harmony in the
concert of love, nor had he perhaps thought me
worth softening that superiority to, but with

this lad I was more on that level which love delights in.

We may say what we please, but those we can be the easiest and freest with are ever those we like, not to say love best. With this stripling, whose art of love was the action of it, I could, without check of awe or restraint, give loose to joy and execute every scheme of dalliance my fancy might put me to, in which he was in every sense a most exquisite companion. My greatest pleasure lay in humouring all the petulancies, all the wanton frolic of a raw novice just fleshed and keen on the burning scent of his game, but unbroken to the sport, and who could better "thread the wood" or stand fairer for the "heart of the hunt" than he? He advanced to my bedside and whilst he faltered out his message I could observe his colour rise and eyes lighten with joy in seeing me in a situation so favourable to his loosest desires.

I smiled and put out my hand towards him which he kneeled down and kissed, a politeness taught him by love alone. After exchanging a few confused questions and answers, I asked him if he would come to bed to me for the short time I could venture to detain him. This was just asking a person dying with hunger to feast upon the dish he most relished on earth. Accordingly, without farther reflection, his clothes were off in an instant, when blushing still more at this new liberty, he got under the bedclothes I held up to receive him, and he was now in bed with a woman for the first time in his life. Then began the usual tender preliminaries, as delicious perhaps as the crowning act of enjoyment itself, which is often lost by an impatience to hurry on to the final period and closing scene of bliss in which the actors are generally too well pleased with their parts not to wish them an eternity of duration. When we had sufficiently graduated our advances towards the main point by toying, kissing, playing with my breasts and feeling of that part of me I might call a furnace mouth from the heat his fiery touches had kindled there, my youngster, emboldened by every freedom he could wish, wantonly takes my hand and placed it on that enormous machine of his that stood up with a stiffness, a hardness and upward bend of erection, and which together with its bottom appendage, the unsurpassed purse of ladies' jewels, formed a grand show of goods indeed! Its dimensions mocking either grasp or span almost renew my terrors. I could not conceive how I could put such a bulk out of sight. I stroked it gently, on which the mutinous rogue seemed to swell and gather a new degree of fierceness and insolence, so that finding it grew in size not to be trifled with any longer, I prepared for it in earnest.

Slipping a pillow under me that I might give him the fairest play, I guided with my hand this furious battering ram, whose ruby head I applied to its proper mark which lay as finely elevated as we could wish; the lips being pointed up and my thighs at their utmost extension, the

gleamy warmth that shot from it made him
feel that he was at the mouth of the flue and
driving forward the lips of my pleasure-thirsty
channel received him. He hesitated a little then,
then settled well into the passage and made his
way up the straits, with a difficulty no more than
pleasing, widening as he went so as to distend
and smooth each soft furrow, our pleasure increasing deliciously in proportion as our points
of mutual contact increased in that vital part of
me in which I had now taken him completely in-
driven and sheathed, and which crammed as it
was, stretched splitting ripe, gave it such a
grateful accommodation, so tight a fold, a
suction so fierce that we both felt unutterable
delight. We had now reached the closest point
of union; but when he backed to come on the
fiercer, as if I had been actuated by a fear of
losing him in the height of my fury, I twisted
my legs around his naked loins and now I had
him in every way encircled and begirt, and
having drawn him home to me I kept him fast
there as if I had sought to unite bodies with
him at that point. This caused a pause of
action, a pleasure stop, whilst that delicate
glutton, my nether mouth, as full as it could
hold, kept palpitating with exquisite relish the
morsel that so deliciously ingorged it. But
nature could not long endure a pleasure that so
highly provoked without satisfying it; so continuing the battery recommenced with redoubled
exertion; nor lay I inactive on my side, but
encountering him with all the impetuosity of

motion I was mistress of, the downy cloth of our
meeting mounts was now of real use to break
the violence of the tilt, and soon, the high-
wrought agitation, the sweet urgency of this
to-and-fro friction raised the titillation in me
to its height, so that finding myself on the point
of going off and loathe to leave the tender
partner of my joys behind me, I employed all
the forwarding motions and arts my experience
suggested to me to promote his keeping me
company to our journey's end. I not only
tightened the pleasure girth round my restless
inmate by a secret spring of friction and com-
pression that obeys the will in those parts, but
stole my hand softly to that storebag of nature's
sweets which is attached to its conduit pipe
from which we receive them; feeling and gently
squeezing those tender globular reservoirs, my
touch took effect instantly and brought on the
symptoms of that sweet agony, the melting
moment of dissolution, when pleasure dies by
pleasure and the mysterious engine of it over-
comes the titillation it has raised in those parts
by playing them with a stream of warm liquid
that is itself the highest of all titillations, and
which they thirstily draw in like the hot natured
leech, which to cool itself extracts all the
moisture within its sphere of suction. Uniting
with me as I melted away, his oily balsamic injection mixed deliciously with the sluices in flow
in me and soothed and blunted all the stings of
pleasure whilst a voluptuous languor possessed
and maintained us motionless and fast locked

in one another's arms. Alas, that these delights should be no longer lived, for now the point of pleasure unedged by enjoyment and all sensations deadened in us, we resigned ourselves to the cruel cares of life. Disengaging myself then from his embrace I made him sensible of the present reasons for his leaving me, on which he put on his clothes with as little hurry, however, as he could help, wantonly interrupting himself between whiles with kisses, touches and embraces I could not refuse myself to. Happily he returned to his master before he was missed, and on his taking leave I forced him to take money enough, for he had enough sentiment to refuse it, to buy a silver watch, that great article of subaltern finery, which he at length accepted as a remembrance he was carefully to preserve of my affections.

And here, madam, I ought perhaps to make you an apology for this minute detail of things that dwell so strongly upon my memory after so deep an impression; but besides that this intrigue bred one great revolution in my life, which historical truth requires I should not keep from you, may I not presume that so exalted a pleasure ought not to be ungratefully forgotten or suppressed by me because I found it a characteristic of low life, where by the by, it is oftener met with purer and more unsophisticated than among the false, ridiculous refinements with which the refined suffer themselves to be so grossly cheated by their pride. The refined! those among whom there exist few

they call vulgar, who are more ignorant or
cultivate less the art of living than they? They,
I say, who forever mistake things the most
foreign to the nature of pleasure itself whose
main object is enjoyment of beauty wherever
that rare gift is found, without distinction of
birth or station. As love never had, and revenge
had no longer any share in my commerce with
this handsome youth, the sole pleasures of enjoyment were now the reasons I held to him,
for though nature had done so well for him in
his outward form, and especially in that superb
piece of furniture she had so liberally gifted
him with and he was thus qualified to give the
senses their richest feast, still there was something more wanting to create in me the passion
of love. Yet Will had very good qualities,
being gentle, tractable, grateful and above all
silent, speaking very little at any time, but
making it up with action; and to do him justice
he never gave me the least reason to complain
either by any tendency to encroach upon me for
the liberties I gave him, or indiscretion in blabb-
ing of them. There must be then a fatality in
love or I would have loved him, for he really
was a treasure and a bit for the "bonne bouche"
of a duchess, and to tell the truth I liked him
so well, that it was distinguishing very nicely
to deny that I loved him.

My happiness, however, did not last long,
but found an end from my own imprudent
neglect. After having taken superflous precautions against a discovery, our success in

repeated meetings emboldened me to omit the
barely necessary ones. About a month after
our first intercourse, one fatal morning, the
time Mr. H. rarely or never visited me in, I
was in my closet in nothing but my shift with
Will with me. Both of us always too well
disposed to miss an opportunity, and for my
part a whim taking me, I challenged my man to
execute it on the spot, who did not hesitate to
comply with my wanton humour. I was set in
the arm chair, my shift up and my thighs wide
spread and mounted over the arms of the chair,
presenting the fairest mark to Will's drawn
weapon which he stood in the act of plunging
into me; when, having neglected to secure the
chamber door, Mr. H. stole in upon us before
either of us was aware and saw us in these
convicting attitudes. I gave a scream and
dropped my shift, the thunder struck lad stood
trembling and pale waiting his sentence of
death. Mr. H. looked sometimes at one, sometimes at the other with a mixture of indignation
and scorn, and without a word spun on his heel
and went out. As confused as I was, I heard
him turn the key and lock the chamber door
upon us, so that there was no escape but through
the dining room where he himself was walking
about with angry strides, stamping in a great
chafe and doubtless debating what he should do
with us. In the meantime poor William was
frightened out of his senses, and as much need
as I had of spirits myself, I was obliged to
employ them all to keep his a little up. The

misfortune I had brought upon him endeared him the more to me, and I could have joyfully suffered any punishment he did not share in. I watered plentifully with my tears the face of the frightened youth, who sat, not having strength to stand, as cold and lifeless as a statue.

Presently Mr. H. came in to us again and made us go before him into the dining room, trembling and dreading the issue. Mr. H. sat down on a chair whilst we stood like criminals under examination, and beginning with me, asked me in an even, firm tone of voice, neither soft nor severe, but cruelly indifferent, what I had to say for myself for having abused in so unworthy a manner, with his own servant too, and how he deserved this of me? Without adding to the guilt of my infidelity any audacious defence of it in the style of a common kept mistress, my answer was modest and often interrupted by tears as follows: "That I never had a single thought of wronging him till I had seen him taking every liberty with my servant wench (here he coloured prodigiously) and that my resentment at that had driven me to a course that I did not pretend to justify, but as to the young man he was entirely faultless in view of the fact that I made him the instrument of my revenge and that I had really seduced him to what he had done, and therefore hoped whatever he determined about me, he would distinguish between the innocent and the guilty."

Mr. H. on hearing what I said, hung his head a little, but recovering himself, said to me as near as I can remember: "Madam, I take shame to myself and confess that you have fairly turned the tables upon me. It is not with one of your cast of breeding and sentiments that I should enter into a discussion of the very great difference of the provocations; be it sufficient that I allow you so much reason on your side as to have changed my resolution in consideration of what you reproach me with, and I own too that your clearing that rascal there is fair and honest of you. Renew with you I cannot, the affront is too gross. I give you a week's warning to go out of these lodgings; whatever I have given you remains yours, and as I never intend to see you more, the landlord will pay you fifty pieces on my account with which, every debt paid, I hope you will blame only yourself that your condition is no better; for I do not leave you in any worse condition than I found you in or than you deserve."

Then, without giving me time to reply, he addressed himself to the young fellow: "For you, spark, I shall for your father's sake take care of you. The town is no place for such an easy fool as you are, and tomorrow you shall set out under the charge of one of my men, well recommended to your father not to let you return and be spoiled here." With these words he went out after my vainly attempting to stop him by throwing myself at his feet. He shook me off, though he seemed greatly moved too, and took Will away with him, who I dare say, thought himself very cheaply off.

I was now once more adrift and left upon my own hands by a gentleman whom I certainly did not deserve. All the letters, arts, friends, and entreaties that I employed within the week of grace in my lodgings could not win him so much as to see me again. He had irrevocably pronounced my doom and submission to it was my only part. Soon after he married a lady of birth and fortune, to whom he proved an irreproachable husband. As for poor Will, he was immediately sent down to the country to his father, who was a farmer, where he was not four months before an innkeeper's buxom young widow, with a very good stock both in money and trade, fancied and perhaps not unacquainted with his secret excellencies, married him, and I am sure there was at least one good foundation for their living happily together. Though I should have been charmed to see him before he went, such measures were taken by Mr. H. that it was impossible, otherwise I should certainly have endeavoured to detain him in town, and would have spared neither effort nor expense to have procured myself the satisfaction of keeping him with me. He had such powerful hold upon my inclinations as was not easily to be shaken off or replaced; as to my heart, it was out of the question; glad, however, I was that nothing worse, and as things turned out, probably nothing better could have happened to him. As to Mr. H., though views of conveniency made me at first exert myself to regain his affection, I was giddy and thoughtless enough to be much easier reconciled to my failure than I should have been; but as I never had loved him, and his leaving me gave me a sort of liberty I longed for, I was soon comforted and flattering myself that the youth and beauty I was going into trade with could hardly fail of procuring me a maintenance and I saw myself under the necessity of trying my fortune with them, rather with pleasure and gaiety than with the least idea of despondency. In the mean time several of my acquaintances among the sisterhood, who had soon got wind of my misfortune, flocked to insult me with their malicious consolations. Most of them had long envied me the affluence and splendour I had been maintained in, and though there was scarce one of them that did not deserve to be in my case, and would probably sooner or later come to it, it was easy to see in their affected pity, their secret pleasure at seeing me thus discarded, and their pretended grief, the uncountable malice of the human heart, which is not confined to the class of life they were of by any means.

As the time approached for me to come to some resolution how to dispose of myself and I was considering where to shift my quarters to, Mrs. Cole, a middleaged, discreet sort of woman, who had been brought into my acquaintance by one of the mistresses that visited me, upon learning of my situation came to offer her advice and service to me, and as I had always taken to her more than any of my female acquaintances, I listened the easier to her pro-

posals. As it happened I could not have put
myself into worse or better hands in all London;
into worse because keeping a house of conveniency, there were no lengths in lewdness she
would not advise me to go in compliance with
her customers; no schemes of pleasure or unbounded debauchery she did not take even a
delight in promoting; into a better because
nobody having had more experience of the
wicked part of the town than she had, was
fitter to advise and guard one against the worst
dangers of our profession, and what was rare
to be met with in those of her kind, she contented herself with a moderate living profit upon
her industry and good offices and had nothing
of their greedy rapacious turn. She was in
reality born and bred a gentlewoman, but
through a chain of accidents reduced to this
course, which she pursued partly through a
necessity and partly through choice, as never
woman delighted more in encouraging a brisk
circulation of the trade for the sake of the trade
itself, or better understood all the mysteries and
refinements of it than she, so that she was at
the top of her profession and dealt only with
customers of distinction, to answer the demands
of whom she kept a competent number of her
daughters in constant recruit, so that she called
those whose youth and personal charms recommended their adoption and management, several
of whom by her means and through her tuition
succeeded well in the world.

This useful gentlewoman, upon whose pro-

tection I now threw myself, sent a friend of
hers on the day appointed for my removal to
conduct me to my new lodgings in R. street,
Covent Garden, the very next door to her own
house, where she had no convenience to lodge
me herself. My lodgings having been for
sometime tenanted by ladies of pleasure the
landlord of them was familiar with their ways,
and provided the rent was paid, everything else
was as easy and commodious as one could wish.
The fifty guineas promised me by Mr. H. at
his parting with me having been duly paid me
and all my clothes and movables packed up,
which were at least two hundred pounds value,
I had them conveyed into a coach where I soon
followed them after taking leave of the landlord and his family with whom I had never
lived in a degree of familiarity enough to regret
my removal, but still the very circumstance of
it being a removal drew tears from me. I left
too a letter of thanks for Mr. H. from whom I
was now irretrievably separated, and discharged
my maid, not only because I got her from Mr.
H., but because I suspected her of having some-
how or other been the cause of his discovering
me, in revenge perhaps for not having trusted
her with it.

I soon got to my lodgings, which though not
so handsomely furnished nor showy as those I
left, were full as convenient and half the price.
My trunks were safely landed and stowed in my
apartment where my neighbour and govern-
ante, Mrs. Cole, was ready with the landlord

to receive me, with whom she took care to set me out in the most favourable light, that of one from whom there was the best reason to expect the regular payment of his rent having more weight with him than all other virtues which possibly could have been attributed to me. I was now turned loose upon the town and the consequences and adventures which befell me will compose the matter for another letter, for surely it is time to put a period to this.

I am, Madam, yours, etc., etc.,

Fanny.

LETTER THE SECOND

MADAME:

If I have delayed the sequel of my
story it has been purely to allow myself a little
breathing time, not without some hopes that
instead of pressing me to a continuation, you
would have relieved me of the task of continuing
a confession in which my self esteem has so
many wounds to sustain. I imagined, indeed,
that you would be cloyed and tired with the
uniformity of adventures and expressions inseparable from a subject of this sort, whose
foundation being in the nature of things
eternally one and the same, whatever the variety
of forms and modes, the situations are suscep-
tible of, there is no escaping a repetition of
nearly the same images, the same figures, the
same expressions, with the further incon-
venience added to the disgust it creates that the
words joys, ardours, transports, ecstacies and
the rest of those pathetic terms so congenial
to, and received in the practice of pleasure,
flatten and lose much of their due spirit and
energy by the frequency they indispensably
recur with in a narrative of which that practice
professedly composes the whole basis. I must
therefore trust to the candour of your judgment for your allowing for the disadvantage
I am necessarily under in that respect; and to

your imagination and sensibility the pleasing
task of repairing it by supplements of your own
where my descriptions fag or fail; the one will
readily place the pictures I present before your
eyes, the other give life to the colours where
they are dull or worn with too frequent
handling. What you say besides by way of
encouragement concerning the extreme difficulty
of continuing so long in one strain in a mien
tempered with taste between the revoltingness
of gross, and vulgar expressions and the ridicule of mincing metaphors and affected cir-
cumlocutions, is so sensible, that you greatly
justify me to myself for a compliance with a
curiosity that is to be satisfied so extremely at
my expense.

Resuming now where I broke off in my last
letter, Mrs. Cole, after helping me to arrange
my things, spent the whole evening with me in
my apartment, where we supped together, in
giving me the best advice and instruction with
regard to this new stage of my profession I
was now to enter upon, passing thus from a
private devotee to pleasure to a public one, with
all the knowledge requisite to put my person
out to use, either for money or pleasure, or both.
She remarked that as I was a kind of new face
upon the town, that it was an established rule
and mystery of the trade for me to pass for a
maid and dispose of myself as such on the first
good occasion, without giving up, however, any
diversions as I might have a mind to in the
meantime, for there was no use in the losing of

profitable time. She would in the mean while
do her best to find a person and would under-
take to manage this nice point for me if I would
accept her aid and advice to such good purpose
that in the loss of a fictitious maidenhead, I
should reap all the advantages of a real one.

As too great a delicacy of sentiments did not
belong to my character at that time, I confess
that I perhaps too readily closed with a proposal
which my candour gave me some repugnance
to, but not enough to contradict the intention
of one to whom I had now entirely left the
direction of all my steps, for Mrs. Cole had, I
do not know how, unless by one of those un-
accountable sympathies that nevertheless form
the strongest links, especially of female friendship, won and got entire possession of me. On
her side she pretended that a resemblance to
an only daughter whom she had lost at my
age was the first motive of her taking to me so
affectionately. It might be so, there exist as
slender motives of attachment, which gathering
force from habit and liking have proved often
more solid and durable than those founded on
much stronger reasons; but this I know, that
though I had no other acquaintance with her
than seeing her at my lodgings when I lived with
Mr. H., where she had made some visits to sell
millinery, she had by degrees insinuated herself
so far into my confidence that I threw myself
blindly into her hands, and came at length to
regard, love and obey her implicitly; and to do
her justice I never experienced at her hands

other than sincerity and a care for my interest hardly heard of in those of her profession. We parted that night after arriving at a perfect agreement, and the next morning Mrs. Cole came and took me to her house for the first time.

Here I found everything breathed an air of decency, modesty and order. In the outer parlour, or rather shop, sat three young women very demurely employed on millinery work, which was the cover of a traffic in more precious commodities, and three more beautiful creatures could hardly be seen. Two of them were extremely fair, the eldest not above nineteen, and the third, about that age, was a piquant brunette, whose black sparkling eyes and perfect harmony of features and shape left her nothing to envy in her fair companions. Their dress had more style to it than it at first appeared to have, being of a uniform correct neatness and elegant simplicity. These were the girls that composed the small domestic flock which my governess trained with surprising order and management, considering the giddy wildness of young girls once got upon the loose. But then she never kept in her house any who after a due noviciate she found untractable or unwilling to comply with the rules of it. Thus she had formed a little family of love of which the members found a rare alliance of pleasure and profit, and Mrs. Cole who had picked them as much for their temper as for their beauty, governed them with ease.

She presented me to these pupils of hers as a
new boarder, and one that was to be admitted
immediately to all the intimacies of the house;
upon which these charming girls gave me a
welcome reception and were as pleased with my
figure as I could possibly expect any of my own
sex to be; but they had been brought up to
sacrifice all jealousy or competition of charms
to a common interest, and considered me as a
partner that was bringing no despicable stock
of goods into the trade of the house. They
gathered around me and viewed me on all sides,
and as my admission into the house made a little
holiday, the show of work was laid aside and
Mrs. Cole gave me up to their entertainment.
The sameness of our sex, age, profession and
views soon created as unreserved a freedom and
intimacy as if we had been acquainted for years.
They showed me the house, their respective
apartments which were furnished with every
article of conveniency and luxury, and above
all a spacious drawing room where a select
revelling band met in general parties of
pleasure, the girls supping with their sparks
and acting their wanton pranks with unbounded
licentiousness, whilst a defiance of awe, modesty
or jealousy were their standing rules, and whatever pleasure was lost on the side of sentiment,
it was abundantly made up to the senses in the
poignancy of variety and the charms of ease
and luxury. The supporters of this secret
institution would in the height of their humour
style themselves the restorers of the golden age

with its simplicity of pleasures before its innocence became so unjustly branded with the
names of lewdnes and shame. As soon as
evening began and the show of a shop was shut,
the academy opened and the mask of mock-
modesty was completely taken off and the girls
delivered to their respective calls of pleasure or
profit with their men, none of whom were
admitted promiscuously, but only those whose
character and discretion Mrs. Cole was satisfied
with. In short, this was the safest, politest, and
at the same time, the most thorough house of
accommodation in town; everything was so conducted that decency made no intrenchment upon
the most libertine pleasures, in the practice of
which it is difficult to reconcile all the refinements of taste and delicacy with the grossest
gratifications of sensuality.

After having consumed the morning with
instructions from my new acquaintances, we
went to dinner, where Mrs. Cole presiding at
the head of her flock gave me the first idea of
her management and address in inspiring these
girls with so sensible a love and respect for her.
There was no stiffness, no reserve, no airs of
pique or little jealousies, but all was unaffectedly
gay, cheerful and easy. After dinner Mrs.
Cole acquainted me that there was a chapter to
be held that night in form for the ceremony of
my reception into the sisterhood, and with all
due reserve to my maidenhead which was to be
cooked up for the first proper chapman, I was
to undergo a ceremonial of initation that they

were sure I would not be displeased with.
Captivated with the charms of my new companions I was too much prejudiced in favour
of any proposal they could make to hesitate
giving assent in the style of a carte blanche.

This point adjusted, the young women left
Mrs. Cole to talk over matters with me, when
she explained to me that I should be introduced
that very evening to four of her best friends,
one of whom she had favoured with the pre-
ference of engaging me in the party of pleasure,
assuring me at the same time that they were
all young gentlemen, agreeable in their persons
and being united and held together by the bond
of common pleasures, they composed the chief
support of her house and made very liberal
presents to the girls, so that they were, properly
speaking, the founders and patrons of this little
seraglio. Not that she did not have other
customers to deal with whom she stood less
upon ceremony with than these; for instance
she could not attempt to pass me for a maid on
one of them, for they were not only to knowing
and too town-bred to bite at such bait, but they
were such generous benefactors to her that it
would be unpardonable to think of it. Amidst
all the flutter and emotion which this promise
of pleasure stirred up in me, I preserved enough
of the woman as to feign just reluctance enough
in giving in to the influence of my patroness,
and reminded her perhaps I should go home
and dress in order to make a good first impression. But Mrs. Cole assured me that the

gentlemen I should be presented to were by their rank and birth superior to being touched with any glare of dress or ornaments such as silly women rather confound and overlay, than set off their beauty with. These veteran voluptuaries knew better than not to hold them in the highest contempt, and pure native charms alone could pass muster; who would not leave any time a shallow, painted duchess for a ruddy, healthy, firm fleshed country maid, and as for me nature had done enough for me to put me above owing the least favour to art, concluding with that for this occasion there was no dress like undress. I thought my governess too good a judge of these matters not to be easily overruled by her, after which she went on preaching the doctrine of passive obedience and nonresistance to all those arbitrary tastes of pleasure which are by some styled the refinements and by others the depravations of it, between which it was not the business of a girl who was to profit by pleasing, to decide, but to conform to.

While I was profiting by this good advice, tea was brought in and the young ladies, returning, joined company with us. After a great deal of chat, frolic and humour, one of them observing there would be a good deal of time on hand before the assembly hour, proposed that each girl should entertain the company with that critical period of her personal history in which she first exchanged the maiden state for womanhood. The proposal was approved, with the exception of Mrs. Cole on account of her age, and I on account of my titular maidenhead, should be excused till I had undergone the forms of the house. This obtained me dispensation and the promptress of this amusement was asked to begin. Her name was Emily, a girl fair to excess, and whose limbs were, if possible, too well made, since their plump fullness was rather to the prejudice of that delicate slimness required by the nicer judges of beauty; her eyes were blue and streamed inexpressible sweetness, nothing could be prettier than her mouth and lips which closed over a range of the evenest, whitest teeth. Thus began:

"My father and mother were, and for aught I know, are still, farmers in the country not over forty miles from town. Their barbarity to me in favour of a son on whom alone they vouchsafed to bestow their tenderness, had a thousand times determined to me to fly their house and throw myself on the wide world, and at length an accident forced me to this desperate course at the age of fifteen. I had broken a china bowl, the pride and idol of both their hearts, and as an unmerciful beating was the least I could expect at their hands, in the silliness of those tender years I left the house and took the road to London. How my loss was resented I do not know, for till this instant I have never heard a syllable about them. My whole stock was two broad pieces of my godmother's, a few shillings, silver shoe-buckles and silver thimble. Thus equipped with no other clothes

than the ordinary ones I had on my back, and
frightened at every noise I heard behind me,
I hurried on, and I dare swear, walked a dozen
miles before I stopped through mere weariness
and fatigue. At length I sat down on a stile
and wept bitterly, for I was still rather under
the impression of fear on account of my escape,
and I dreaded worse than death going back and
meeting my unnatural parents face to face.
Refreshed by this little repose and relieved by
my tears, I was proceeding onward when I was
overtaken by a sturdy country lad who was
going to London to see what he could do for
himself there, and like me had given his friends
the slip. He could not have been above seventeen, was ruddy, well featured, with uncombed
flaxen hair, a little flapped hat, kersey frock,
yarn stockings—in short a perfect cow. I saw
him come whistling behind me with a bundle
tied to the end of a stick, his travelling
equippage. We had walked along by one another
for some time without speaking; at length we
joined company and agreed to keep together till
we got to our journey's end; what his designs
or ideas were I know not, the innocence of mine
I can solemnly vouch for.

"As night drew on it became us to look out
for some inn or shelter, to which perplexity was
added that of what we should say for ourselves
if we were questioned. After some puzzling the
young fellow made a proposal which I thought
the finest that could be, and that was that we
pass for man and wife. I never once dreamed

of the consequences. We soon came, after
having agreed on this notable expedient, to one
of those hedge accomodations for foot passengers, at the door of which stood an old crazy
beldam, who seeing us trudge by, invited us to
lodge there. Glad of any cover we went in, and
my fellow traveller, taking upon him, called for
what the house afforded and we supped together
as man and wife, which considering our figures
and ages could not have passed on anyone but
such ones as anything could pass on. When bed
time came on we had neither of us the courage
to contradict the first account of ourselves and
the young lad seemed as perplexed as I was
how to evade lying together, which was so
natural for the state we had pretended to.
Whilst we were in this quandary the landlady
took the candle and lighted us to our room
through a long yard, at the end of which it
was located separate from the body of the
house. Thus we suffered ourselves to be conducted without saying a word in opposition to
it, and there in a wretched room we were left
to pass the night together as a thing quite of
course. For my part, I was so incredibly innocent as not even then to think of any more harm
in going to bed with the young lad than with
one of our dairy wenches; nor had he perhaps
any other notions than those of innocence, until
such a fair occasion put them into his head.

"Before either of us undressed, however, he
put out the candle, and the bitterness of the
weather made it a necessity for me to get into

bed. Slipping off my clothes, I crept under the bed clothes where I found the stripling already nestled, and the touch of his warm flesh rather pleased than alarmed me. I was, indeed, too much disturbed with the novelty of my condition to be able to sleep, and besides I had not the least thought of harm. But, oh, how powerful are the instincts of nature! and how little is there wanting to set them in action! The young man, sliding his arm under my body, drew me gently towards him as if to keep himself and me warmer, and the heat I felt from joining our bodies kindled another that I had hitherto never felt, and was even than a stranger to the nature of. Emboldened, I suppose by my easiness, he ventured to kiss me and I insensibly returned it without knowing the likely consequence; for on this encouragement, he slipped his hand down from my breast to that part of me where the sense of feeling is so exquisitely critical, as I then experienced by its instantly taking fire upon his touch, and glowing with a strange tickling heat; he then pleased himself and me by playing and feeling there, till growing a little too bold, he hurt me and made me complain. Then he took my hand and guided it, not unwilling on my part, between his thighs where he lodged and pressed it, till raising it by degrees he made me feel the proud distinction of his sex from mine. I was frightened at the novelty and drew back my hand, yet spurred on by sensations of a strange pleasure, I could not help asking him what that was for. He told me he would show me if I would let him, and without waiting for my answer, which he prevented by stopping my mouth with kisses I was far from disliking, he got upon me, and inserting one of his thighs between mine opened them so as to make way for himself and fix me for his purpose; whilst I was so much out of my usual senses and so subdued by the present power of a new one, that between fear and desire, I lay utterly passive, till a piercing pain aroused me and made me cry out. But now it was now too late; he was too firmly fixed in the saddle for me to be able to throw him off with all the struggles I could use, some of which only served to further his point, and at length an irresistable thrust murdered at once my maidenhead and almost me, and I lay a bleeding witness of the necessity imposed on our sex to gather the first honey of the thorn.

"But the pleasure rising as the pain subsided, I was soon reconciled to fresh trials, and before morning nothing on earth could be dearer to me than this rifler of my virgin sweets; he was everything to me now. How we agreed to join fortunes, how we came up to town where we lived together till necessity parted us and drove me into this course of life which would have long ago battered and torn me to pieces had it not been for my finding refuge in this house are all circumstances which pass the mark I proposed, so here my narrative ends."

In the order of our sitting it was Harriet's turn next. Among all the beauties of our sex

that I had before or since seen, few indeed were
the forms that could dispute excellence with
her's; it was not delicate, but delicacy itself incarnate, such was the symmetry of her small but
perfectly fashioned limbs. Her complexion, fair
as it was, appeared yet more fair from the effect
of her black eyes, the brilliancy of which gave
her face more vivacity than belonged to the
colour of it, which was defended from paleness
by a sweetly pleasing blush in her cheeks that
grew fainter and fainter, till at length it died
away insensibly into the overbearing white.
Her miniature features joined to finish the extreme sweetness of it, which was not belied
by that of a temper turned to indolence, languor
and the pleasures of love.   Pressed to tell her
story, she smiled, and blushing, thus complied
with our desires:

"My father was a miller near the city of
York; both he and my mother dying while I
was an infant, I fell under the care of a widow
and childless aunt, housekeeper of Lord N., at
his seat in the county of ————, where she
brought me up with all imaginable tenderness.
I was not seventeen before I had on account
of my person, for I had no fortune, several
advantageous proposals; but whether nature
was slow in making me sensible in her favourite
passion, or because I had not seen any of the
other sex who had stirred up the least emotion or
curiosity to be better acquainted with it, I had
till that age preserved a perfect innocence even
in thought, whilst my fears of what I did not

well know what made me no more desirous of
marrying than of dying. My aunt, good
woman, favoured my timidity, which she looked
on as childishness which she knew from her
own experience would wear off in time and
make me give my suitors the proper answer.
The family had not been down at that seat for
years, so that it was neglected and given entirely to my aunt and two old domestics to take
care of. Thus I had full range of a spacious
lonely house and gardens, situated at about half
a mile distant from any other habitation, except,
perhaps, a straggling cottage or so. Here in
tranquility and innocence I grew up without
any memorable accident, till one fatal day I left
my aunt to sleep for some hours after dinner,
and went out to an old summer house at some
distance from the house, carrying my work
with me and sitting over a rivulet which the
doors and windows of the summer house faced.
Here I fell into a gentle slumber which stole
over my senses as they fainted under the excessive heat of the season at that hour; a cane
couch with my work basket for a pillow were
all the conveniences of my short repose, for I
was soon awakened and alarmed by a flounce
and plashing in the water. I got up to see
what was the matter, and what indeed should
it be but the son of a neighbouring gentleman,
as I afterwards found out, for I had never seen
him before, who had strayed that way with his
gun, and heated by his sport and the sultriness
of the weather, had been tempted by the fresh-

ness of the clear stream, and stripping, he
jumped into it on the other side which was
wooded down to the water forming a pleasant
shady place to undress and leave his clothes in.

"My first emotions at the sight of this youth
naked in the water were those of surprise and
fear, and I should have immediately run out had
not my modesty, fatally for itself, prevented
me on account of the door and window being so
situated that it was impossible to get out and
make my way along the bank to the house without his seeing me, which I could not bear the
thought of being so ashamed and confused at
seeing him. Obliged then to stay until his departure released me, I was greatly embarrassed
how to dispose of myself. I was kept some
time between terror and modesty even from
looking through the window, which being an
old fashioned casement without any light behind me, could hardly betray anyone's being
there to him; then the door was so secure that
without my consent there was no opening it
from without. But now I found that objects
which affright us when we cannot go from
them, draw our eyes as forcibly as those that
please us. I could not long withstand that
nameless impulse which without any desire to
see this novel sight, compelled me towards it;
emboldened too by my certainty of being unseen
and safe, I ventured by degrees to cast my eyes
on an object so terrible and alarming to my
virgin modesty as a naked man. But as I
snatched a look the first thing that struck me

was the dewy lustre of the whitest skin imaginable, which the sunbeams playing upon made
the reflection of it perfectly gleaming. His
face, in the confusion I was in, I could not well
distinguish the features of further than there
was a good deal of youth and freshness in it.
The frolic and play of all his limbs as they
appeared above the surface in the course of his
swimming, amused and insensibly delighted me;
sometimes he lay motionless on his back, floating and dragging after him a fine head of hair
which made a floating bush of black curls. At
the bottom of his glossy white belly I could not
help observing so remarkable a distinction as a
black, mossy tuft, out of which appeared to
emerge a round, softish, limber, white something, that played every way with the least
motion or whirling eddy. I cannot say but that part
chiefly, by a natural instinct, attracted, detained,
and captivated my attention; it was out of all
power of my modesty to take my eye away
from it! and seeing nothing so very dreadful
in its appearance, I insensibly looked away all
my fears, but as fast as they gave way, new
desires and strange wishes took their place and
I melted away as I gazed. The fire of nature
which had so long lain dormant and concealed
began to break out and make me feel my sex
for the first time. He had now changed his
posture and swam prone on his belly, striking
out with his legs and arms whilst his floating
locks played over a neck and shoulders whose
whiteness they delightfully set off.

"By this time I was so affected by this in-
ward revolution of sentiments, so excited by
this sight, that now, betrayed into a sudden
transition from extreme fear to extreme desire,
I found the last so strong upon me that nature
almost fainted under it. Not that I so much
as knew precisely what was wanting to me; my
only thought was that so sweet a creature as
this youth seemed to me could only make me
happy, but then the little likelihood there was of
compassing an acquaintance with him, or perhaps of ever seeing him again, dashed my desires and turned them into torments. I was still
gazing with all the powers of my sight on this
bewitching object, when in an instant, down he
went. I had heard of such things as a cramp
seizing on even the best swimmers and causing
their being drowned; and imagining this sudden
disappearance due to that, I was distracted
with the most killing terrors, and my concern
and inconceivable fondness for this unknown
giving me wings, I flew to the door, opened it
and ran down to the canal guided by the madness of my fears for him and the intense desire
of trying to save him, though I was ignorant
how or by what means to effect it. All this took
up scarce the space of a minute. I had just
life enough to reach the green borders of the
brook, where wildly looking around for the
young man and still missing him, my fright
and concern made me faint away in a deep
swoon which must have lasted some time, for
I did not come to myself till I roused out of it

by a sense of pain that pierced me to my very
vitals and awakened me to the most surprising
circumstance of finding myself not only in the
arms of the very same young man I had been
so solicitous to save, but taken at such an advantage in my unresisting condition, that he
had actually completed his entrance into me so
far, that weakened as I was by all the preceding
conflicts of mind I had suffered and struck
dumb by surprise, I had neither the power to
cry out nor the strength to distangle myself
from his strenuous embraces before, urging his
point, he had forced his way in and completely
triumphed over my virginity, as he could now
well see by the streams of blood that followed
his drawing out as well as by the difficulties he
had met with in consumating his penetration.
But the sight of that blood and the sense of my
condition affected him so, now that the ungovernable rage of his passion was somewhat
appeased, that he could not find it in his heart
to leave me and make off as he might easily
have done. I still lay in bleeding ruin, palpitating, speechless, unable to get up, and frightened
and fluttering like a poor wounded partridge,
ready to faint away again at the sense of what
had befallen me. The young man was kneeling
by me, kissing my hand and with tears in his
eyes beseeching me to forgive him and offering
all reparation in his power. It is certain that
could I at the instant of regaining my senses
have taken the bloodiest revenge I would not
have stopped at it, his violation was attended

with such aggravating circumstances, though he was ignorant of them since it was to my concern for his life that I owed my ruin.

"But how quick is the shift of passions from one extreme to the other. I could not see this amiable criminal, so suddenly the first object of my love and as suddenly of my just hate, on his knees bedewing my hand with his tears without relenting. He was still stark naked but my modesty had been already too much wounded in essentials to be so much shocked as I should have been otherwise with appearances only; and my anger ebbed so fast, and the tide of love returned so strong upon me, that I felt it a part of my own happiness to forgive him. The reproaches I made him were murmured in so soft a tone, my eyes met his in glances expressing more languor than resentment, that he could not but presume his forgiveness was at no great distance, but still he would not quit his posture of submission till I had pronounced his pardon in form, which after the most fervent entreaties, protestations, and promises, I had not the power to withhold; on which, with the utmost marks of a fear of again offending he ventured to kiss my lips, which I neither declined or resented; but on my mild expostulation with him upon the barbarity of his treatment, he explained the mystery of my ruin, if not entirely to the clearance, at least much to the alleviation of his guilt in the eyes of a judge so partial in his favour as I had grown. It seems that his going down, or sinking, was nothing but a trick of diving,

which I in my ignorance had mistaken for
something fatal; and he was so long-breathed
at it that in the few moments in which I ran out
to save him he had not yet emerged before I
fell into the swoon, in which as he came up he
saw me extended on the bank. His first idea
was that some young woman was upon some
design of frolic or diversion with him, for he
knew I could not have fallen asleep there without his having seen me before; agreeable to this
notion he had ventured to approach, and finding
me without sign of life and still perplexed as
to what to think of the adventure, he took me in
his arms and carried me to the summer house;
there he laid me down on the couch and tried in
good faith by several means to bring me to
myself again, till fired beyond all bearing by
the sight and touch of several parts of me which
were unguardedly exposed to him, he could no
longer govern his passion, the less so, as he
was not quite sure that his first idea of this
swoon being a feint was not the truth of the
case. Seduced then by this flattering notion
and overcome by superhuman temptations
combined with the solitude and seeming safety
of the attempt, he was not enough his own
master not to make it. Leaving me only while
he fastened the door, he returned with redoubled
eagerness to his prey and finding me still en-
tranced he placed me as he pleased, whilst I felt
no more than the dead what he was about till
the pain he put me to roused me just in time to
be witness of a triumph I was not able to defeat

and now scarce regretted. As he talked the tone
of his voice sounded so sweetly in my ears, the
nearness of so new and interesting an object
to me affected me so powerfully, that in seeing
things in this light I lost all sense of the past
injury. The young man soon discerned the
symptoms of a reconciliation in my softened
looks and hastening to receive the seal of it
from my lips pressed them tenderly with his in
a kiss which grew so meltingly fiery, that I felt
it go to my heart and then to my new discovered
sphere of joy and I was melted into a softness
that could not refuse him anything. He now
managed his caresses and endearments so artfully as to insinuate the most soothing consolations for the past pain and the most pleasing
expectations for future pleasure, but whilst
mere modesty kept my eyes from looking at
him, I had a glimpse of that instrument of mischief which was now obvious even to me who
had scarce had a chance for observation of it,
to be resuming its capacity for more mischief
and grew greatly alarming with its increase in
size, as he bore it hard and stiff against one of
my hands; but he employed such tender pre-
facing, such winning progressions, that my
returning passion of desire being now so strongly prompted by the engaging sight and incen-
diary touch of his naked glowing beauty, I
yielded at length to the force of the present
impressions and he obtained my blushing consent to all the gratifications of pleasure left in
the power of my poor person to bestow after

my suspension of life and unability to guard it. Here I should stop, and I shall only add that I got home without the least discovery or suspicion of what had happened. I met my young ravisher several times after, who I grew to love passionately and who would have married me, but as the accident that prevented it and its consequences which threw me on the public contain matters too serious to introduce at present, I will stop here."

Louisa, the brunette, now took her turn to treat the company with her history. I have already hinted to you the graces of her person and will proceed to give you her narrative as follows:

"According to social maxims of life I ought not to boast of my birth, since I owe it to pure love, without marriage; but this I know, it was not possible to inherit a stronger propensity for that cause of my being than I did. I was the rare production of the first essay of a journeyman cabinet-maker on his master's maid, the consequence of which was a big belly and the loss of a place. He was not in circumstances to do much for her, and yet after all this blemish she found means after she had dropped her burden and disposed of me to a poor relation in the country, to repair it by marrying a pastry cook here in London in thriving business, on whom she soon under favour of the complete hold he had given her over him, passed me for a child she had by her first husband. I had, on that footing, been taken home and was now six

years old when this father-in-law died and left
my mother in tolerable circumstances and without children by him. As to my natural father,
he had betaken himself to sea, where when the
truth of things came out, I was told that he
died, not immensely rich you may think, since
he was no more than a common sailor. As I
grew up under the eyes of my mother, who kept
on with the business, I could not but see in her
severe watchfulness the marks of the slip which
she did not care should be hereditary; but we
no more choose our passions than our features
or complexions, and the bent of mine was so
strong to the forbidden pleasure, that it got the
better of all her care and precaution.   I was
scarce twelve years old before that part which
she wanted so much to keep out of harm's way,
made me feel its impatience to be taken notice
of and come into play; already it had put forth
the signs of forwardness in the sprout of a soft
down over it, which had often flattered and I
might add, grown under my constant touch, so
pleased was I with what I took to be a kind of
title to womanhood, the state I pined to reach
for the pleasures I conceived were annexed to
it; and now the growing importance of that part
of me and the new sensations in it demolished
at once all my girlish playthings and amuse-
ments. Nature now pointed me strongly to
more solid diversions, and while stings of desire settled so fiercely in that little center of
them I could not mistake the spot I wanted a
playfellow in.

"I now shunned all company in which there was no hopes of coming at the object of my longings, and used to shut myself up, to indulge in solitude some tender meditation on the pleasures I strongly felt the beginning of in feeling and examining what nature assured me must be the chosen avenue, the gates for the unknown bliss to enter at which I longed for. But these meditations only increased my desire and fanned the fire that consumed me. I was still worse when yielding to the insupportable irritations of the little fairy charm that tormented me, I seized it with my fingers, teasing it to end. Sometimes in the furious excitations of desire, I threw myself on the bed, spread my thighs apart, and lay as if expecting the long-looked for relief, till finding my illusion, I shut and squeezed them together, burning and fretting. In short, this devilish thing with its impetuous moods and itching fires, led me such a life that I could neither, night or day, be at peace with it or myself. In time, however, I thought I had gained a prodigious prize, when figuring to myself that my fingers were something of the shape of what I pined for, I worked my way in with one of them with great agitation and delight, yet not without pain did I deflower myself, proceeding with such a fury of passion in this solitary pleasure as at length to leave myself breathless on the bed in an amorous melting trance. But frequency of use dulling the sensation, I soon began to perceive that this work was but a paltry expedient that went but a little way to relieve me and rather raised more flame than its dry and insignificant titilation could rightly appease.

"Man alone, I almost instinctively knew, as well as by what I had industriously picked up at weddings and christenings, was possessed of the only remedy that could reduce this rebellious disorder; but watched and looked over as I was, how to come at it was the point and it seemed impossible, not that I did not rack my brain and ingenuity how to elude my mother's vigilance and procure myself the satisfaction of my impetuous curiosity and longings for this untasted pleasure. At length, however, a singular chance did the work of a long course of watchfulness. One day we dined at an acquaintance's over the way together with a gentlewoman lodger who occupied the first floor of our house; after dinner there arose a necessity for my mother's accompanying her down to Greenwich and the party was settled, when I do not know what genius whispered to me to plead a headache against my being included in a jaunt that I had not the least relish for. The pretex passed and my mother with much reluctance decided to go without me, but took particular care to see me safe home, where she consigned me into the hands of an old trusty maid servant who served in the shop, for we had not a male creature in the house.

"As soon as she was gone I told the maid I would go up and lie down on our lodger's bed, mine not being made, with a charge to her not to disturb me as I wanted to rest. This injunction probably proved of eminent service to me. As soon as I had got into the bed chamber I unlaced my stays and threw myself on the outside of the bed in the loosest undress. Here I gave myself up to the old insipid privy shifts of self-viewing, self-touching, self-enjoying, in fact to all the means of self knowledge I could devise in search of the pleasure that lay before me and tantalised with that unknown something that was out of my reach; all this only served to enflame me and violently provoke my desires, whilst the one thing needful to their satisfaction was not at hand and I could have bitten my fingers for representing it so ill. After wearying and fatiguing myself with grasping shadows whilst that most sensitive part of me disdained to content itself with less than realities, the strong yearnings, the urgent struggles of nature towards the melting relief and the extreme self-agitations I had used to come at it had wearied and thrown me into a kind of unquiet sleep; for if I tossed and threw about my limbs in proportion to the distraction of my dreams, as I had reason to believe I did, a by-stander could not have helped seeing all I had for love. And one there was it seems, for waking out of my very short slumber I found my hand locked in that of a young man who was kneeling at my bedside and begging pardon for his boldness; but that being the son of the lady to whom the bed chamber belonged, he had slipped by the servant in the shop unperceived, and finding

me asleep was going to withdraw, but was held
by a power he could neither account for nor
resist.

"What could I say? my feelings of fear and
surprise were instantly subdued by those of the
pleasure I hoped for in turn this adventure
might take. He seemed to me no other than a
pitying angel dropped out of the clouds, for
he was young and handsome, which was more
than I asked for, man in general being all that
my utmost desires had pointed at. I thought
then I could not put too much encouragement
into my eyes and voice, I omitted no leading
advances, no matter what his after opinion of
my forwardness was so long as it might bring
him to the point of answering my pressing
demands for present ease; it was not now with
his thoughts but his actions that my business
lay. I raised my head and told him in a soft
tone that his mother had gone out and would
not return till late at night, which I thought
no bad hint, but as it proved, I had no novice
to deal with. The impressions I had made on
him during his view of my charms in my disordered sleep had so worked upon him, as he
afterwards told me, that had I known his in-
tentions, I would have had more to hope for
from his violence than from his respect, and
even less than the tenderness which I threw
into my voice and eyes would have served to
encourage him to make the most of the opportunity. Finding that his kisses imprinted on
my hand were taken as tamely as he could wish,

he rose to my lips, and glueing his to them, made me so faint with overcoming joy and pleasure that I fell back, he with me of course, on the bed upon which I had by imperceptable shifting from the side to near the middle, invitingly made room for him. He then lay down by me and the minutes being too precious to consume in untimely ceremony or dalliance, my youth proceeded immediately to those extremities which all my looks, sighing and palpitations had assured him he might attempt without fear of a repulse; those rogues the men read us admirably on those occasions. I lay then panting for the imminent attack, with desire far beyond my fear, for it was scarcely possible of a girl barely thirteen, tall and well grown, to be better developed than I. He threw up my petticoat and shift, whilst my thighs were by an instinct of nature opened to their widest, and my desires had so thoroughly destroyed all modesty in me that even their being now naked and laid wide open to him caused my blushes to deepen more from pleasure than from shame. What an immensely different sense of feeling did I feel in my center from his wanton handling of it than from my own insipid handling! Now he unbuttoned his waistcoat, and, released from the confinement of his breeches, out burst to view the amazing, pleasing object of all my dreams, all my love, the king indeed. I gazed at it, I devoured it with my eyes, till his getting upon me and placing it between my thighs took from me the enjoyment of its sight to give me a far

more exquisite one in its touch in that part
where its touch is most delightful. Applying
it to my minute opening, for such at that age it
certainly was, I met it with too much good will
and felt too great a rapture of pleasure at the
first insertion of it to heed much the pain that
followed. I thought nothing too dear to pay
for this, the richest treat of the senses, so that
split up, torn, bleeding, mangled, I was still so
pleased that I hugged the author of .all this
delicious ruin. But when soon after he made
his second attack, sore as everything was, the
smart was soon eased by the sovereign cordial,
all my soft complainings were silenced, and the
pain melting fast away into pleasure I
abandoned myself over to all the transports of
love and gave them the full possession of my
whole body and soul, for now all thought was
at an end with me, I lived in what I felt only.
And who could describe those feelings, those
agitations, exalted by the charm of their novelty
and surprise, when that part of me which had
so long hungered for the dear morsel that now
so delightfully crammed it, forced all my vital
sensations to fix their home there during the
stay of my beloved guest, who too soon paid me
for his hearty welcome with a nectar far richer
than I have heard of any queen treating her
paramour with, a liquified peal which lavishly
poured into me where now I myself was too
much melted to give it a dry reception and I
hailed it with the warmest confluence on my
side amidst all those ecstatic raptures not un-

familiar I presume to this good company. Thus,
I arrived at the very top of all my wishes by
an unexpected accident indeed, but not so
strange, as this young gentleman had just
arrived in town from college and came to call
on his mother at her apartment where he had
been before, though by chance I had not seen
him so that we knew each other by hearing only,
and when finding me stretched out on his
mother's bed, he readily concluded from her
description who I was. Our affair had no serious consequences, the young gentleman escaping undiscovered this time and more others.
But the warmth of my nature that made the
pleasures of love a necessity of life to me having
betrayed me into indiscretions fatal to my best
interests, I fell at length to the public, from
which it is probable I should have met with the
worst of ruin if my good fortune had not
thrown me into this safe and agreeable refuge."

Here Louisa ended, and these stories having
brought the time for the girls to retire and prepare for the revels of the evening, I stayed with
Mrs. Cole till Emily came and told us the
company had come and awaited us. On this,
Mrs. Cole taking me by the hand with a smile
of encouragement, led me up stairs. On the
landing of the first flight we were met by a
young gentleman extremely well dressed to
whom I was to be indebted for the first pleasures
of the house. He bowed to me with great
gallantry and handed me into the drawing room,
the floor of which was covered with a Turkish

carpet and its furniture adapted to every demand of the most voluptuous luxury, the room was livened by lights soft and pleasing for the joys of love.

On my entrance into the room I had the satisfaction to hear a buzz of approbation run through the whole company, which now consisted of four gentlemen, including my "particular", this was the cant term of the house for one's gallant for the time, the three young women in neat dishabille, the mistress of the academy, and myself. I was welcomed and saluted by a kiss all around, in which it was easy to discover by the superior warmth of those of the men the distinction of the sexes. Awed as I was at seeing myself surrounded, caressed and made court to by so many strangers, I could not immediately familiarise myself to the air of gaiety and joy which dictated their compliments and animated their caresses. They assured me that I was so perfectly to their taste as to have only one fault, and that was my modesty; this they observed might pass for a favourable point with those that wanted it, but their maxim was that it was an impertinent mixture and dashed the cup so as to spoil the sincere draught of pleasure; they considered modesty as their mortal enemy and gave it no quarter whenever they met with it. This prologue was not unworthy of the revels that ensued. In the midst of the frolic and wantonnesses which this joyous group were indulging in, an elegant supper was served and we sat down to it, my spark-elect placing himself next to me and the other couples as they pleased. The cheer and warmth of the good wine soon banished all reserve and the conversation grew as lively as could be wished without taking too loose a turn; these professors of pleasure knew too well to stale the impressions of it or evaporate the imagination of words before the time of action. Kisses were snatched at times and when a handkerchief round the neck interposed its feeble barrier it was not greatly respected; the hands of the men went to work with their usual petulance till the provocations on both sides rose to such a pitch that my particular's proposal for beginning the dances was received with instant assent, for as he laughingly added, he fancied the instruments were in tune. This was a signal for preparation that the complaisant Mrs. Cole, who understood life, took for her cue to disappear, being no longer fit for personal service herself and content with having planned the battle she left the field for the combatants to fight it out at their discretion.

As soon as she was gone the table was removed from the middle of the room and became a side-board, a couch was brought in, for which I whisperingly asked of my particular the reason; he told me that as it was chiefly on my account that this party was held, the couples intended to satisfy their tastes of variety in pleasure and by an open public enjoyment to break me of any taint of reserve or modesty, which they looked on as the poison of joy; that

though they occasionally preached their idea
of pleasure and lived up to its text, they did not
enthusiastically set up for missionaries and only
indulged themselves in the delights of a prac-
tical instruction of the pretty women they liked
well enough to teach and who desired to be
taught; but as such a proposal might be too
shocking for a young beginner, the old timers
were to set an example which he hoped I would
not be averse to follow, as I was at liberty to
refuse the party if I wished. My countenance
no doubt expressed my surprise as my silence
did my acquiescence to embark on any voyage
the company desired to take me on.

The first couple that stood up to open the ball
was a colonel and the soft and amourous Louisa.
He led her to the couch, nothing loth, on which
he gave her the fall and extended her at length
with an air of vigour relishing high of amourous eagerness and impatience. The girl spreading herself to the best advantage, with her head
on the pillow, was so concentrated in what she
was about that our presence was the least of
her care and concern. Her petticoats thrown
up showed the company the finest shaped legs
and thighs that could be imagined, and in full
view that delicious cleft of flesh over which the
pleasing hair parted and presented a most
inviting entrance between two close hedges
delicately soft and pouting. Her gallant was
now ready having disencumbered himself from
his clothes and showing us his forces in high
plight and ready for action. But giving us no

time to consider the dimensions of it, he threw
himself instantly upon his charming antagonist,
who received him as he pushed dead at the mark
like a heroine without flinching; for surely
never had a girl a truer taste for joy, nor
sincerer in the expressions of its sensations than
she; we could observe pleasure lighten in her
eyes as he introduced his plenipotentiary instrument into her till, having inflated her to its
utmost, its irritations grew so violent and gave
her the spurs so furiously that she was lost to
everything but the enjoyment of her favourite
feelings and she returned his thrusts with a
concert of springy heaves, keeping time with
the most pathetic sighs so exactly that one
might have counted their strokes by her distinct
murmurs, whilst her active limbs kept wreathing and intertwining with his in convulsive
folds; then the kisses and poignant painless love
bites which they both exchanged in a rage of
delight all conspired towards the melting point.
It soon came on, when Louisa in the ravings of
her pleasure frenzy and beyond all restraint,
cried out: "Oh! Oh! Sweetheart! Don't
spare me! ah! ah! a-h-h-h-!" her accents faltering into heart-fetched sighs while her eyes
closed in sweet death, at the same time she was
embalmed by an injection of which we could
easily see the signs in the quiet, dying, languid
posture of her late so furious driver, who now
suddenly stopped, breathing short, panting and
for that time giving up the spirit of pleasure.
As soon as he had dismounted Louisa sprung

up, shook her petticoats and running up to me
gave me a kiss and drew me to the side-board
where she and her gallant made me pledge them
in a glass of wine and toast a droll health.

By this time the second couple was ready to
enter the lists, which was a young baronet and
that most delicious of charmers, the winning,
tender Harriet. And surely never did one of
her profession play the bareface part she was
engaged to play with such grace, sweetness,
modesty and yielding coyness as she did. Her
air and motions breathed only unreserved,
unlimited compliance without the least mixture
of imprudence or prostitution. But what was
more surprising, her spark-elect in the midst of
this open public enjoyment, doted on her to
distraction and had by dint of love and sentiment touched her heart, though for awhile restraint of her duty to the house laid him under
a kind of necessity of complying with an institution which he himself had had the greatest
share in establishing. Harriet was then led to
the vacant couch by her gallant, blushing as she
looked at me and with eyes tenderly asking of
me the most favourable construction of the step
she was thus irresistibly drawn into. Her
lover, for such he was, sat by her at the foot
of the couch, and passing his arm around about
her neck, preluded with a kiss fervently applied
to her lips, which visibly gave her life and spirit
to go through with the scene, and as he kissed
her they gently fell back on the couch their
heads resting on the pillow. Then as if he had

guessed our wishes, or meant to gratify at once
his pleasure and pride in being the master by
title of present possession of beauties delicate
beyond imagination, he uncovered her breasts
to his touch and our view; oh how delicately
moulded they were, small, firm, round and exquisitely white, the grain of their skin so soft
and soothing to the touch, and the nipples which
crowned them the sweetest buds of beauty.
When he had feasted his eyes and touch with
them, and his lips with kisses of the highest
relish imprinted on those most delicious twin
buds, he proceeded downwards. Her feet were
still on the floor, and with the tenderest attention
not to shock or alarm her too suddenly he by
degrees rather stole than rolled up her petticoats, at which as if a signal had been given
Louisa and Emily took hold of her legs in pure
wantoness and stretched them wide apart, exposing to our view the finest exhibtion of female
charms even seen. The whole company who
had often seen them, except myself, seemed as
much dazzled and delighted as one would be who
beheld them for the first time. Beauties so excessive could not but enjoy the privilege of
eternal worship. Her thighs were so exquisitely
fashioned that either more or less flesh than
they had would have reduced them in perfection.
But what infinitely enriched and adorned them
was the sweet intersection formed where they
met, at the bottom of the smoothest, roundest,
whitest belly, between two soft pouting lips
which were in perfect symmetry with the rest

of her frame, and arched over with a dark, downy moss.

Her enamoured gallant who remained absorbed and engrossed by the pleasure of the sight long enough to afford us time to feast our eyes, now prepared himself for more material enjoyment, and drawing the curtain that hung between us and his master member of the revels, exhibited one whose size proclaimed him a true woman's hero. Standing between Harriet's legs, which were still supported at their widest extension by her two companions, he gently opened the lips of that luscious mouth of nature and steered his mighty machine to its lair from the end of his stiff stand-up to his belly; the lips kept open by his fingers received its broad shelving head of coral hue, then pausing there a little he nestled it in and the girls delivered over to his hips the agreeable task of supporting her thighs; and now as if he meant to give his pleasure the longest play for its life, he inserted his instrument so slowly that we lost sight of it inch by inch, till at length it was wholly taken into the soft laboratory of love and the mossy mounts of each met fairly together. In the meantime we could plainly see the prodigious effect the progressions of this delightful machine wrought in this delicious girl, gradually heightening her beauty as it heightened her pleasure. Her countenance grew animated, the faint blush of her cheeks gaining ground on the white, deepened into a vivid vermillion glow and her naturally brilliant eyes now sparkled

with ten-fold lustre; her languor vanished and
she became lively and spirited. He had now
fixed and nailed this tender creature with his
home driving wedge so that she lay passive by
force and unable to stir, till beginning to urge
the to-and-fro motion he awakened and roused
her so that unable to contain herself she could
not but reciprocate to his motions briskly, till
the raging stings of pleasure rising toward the
climax made her wild with the intolerable sensations of it and she threw her legs and arms
about at random as she lay lost in the sweet
transport; which on his side declared itself by
quicker eager thrusts, convulsive gasps, burning sighs, swift laborious breathing, eyes dart-
ing humid fires and all the faithful tokens of the
imminent approaches of the last gasp of joy.
It came on at length, the baronet led the ecstacy
which she joined in as she felt the melting
symptoms from him, in the midst of which,
gluing his lips to hers more ardently than ever,
he showed all the signs of that agony of bliss
being strong upon him and he gave her the
finishing titillation, inwardly thrilled with which
she answered with all the effusion she was
mistress of whilst a soft shudder ran through
her limbs and she stretched out and lay motionless, breathless, dying with delight, the nearly
closed lids of her eyes showing just the edges
of their iris and her sweet lips parted and showing the tip of her tongue while their natural
ruby colour glowed with heightened life. Was
this not a subject to dwell upon? and accordingly

her lover still kept upon her in joyful bliss, till compressed, squeezed and drained to the last drop he took leave with one fervant kiss expressing satisfied desires but unextinguished love. As soon as he was off I ran to her and sitting down on the coach by her raised her head which she inclined on my bosom to hide her blushes and confusion at what had passed, till by degrees she composed herself and accepted a glass of wine from my spark whilst her own was adjusting his affair and buttoning up, after which he led her leaning languishing upon him to a place to view the couch.

And now Emily's partner had taken her out for her share in the dance. This fair and sweet tempered creature had a complexion that would put the rose and lily out of countenance; extremely pretty features and that florid health and bloom for which the country girls are so lovely; she certainly was a beauty and one of the most striking of the fair ones. Her gallant began first to disengage her breasts as she stood up and restore them to the liberty of nature. On their coming out to view we thought a new light was added to the room, so superiorly shining was their whiteness, and they rose in so nice a swell as to give her a perfect formed fullness of bosom that seemed like flesh hardened into marble, of which it emulated the polish gloss and far surpassed even the whitest in the life and lustre of its colours veined with blue. Who could refrain from such provoking enticements in reach? He caressed her breasts, first

lightly and the glossy firmness of the skin eluded
his hand and made it slip along the surface;
he pressed them and the springy flesh thus
dented by force, rose again reboundingly; and
indeed this was the consistency of all parts of
her body where the fullness of her flesh con-
stituted that fine plumpness which the touch is
so greatly attracted to. When he had thus
greatly pleased himself with all forms of dalliance and delight, he trussed up her skirt and
tucking it in, she stood fairly naked on every
side; at this a blush overspread her lovely face
and her eyes downcast to the ground seemed
to ask for quarter when she had so great a right
to triumph in all the treasures of youth and
beauty which she now displayed. Her legs were
perfectly shaped and her thighs which she kept
pretty close, showed so white, so substantial and
abounding in firm flesh, that nothing could offer
a greater luxury to the touch, which he did not
fail to indulge himself in. Then gently removing
her hand which in the first emotion of modesty
she had carried to her treasure, he gave us a
view of that soft furough running its little
length downwards and hiding the remains of
it between her thighs with a fringe of light
brown curls in beauteous growth over it, which
with their silky gloss created a pleasing variety
from the surrounding whiteness and added to
its lustre. Her spark then endeavoured, as she
stood, to give us a complete sight of that central
charm of attraction by unclosing her thighs, but
not obtaining it so conveniently in that attitude

he led her to the couch and bringing to it one
of the pillows, gently rested her head on it, so
that as she leaned over on it still standing and
straddling with her thighs wide spread she presented a full back view of her naked person.
Her posteriors, plump, smooth and prominent,
formed luxuriant tracts of animated snow, that
splendidly filled the eye till it was drawn down
the parting or separation of those exquisite
white cliffs by their narrow vale, and was there
stopped, attracted by love's grotto which stood
moderately gaping from the influence of her
bended posture, so that the interior red of the
sides of the orifice came into view and contrast-
ing with the white that dazzled around it, gave
somewhat the idea of a pink sash in the glossiest
white satin. Her gallant, a gentleman about
thirty and somewhat inclined to stoutness, taking the hint thus tendered him of this mode of
enjoyment and encouraging Emily with kisses
and caresses, drew out his affair already erect,
the extreme length of which rather dispro-
portionate to its breadth was the more surprising, as that is not often the case with those
of his corpulency, and taking careful aim he
drove it up to the guard, whilst the round bulge
of her bottom fitted into the hollow made with
the bend of his belly and thighs, brought their
parts surely and delightfully into warm and
close conjunction while his hands he kept passing over her body and toying with her enchant-
ing breasts. As soon as she felt him as far
home as he could reach, she lifted her head a

little from the pillow and turning her neck met
the kiss he pressed forward to give her as they
were thus closely joined, and then leaving him
to pursue his delights, she hid again her face
and blushes in the pillow, and thus stood
passively whilst he kept laying at her with repeated thrust, making the meeting flesh resound
with the violence of them; as he backed from
her we could see between them part of his
long white staff foamingly in motion, till,
driving it in her again her white hillocks hid it
from sight. Sometimes he took his hand from
the semi-globes of her bosom and tranferred the
pressure of them to those large ones, the present
subjects of his soft blockade, which he squeezed,
grasped and played with till at length a spell
of driving, hotly urged, brought on the height
of their joy with such overpowering pleasure
that his fair partner had to support him as
panting, fainting and dying, he discharged, and
she feeling the killing sweetness of it yielded
to the mighty intoxication and fell fainting
forward on the couch, making it necessary for
him if he would preserve his warm pleasure hold
in her to fall upon her, where they continued in
conjunction of body and ecstatic flow their joys
for that time.

As soon as he had disengaged, the charming
Emily got up and we crowded around her with
congratulations and other officious little services,
for it is to be said that though all modesty and
reserve were banished from the transaction of
these pleasures, good manners and politeness

were invariably observed; there was no gross
ribaldry, no offensive or rude behaviour or ungenerous reproaches to the girls for their compliance with the humours and desires of the
men. On the contrary nothing was wanting to
soothe, encourage and soften the sense of their
condition to them. Men know not in general
how much they destroy of their own pleasure
when they break through the respect and tenderness due to our sex, even to those of it who live
by pleasing them. This was a maxim perfectly
well understood by these voluptuaries, these
profound adepts in the great art and science of
pleasure, who never showed their mistresses a
more tender respect than at the time when they
unlocked their treasures of concealed beauty and
showed out in the pride of their naked charms.

The frolic had now come around to me, it
being my turn of submission to the will and
pleasure of my partner as well as to that of the
company, and he coming to me with a flattering
eagerness, reminded me of the compliances my
presence there gave him hopes of; he told me,
however, that if the preceding examples had not
surmounted any repugnance I might feel in
concurring with the humours and desires of the
company, and though his own disappointment
would be great, he would suffer anything rather
than be the instrument of imposing a disagreeable task on me. To this I replied, that even
if I had not contracted a kind of engagement to
be at his disposal without the least reserve, the
example of such agreeable companions would

alone determine me and that I only regretted
appearing to so great a disadvantage after such
superior beauties. The frankness of the answer
pleased them all and my particular was compli-
mented on his acquisition, while Mrs. Cole could
not have shown me a greater mark of her regard
than in arranging for me the choice of this
young gentleman for my master of ceremonies,
for besides his noble birth and the great fortune
he was heir to, his person was uncommonly
pleasing, tall and well shaped; his face marked
with small-pox but only enough to add a grace
of more manliness to his features which were
enlivened by eyes of sparkling black, in fact
one any woman would, in the familiar style,
call a very pretty fellow.

I was now handed by him to the cockpit of
our match, where as I was dressed in nothing
but a white morning gown, he vouchsafed to
play the male Abigail on the occasion and
spared me the confusion that would have
attended the forwardness of undressing myself;
my gown was loosened in a trice and I divested
of it; my stays next offered an obstacle which
readily gave away, Louisa furnishing a pair of
scissors to cut the string, off went that shell
and dropping my petticoat I was reduced to
my shift, the open bosom of which gave the
hands and eyes all the liberty they could wish.
Here I imagined the stripping was to stop, but
I reckoned short, my spark desiring the rest
off, tenderly begged that I would not suffer the
small remains of a covering to rob them of a

full view of my whole person, and I who was too willing to please them to dispute any point, and considered the little that remained as very immaterial, assented to whatever he pleased. In an instant then my shift was drawn over my head, my cap coming with it and letting all my hair down, of which I had a very fine head.

I now stood before my judges in stark nakedness, to whom I could not appear a very disagreeable figure if you please to recollect what I have said before of my person, which time had at that period greatly improved into full and open bloom, for I still lacked some months of being eighteen. My breasts now developed to a graceful plentitude, maintained a firmness and a steady independence of any stay or support that dared and invited the test of touch. I was as tall and as slim shaped as could be consistent with that juicy plumpness of flesh which is so delightful to the senses of sight and touch. I had not, however, so thoroughly renounced all shame as not to suffer great confusion at the state I was in; but the whole troupe around me, men and women, relieved me with every mark of applause and satisfaction and flattering attention to raise and inspire me with sentiments of pride on the figure I made, which my friends gallantly protested infinitely outshone all other birthday finery ever seen, and I flatter myself on having passed this examination with the approbation of connoisseurs.

My friend, who for this time had the disposal of me humoured their curiosity and his own in placing me in all the variety of postures and lights imaginable, pointing out every beauty from every view of me with such inflammatory liberties of his roving hands and passionate kisses that made all shame fly before them, my blushing glow giving place to a warmer one of desire which led me to find some relish in the present scene. But in this general survey you may be sure the most material spot of me was not excused the strictest visitation, and it was agreed that I had not the least reason to be diffident of passing for a maid, so little flaw had my preceding adventures created there and so soon had the blemish of an over-stretch been repaired at my age in the natural smallness of that part.

Now whether my partner had exhausted all the modes of regaling the touch and touch, or whether he was now ungovernably wound up to strike, I know not, but briskly throwing off his clothes and his breeches now loosened disclosed their contents to view and showed in front the enemy I had to engage with, stiffly bearing up its head unhooded and glowing red. I then plainly saw what I had to deal with; it was one of those just-true-to-size instruments of which the masters have better command than those having the more unwieldly, inordinate sized ones. Straining me close to his bosom as he stood up against me, he applied to its obvious niche its peculiar idol and attempted to insert it which with my help he effected at once by placing my thighs around his naked hips and I received every inch close home; so that stuck upon the pleasure-pivot and clinging around his neck with my bosom glued to his, he carried me once around the couch on which he then laid me down without losing his middle hold or unsheathing and began the pleasure-grist. But so provokingly predisposed and primed as we were by all the moving sights of the night, our imagination was too much heated not to melt us immediately and I no sooner felt the warm spray from him dart up my inwards than I was at once on flow, sharing the momentary ecstacy; but I had yet greater reason to boast of our harmony, for finding that all the flames of desire were not yet quenched within me, but that rather like wet coals I glowed the fiercer for this sprinkling, my hot-mettled spark sympathising with me and loaded for a double fire, continued the sweet battery with undying vigour, accomodating all my motions to his best advantage and delight, kisses, squeezes, tender murmurs all came into play, till our joys growing more turbulent and riotous threw us into a fond disorder and as they raged to a climax, bore us far from ourselves on an ocean of pleasures into which we both plunged together in a transport of bliss. All the impressions of burning desire from the lively scenes I had witnessed, ripened by my heat, throbbed and agitated me with insupportable irritations and perfectly fevered and maddened with their excess I felt the power of such rare and exquisite provocatives as the

examples of the night had proved towards thus
exalting our pleasures, which I found with joy
my gallant shared in and expressed by his eyes
flashing eloquent flames and his action infuriated with the stings of it, which all conspired
to raise my delight by assuring me of his. Lifted
to the utmost pitch of joy that human life can
experience I reached that sweetly critical point
when scarcely preceeded by the injection of my
partner, I dissolved, and with a deep drawn sigh
sent my whole soul down to that passage where
escape was denied it by its being so deliciously
plugged and choked up. Thus we lay a few
blissful m o m e n t s , overpowered, still, and
languid, till as the sense of pleasure left us we
recovered from our trance and he slipped out
of me, not, however, before he had protested
his extreme satisfaction by the tenderest kiss
and embrace, as well as by the most cordial expressions. The company who had stood around
us in the most profound silence, when all was
over helped me hurry on my clothes and compli-
mented me on the sincere homage they could
not escape observing had been done to the
sovereignty of my charms in my receiving a
double payment of tribute at one juncture. My
partner, now dressed, showed a fondness unabated by the circumstances of our recent enjoyment and the girls also kissed and embraced
me, assuring me I need go through no further
public trials as I now was initiated and one of
them.

As it was an inviolable law for every gallant

to keep to his partner for the night especially,
or till he had relinquished possession over to
the house in order to preserve a pleasing pro-
priety and to avoid the disgust and indency of
another engagement; the company after a re-
past of biscuits, wine, tea and chocolate served
at about one in the morning, broke up and went
off in pairs. Mrs. Cole had prepared for me and
my spark an emergency folding cot to which
we retired and there ended the night in one
continued round of pleasure which we wished
might never have an end. In the morning after
breakfast in bed he got up and with very tender
assurance of his regard for me, left me to the
composure and refreshment of a sweet slumber,
on waking out of which and getting up to dress,
I found in one of my pockets a purse of guineas
which he had slipped there; and as I was musing
on a liberality I had not expected, Mrs. Cole
came in to whom I immediately told of the
present and naturally offered her whatever
share she pleased, but assuring me that the
gentleman had very nobly rewarded her she
would on no terms, or entreaties receive any
part of it. Her refusal she said was final and
she then proceeded to read me such admirable
lessons on the economy of my person and purse
that I was well paid for heeding and conforming to them in the course of my acquaintance
with the town. Then changing the conversation
to the pleasures of the preceding night, I learned
without much surprise that she had seen everything that had passed from a convenient place

arranged solely for that purpose and of which she readily made me the confidante. She had scarcely finished when the little troupe of girls, my companions, broke in and renewed their compliments and caresses. I observed with pleasure that the fatigues and excesses of the night had not affected in the least their complexions or the freshness of their bloom; this I found by their confession was due to the management and advice of our rare directress. They then went down to talk it over in the shop while I repaired to my lodging where I employed myself till I returned to dinner at Mrs. Cole's.

I stayed at Mrs. Cole's till about five in the evening with one or another of these charming girls, till seized with a sudden drowsy fit I was prevailed to go up and doze it off on Harriet's bed who left me on it to my repose. I lay down in all my clothes and fell fast asleep for about an hour's rest when I was surprisedly awakened by my new and favourite gallant, who inquiring for me was readily directed where to find me. Coming into my chamber and seeing me alone with my face turned from the light towards the inside of the bed he without more ado slipped off his trousers for the greater ease and enjoyment of the naked touch and gently turning up my petticoats behind, opened the prospect of the back avenue to the cozy seat of pleasure, where as I lay on my side at length rather inclining face downwards, I appeared full fair and liable to be entered. Laying himself down gently by me he started to plug in from behind when, feeling the warmth from his thighs and belly close against me and the endeavours of his machine to make its way well into me, I awakened pretty much startled at first, but seeing who it was I started to turn to him when he gave me a kiss and desired me to keep my posture and lifting up my upper thigh and ascertaining the right angle he soon drove it in to the farthest point, satisfied with which and solacing himself with lying closely in touch with the bare flesh of those parts he suspended motion and thus steeped in pleasure, kept me lying on my side against him, spoon-fashion, as he termed it from the snug fit of the back of my thighs into the curve of his belly and thighs; after some time that restless and turbulent inmate impatient of longer quiet, urged him to action which now proceeding to with toying, kissing and the like ended at length in liquid proof on both sides that we had not been exhausted or were quickly recovered from the night's draughts of pleasure on us.

With this agreeable youth I lived in perfect joy and constancy. He was bent on keeping me to himself, for the month at least, but his stay in London was not even so long, his father, who had a post in Ireland, taking him abruptly with him on his returning thither. Even then I nearly kept hold of his affection and person as I had consented to follow him to Ireland as soon as he was settled there, but meeting with an agreeable and advantageous match in that

kingdom he chose the wiser course and forbore
sending for me, but at the same time took care
that I should receive a very magnificent present,
which did not, however, compensate for my
deep regret in losing him.

This event created a chasm in our little
society, which Mrs. Cole with her usual caution
was in no haste to fill up, but then it redoubled
her efforts to procure me a sale for my counter-
feit maidenhead as some consolation for the sort
of widowhood I had been left in, and this was
a scheme she had never lost hope of and only
waited for a proper person to try it on.   But
I was, it seems, fated to be my own caterer in
this as I had been in my first trial on the market.
I had now passed nearly a month in the enjoyment of all the pleasures of familiarity and
society with my companions, who had all solicited the gratification of their taste for variety in
my embraces except the baron who had taken
Harriet home with him, but I had with the utmost art and skill on various pretexts eluded
their pursuit without giving them cause to
complain; this reserve was neither out of dislike
of them or disgust of the thing, but was my
attachment for my own spark and the dislike
of going with the friend of another girl who
though they seemed outwardly exempt from
jealousy, could not but in secret like me the
better for the regard I had for them.   Thus
liked by the whole family I continued to live
along easily till one day about five in the afternoon I stepped over to a fruit shop in Covent

Garden to get some fruit for the girls and myself when I met with the following adventure.

While I was chaffering for the fruit I wanted,
I observed myself followed by a young gentleman, whose rich dress first attracted my notice,
for the rest he had nothing remarkable in his
person except that he was pale, thin made and
ventured himself upon the slenderest legs. It
was easy to perceive without seeming to, that
it was I he wanted to be at and he kept his eyes
fixed on me till he came to the same basket
that I stood at, and giving the first price asked
for the fruit, he began his approaches. Now
certainly I was not at all out of figure to pass
for a modest girl. I had neither the feathers nor
appearance of a tawdry town miss; a straw
hat, a white gown, clean linen, and above all a
certain natural and easy air of modesty which
never forsook me even on those occasions I
most broke in upon it in pleasure, were all signs
that gave him no opening to conjecture my
condition. He spoke to me and this address
from a stranger making me blush, set him still
wider of the truth and I answered him with an
awkwardness and confusion the more apt as
there really was a mixture of the genuine in
them. But when proceeding on having broken
the ice into other leading questions, I put so
much innocence, simplicity and even childishness into my answers that on no better foundation, and liking my person as he did, he would
have sworn to my modesty. There is a fund
of gullibility in men that their lordly wisdom

little dreams of, and by virtue of which the most sagacious of them are often made our dupes. Amongst other queries he put to me was whether I was married. I replied that I was too young to think of that for many a year and told him I was seventeen. As for my mode of living I told him I was serving an apprenticeship to a milliner in Preston and had come to town after a relation who on my arrival I found was dead, and that I now was a journey-woman to a milliner in town. This last was not far from what I did pretend to pass for and it passed with him under favour of the increasing passion I inspired him with. After he had next got out of me very dexterously, as he thought, my name, the name of my mistress and where I lived, all of which I had no idea of keeping from him, he loaded me down with the rarest fruit and sent me home pondering on what might be the consequence of this adventure. As soon as I got to Mrs. Cole's I related to her all that had passed, on which she judiciously concluded that if he did come after me there was no harm done, and that if he made her any proposition his character and means would be well sifted so as to know whether the game was worth the candle; in the mean time all there was for me to do was to follow her cue and advice till the last act.

The next morning, after an evening spent on his part as we afterwards learned, in perquisitions into Mrs. Cole's character in the neighbourhood, of which everything he learned was most favourable to our designs upon him, my gentleman came in his cab to the shop where Mrs. Cole alone had an inkling of his errand. Asking for her he easily made her acquaintance by asking for some millinery while I sat without lifting up my eyes working on the hem of a ruffle with the utmost composure and simplicity. Mrs. Cole took care that the first impressions I made on him ran no risk of being destroyed by those of Emily and Louisa who were working with me. After vainly endeavouring to catch my eyes with his, he gave Mrs. Cole directions where to bring the things to him herself, and he went out with some goods which he paid for liberally.

The girls all this time did not in the least smell the mystery of this new customer, but Mrs. Cole as soon as we were conveniently alone assured me by virtue of her long experience in these matters that my charms had not missed fire, for by his eagerness, his manner and looks she was sure he was caught; the only point now in doubt was his character and circumstances, which her knowledge of the town would soon gain her sufficient knowledge of to take the next step. In a few hours she learned that this conquest of mine was no other than Mr. Norbert, a gentleman originally of great fortune, which with a constitution naturally not the best he had vastly impaired by his over violent pursuit of the vices of the town, in the course of which having worn out and staled of all the more common mode of debauchery, he had fallen

into a taste of maiden hunting, in which chase
he had ruined a number of girls sparing no
expense to compass his ends and generally using
them well till tired or cooled by enjoyment; or
seeing a new face he could easily disembarrass
himself of the old ones and resign them to their
fate as his sphere of achievements lay only
amongst such as he could proceed with by way
of bargain and sale. Concluding from these
facts that a character of this sort was ever a
lawful prize, and the sin would be not to make
the best of our opportunity, Mrs. Cole remarked
that she only thought that such a girl as I was
too good for him anyway and on any terms.

She went at the hour appointed to his
lodgings at one of the court inns, which were
furnished in a taste of grandeur that had an
eye to all the conveniences of luxury and
pleasure. Here she found him waiting and
after finishing her pretence of business and a
long discussion concerning her trade, the qualities of her servants, 'prentices, and journey-
woman, the talk naturally came at length to me,
when Mrs. Cole acting admirably the good old
prattling gossip who lets everything escape her
when her tongue is set in motion, cooked him up
a story so plausible of me, throwing in every
now and then such strokes of art with the sim-
plest air in praise of my person as finished him
for her purpose, whilst nothing could be better
counterfeited than her innocence of his object.
When now fired and on edge he proceeded to
drop hints of his design upon me after he had

with much confusion and trouble brought her
to the point, and she kept as long aloof as she
thought proper from understanding him, without affecting to pass for a goddess of virtue and
flying into one of those violent and ever
suspicious passions, she with better grace
affected the character of a plain, good sort of
woman that knew no harm and was made of
stuff easy and flexible enough to be wrought
upon to his ends by his superior skill and
address; but she managed so artfully that three
or four meetings took place before he could
obtain the least favourable hope of her assistance without which he had by a number of
fruitless messages and letters convinced himself
there was no getting at me, all of which also
raised my character and price with him. Regardful, however, not to carry these difficulties
to such length as might afford time for startling
discoveries or accidents unfavourable to our
plan, she at last pretended to be won over by
mere dint of entreaties, promises and above all
by the dazzling sum she took care to have agreed
on, and she now feigned her yielding to the
allurement of a large sum as a pretext for
yielding at all, in such a manner that he might
think she had never dipped her virtuous fingers
in an affair of this sort before.

Thus she led him through all kinds of difficulties and obstacles necessary to enhance the
value of the prize he aimed at, and in conclusion
he was so struck with the beauty I was mistress
of, and so eagerly bent on gaining his ends with

me, that he left her no room to boast of her
management in bringing him up to the point,
he fell for the bait so easily.   In other respects
Mr. Norbert was clear sighted enough and knew
the town perfectly, and by previous experience
even the very same imposition we were now
practicing upon him; but we had his passion for
our friend and he was so blinded by it that he
would have thought the truth a harm done to
his pleasure.   Thus brought to the point we
wanted him at, he was ready to hug himself on
the cheap bargain he considered the purchase of
my imaginary jewel was to him at three hundred
guineas to myself and a hundred to Mrs. Cole,
being a slender recompense for all her pains and
scruples she had sacrificed for the first time in
her life; the sums were to be paid down on the
spot upon delivery of my person, exclusive of
some no inconsiderate presents that had been
made in the course of the negotiations, during
which I had occasionally seen him but at proper
times and hours, when with little effort I passed
upon him for a real maid, my looks and gestures
never breathing anything except that innocence
which all men so ardently desire in us for no
other reason than to feast themselves with the
pleasure of destroying it, and which they are
so grievously with all their skill often mistaken
in.   When the articles of the treaty had been
fully agreed on and the stipulated payments
duly made, nothing remained but the execution
of the final point which was the surrender of my
person up to his free disposal and use; Mrs.

Cole managed her objections, especially to his lodgings, so nicely that it became his own notion and urgent request that this wedding should be finished at her house, but not for a thousand pounds would he have any of the servants know it and besides her good name would be gone forever; and at last it was decided that her house would be the place.

The night was then fixed with all due respect to his eagerness and impatience, and in the meantime Mrs. Cole had omitted no instructions that might enable me to come off with honour in regard to the appearance of my virginity, and favoured as I was by nature with all the narrowness and tightness necessary in that part requisite to carry out my designs, I had no occasion to borrow those auxiliaries of art that create a momentary one easily discovered by the test of a warm bath, and as to the usual sanguinary symptoms of defloration which are generally if not always attendant on it, Mrs. Cole had made me an invention of her own which could hardly miss its effect, of which more will be said in its place. Everything then being ready for Mr. Norbert's reception, he arrived at the hour of eleven at night and was let in with all the mystery of silence and secrecy by Mrs. Cole herself and brought into her bedchamber where in an old fashioned bed of hers I lay fully undressed and panting, if not with the fears of a real maid, at least with those perhaps greater of a dissembled one which gave me an air of confusion and bashfulness that maiden modesty had all the honour of and was indeed scarce distinguishable from it even by less partial eyes than those of my lover, as I will call him, for I always thought the term "cully" too cruel a reproach to the men for their abused weakness for us.

As soon as Mrs. Cole had told me the old story used on these occasions with young women abandoned for the first time to the will of man, she left us alone in her room, which by the way was well lighted up at his desire, which seemed to bode a stricter examination than he afterwards made; Mr. Norbert, still dressed, sprang towards the bed where I got my head under the clothes and defended myself a good while before he could even get at my lips to kiss them, so true is it that a false virtue on occasion even makes a greater resistance than a true one. From thence he descended to my breasts, the feel of which I disputed tooth and nail with him, till tired with my resistance and thinking probably to give a better account of me when in bed with me, he hurled off his clothes in an instant and came into bed. Meanwhile by the glimpse I stole of him, I could easily discover a person far from promising any such doughty performances as the storming of maidenheads generally requires, and whose flimsy consumptive texture gave him more the air of an invalid that was pressed, than of a volunteer on such hot service. At scarce thirty he had already reduced his strength of appetite down to a wretched dependence on forced provocatives very little seconded by the natural power of a body jaded and racked off to the lees by constant repeated over draughts of pleasure which had done the work of sixty winters on his springs of life, leaving him at the same time all the fire and heat of youth in his imagination, which served at once to torment and spur him down the precipice.

As soon as he was in bed, he threw off the bed clothes, which I suffered him to force from my hold, and I now lay as exposed as he could wish, not only to his attacks but his examination of the sheets where in the various agitations of my body through my endeavours to defend myself, he could easily assure himself there was no preparation, though to do him justice, he seemed less strict in examination than I had apprehended from so experienced a practitioner. My shift he fairly tore open, finding I made too much use of it to barricade my breasts as well as the more important avenue, yet in everything else he proceeded with all the marks of tenderness and regard for me, whilst the art of my play was to show none to him. I acted all the niceties, apprehensions and terrors supposable for a perfectly innocent girl to feel at so great a novelty as a naked man in bed with her for the first time. He scarce even obtained a kiss but what he ravished it; I put his hand away twenty times from my breasts, where he had satisfied himself of their hardness and consistence with passing for hitherto unhandled goods. But growing impatient for the main

point, he now threw himself upon me, first
trying to examine me with his finger and sought
to make himself further way; I complained of
his usage bitterly: "I did not think he would
treat a person so; I was ruined; I did not know
what I had done; I would get up, so I would;"
and at the same time kept my thighs so fast
locked that it was not for strength like his to
force them open. Finding thus my advantage
and that I had both my own and his motions at
command, the deceiving him came so easily that
it was perfectly playing upon velvet. In the
mean time his machine, which was one of those
sizes that slip in and out without being minded,
kept pretty stiffly bearing towards that part
which the shutting of my thighs barred access
to; finding at length he could do no good by
mere dint of bodily strength, he resorted to
entreaties and arguments, to which I only
answered with a tone of shame and fear that,
"I was afraid he would kill me; Lord! I would
not be treated so; I was never used so in my
born days; I wondered he was not ashamed of
himself, so I did;" with such silly infantine
moods of repulse and complaint as I judged best
adapted to express the character of innocence
and affright. Pretending, however, to yield at
length to the vehemence of his insistence in
action and words, I sparingly unclosed my
thighs so that he could just touch the cloven
inlet with the tip of his instrument; but as he
fatigued and toiled to get it in, a twist of my
body so as to receive it obliquely not only

thwarted his admission, but giving a scream as if he had pierced me to the heart, I shook him off me with such violence that he could not with all his might keep the saddle. Vexed indeed at this he seemed, but not in the way of displeasure at me for my skittishness; on the contrary, I dare swear he held me the dearer and hugged himself for the difficulties that even hurt his instant pleasure. Fired, however, now beyond all bearance of delay, he remounted and begged of me to have patience, stroking and soothing me to it by all the tenderest endearments and protestations of what he would moreover do for me; at which, feigning to be somewhat softened and abating my anger which I had shown at his hurting me so prodigiously, I suffered him to lay my thighs aside and make way for a new trial; but I watched the directions and mangement of his point so well that no sooner was the orifice in the least open to it, but I gave such a timely jerk as seemed to proceed not from the invasion of his entry, but from the pain his efforts at it put me to, a circumstance too that I did not fail to accompany with proper gestures, sighs, and cries of complaint, of which "that he had hurt me; he killed me; I should die," were the most frequent interjections. But now, after repeated attempts in which he had not made the least impression towards gaining his object, the pleasure rose so fast upon him that he could not check or delay it, and in the vigour and fury which the approaches of the height of it inspired him, he made one fierce thrust that

almost put me by my guard, and lodged his
machine far enough in me so that I could feel the
warm ejection just within the exterior orifice,
which I had the cruelty not to let him finish
there but threw him out again, not without a
most piercing exclamation, as if the pain had
put me beyond all regard of being overheard.
It was then easy to observe that he was more
satisfied, more highly pleased with the supposed
motives of his balk of consummation than he
would have been at the full attainment of it. It
was for this fact that I felt at ease for all the
falsity I employed to procure him that blissful
pleasure, which most certainly he would not
have tasted in the truth of things. Eased, however, and relieved by one discharge, he now
applied himself to sooth, encourage, and put me
into humour and patience to bear his next
attempt, which he began to prepare and gather
force for from all the incentives of the touch
and sight which he could think of and by
examining every individual part of my whole
body, which he declared his satisfaction with in
raptures of applauses, and kisses which spared
no part of me in all the eagerest wantoness of
feeling, seeing and toying. His vigour, however, did not return so soon, and I felt him more
than once pushing at the door, but in so little
condition to break in that I question whether he
had the power to enter had I held it ever so
wide open; but this he thought me too little
acquainted with to have any confusion about,
and he kept fatiguing himself and me for a long

time before he was in any state to resume his attacks with any prospect of success; and then I resisted him so strongly and kept him so at bay, that before he had made any sensible progress in point of penetration he was exceedingly sweated and worn out indeed, so that it was well in the morning before he achieved his second ejection about half way in me, I all the while crying and complaining of his prodigious vigour and the immensity of what I appeared to suffer being split up with. Tired at length with such athletic drudgery, my champion began now to give out and to gladly embrace the refreshment of some rest. Kissing me then with much affection, he presently fell fast asleep, which, as soon as I had well satisfied myself of, I carefully, so as not to waken him by my movements, played off Mrs. Cole's device for perfecting the signs of my virginity.

In each of the head bed-posts just above where the bedsteads are inserted into them, there was a small drawer so artfully adapted to the mouldings of the wood work that it might have escaped even the most curious search; the drawers were easily opened or shut by the touch of a spring and were each fitted with a shallow glass tumbler full of a prepared fluid blood in which lay soaked a sponge ready for use. All that was required was to gently reach the hand to it and taking it out, properly squeeze it between the thighs, when it yielded a great deal more of the red fluid than would save a girl's honour; after which, replacing it and touching

the spring all possibility of discovery or even
suspicion was gone; this not the work of a
quarter of a minute, and on whichever side one
lay it was equally easy and practicable to do.

Now at ease and out of fear of doubt or
suspicion of me on his part, I sought my repose,
but could obtain none, and in about half an hour
my gentleman waked again and turned towards
me while I feigned a sound sleep which he did
not long respect, but girding himself again to
renew the onset he began to kiss and caress me,
when acting as if I had just awakened, I complained of the disturbance and of the cruel pain
that this little rest had stole my senses from.
Desiring more pleasure as well as to completely
triumph over my virginity, he said everything
that he could to overcome my resistance and
bribe my patience to his end, which I now was
ready to listen to, being secure in the bloody
proof I had prepared of his victorious violence,
though I still thought it good policy not to let
him in yet awhile.   I answered to his impor-
tunities with sighs and moans, "that I was so
hurt I could not bear it, I was sure he had done
me a mischief, that he had, he was such a bad
man!"   At this, turning down the clothes and
viewing the field of battle by the glimmer of a
dying taper, he plainly saw my thighs, shift and
sheets all stained with what he took for a virgin
effusion due to his half penetration of me, at
which nothing could equal his joy and exultation.   The illusion was complete, no other conception entered his head but that of his having

been at work upon an unopened mine, which
idea on such strong evidence redoubled at once
his tenderness for me and his ardour for breaking we wholly in. Kissing me with the utmost
rapture, he comforted me and begged my pardon
for the pain he had put me to, observing withal,
that it was only a thing in course and the worst
was past; with a little courage and constancy
I should get it well over and never afterwards
experience anything but the greatest pleasure.
Giving in a little to him, I insensibly spread my
thighs and yielded him liberty of access, which
improving, he got a little ways in me, when I
worked the female screw so nicely that I kept
him from the easy mid channel direction and by
dexterous writhing and contortions, created an
artificial difficulty of entrance and made him
win it inch by inch with the most laborious
struggles, I all the while sorely complaining, till
at length with might and main winding his way
in he got it completely home, and gave my
virginity, as he thought, the coup de grace,
furnishing me with the cue of setting up a
terrible outcry, whilst he triumphant, and like a
cock, clapped his wings over his downtrod
mistress, pursued his pleasure which presently
rose in virtue of this idea of a complete victory
to a pitch that made me soon sensible of his
melting period, whilst I now lay acting the
deep-wounded, breathless, frightened, undone,
no longer maid.

You ask me, perhaps, whether all this time I
enjoyed any feeling of pleasure? I assure you,

little or none, till just towards the end a faintish sense of it came on mechanically from so long a struggle and frequent fret in that ever sensitive part; but in the first place I had no taste for the person I was suffering the embraces of on a purely mercenary account; and then, I was not entirely delighted with myself for the jade's part I was playing, whatever excuses I might plead for being brought into it; then this sensibility kept me so much mistress of my own mind and motions that I could the better manage the whole scene of deception. Recovered at length to more signs of life by his tender condolences, kisses and embraces, I upbraided him and reproached him with my ruin in such natural terms as added to his satisfaction with himself for having accomplished it; and guessing by observations of mine to spare him, when he came on again feebly enough to a further assault, I resolutely withstood any further endeavours on a pretext that flattered his prowness, of being so violently hurt and sore that I could not possibly endure a fresh trial. He then graciously granted me a respite, and the morning soon coming I got rid of further trials, for Mrs. Cole being rung for by him, came in, and was acquainted in terms of the utmost joy and rapture with his triumphant certainty of my virtue and the finishing stroke he had given it in the course of the night, of which, he added, she would see in bloody proof on the sheets. You may guess how a woman of her turn of address and experience humoured the jest and played him off with mixed exclamations of shame, anger, compassion for me, and of her being pleased that all was so well over, in which last I believe she was certainly sincere. And now as the objection which she had represented as an invincible one, to my lying the first night in his lodgings on account of my maiden fears and terrors at the thoughts of going to a gentle-man's chambers and being alone with him in bed, was surmounted, she pretended to persuade me that I should go there to him whenever he pleased and still keep up all the necessary appearances of working with her that I might not lose with my character the prospect of getting a good husband, and at the same time her house would be kept the safer from scandal. All this seemed so reasonable, so considerate to Mr. Norbert, that he never once perceived that she did not want him to resort to her house lest he might in time discover certain inconsistencies with the character she had posed in for him; besides this plan greatly flattered his own ease and views of liberty.

Leaving me then to my much wanted rest, he got up, and Mrs. Cole after settling with him all points relating to me, got him un-observed out of the house. When I awakened, she came in, and gave me due praises for my success. Acting with her usual custom she re-fused any share of the sum I had thus earned, and advised me on a secure and easy way of disposing of my affairs which now amounted to a kind of little fortune, so that a child of ten

might have kept the account and property of
them safely in its hands. I was now restored
to my former state of a kept mistress, and used
punctually to wait on Mr. Norbert at his
chambers whenever he sent a messenger for me,
at the same time I managed with so much
caution that he never once guessed the nature
of my connections with Mrs. Cole. In the mean
time, if I may judge from my own experiences,
none are better paid or better treated during
their reign than the mistress of one, who enervated by nature, debaucheries, or age, have
the least employment for the sex, and sensible
that a woman must be satisfied some way, they
ply her with a thousand little tender attentions,
presents, caresses, confidences, and exhaust
their invention of means and devices to make
up for the capital deficiency; and even towards
lessening their inability, what arts, what modes,
what refinements of pleasure have they not recourse to to raise their languid powers and press
nature into the service of their sensuality. But
here is their misfortune, when by a course of
teasing, worrying, handling, wanton postures,
lascivious motions, they have at length accomplished a flashy enervated enjoyment, they
at the same time light up a flame in the object
of their passion, that, not having the means
themselves to quench, drives her for relief into
the next person's arms who can finish their
work; and thus they become bawds to some
favourite, tried and approved of, for a more
vigorous and satisfactory execution; for with

women of our turn especially, there is a controlling spring or queen-seat in us that governs itself by its own maxims of state, amongst which one, in the matter of its dues, is to never accept the will for the deed. Mr. Norbert, though he professed to like me extremely, could but seldom consummate the main joy itself with me, without such a length and variety of preparations as were wearisome. Sometimes he would strip me stark naked on a carpet, by a good fire, where he would contemplate me almost by the hour, disposing me in all the figures and attitudes of body that it was possible to be viewed in, kissing me on every part, the most secret and critical one so far from excepted that it received most of that branch of homage. Then his touches were so exquisitely wanton, so luxuriously diffused and penetrated me at times so that he made me perfectly rage with titillating fires, when after all and much ado, he had gained a short lived erection, he would perhaps melt it away in a sweat, or a premature abortive effusion, that provokingly mocked my eager desires; or, if carried home, how insufficient the sprinkle of a few heartdrops to extinguish all the flames he had kindled!

One evening I remember that returning home from him with a spirit he had raised to a height his wand had proved too weak to lay, as I turned the corner of a street, I was overtaken by a young sailor. I was then in that spruce, neat, plain dress which I ever affected, and perhaps might have had in my walk a certain air

of restlessness unknown to the composure of
cooler thoughts. However, he seized me as a
prize and without further ceremony threw his
arms around me and kissed me boisterously and
sweetly. I looked at him with a beginning of
anger and indignation at his rudeness, that
softened away into other sentiments as I viewed
him, for he was tall, manly-carriaged, handsome of body and face, so that I ended my
stare with asking him in a tone turned to tenderness, what he meant; at which with the same
frankness and vivacity as he had begun with,
he proposed treating me with a glass of wine.
Now it is certain that had I been in a calmer
state of blood than I was, had I not been under
a spell of unappeased irritations and desires, I
should have refused him without hesitation,
but I do not know what it was, my pressing
needs, his figure, the occasion, and if you will,
the powerful combination of all of these with
a little curiosity to see the end of an adventure so novel as being treated as a common
street walker, made me give a silent consent;
in short, it was not my head that I now obeyed,
I suffered myself to be towed along as it were
by this man-of-war, who took me under his arm
as familiarly as if he had known me all his life
and led me into the next convenient tavern,
where we were shown into a little room. Here,
scarce allowing himself patience till the waiter
brought in the wine he called for, he fell directly
on board me, and, untucking my handkerchief
and giving me a snatching kiss, he laid my

breasts bare at once and handled them with a keeness of gust that abridged a ceremony always more tiresome than pleasing on such pressing occasions, and now hurrying towards the main point we found no conveniency for our purpose, two or three disabled chairs and a rickety table composing all the furniture of the room.

Without more ado, he planted me standing with my back against the wall and my petticoats up, and coming out with a splitter indeed, made it shine as he brandished it before my eyes, and going to work with an impetuosity and eagerness bred very likely by a long fast at sea, started to give me a taste of it. I straddled, I changed my posture, and did my best to buckle to it; I got part of it in, but still things did not go to his thorough likening. Changing then in a trice his system of battery, he led me to the table and laid me face down on the edge of it, and canting up my petticoats and shift, bared my naked posteriors to his blind and furious attack and forced his way in between them, and I feeling pretty certain that it was going past the right door and knocking desperately at the wrong one, told him of it. "Pooh! my dear," says he, "any port in a storm." However, altering his course a few points he fixed it right and drove it up with a delicious stiffness, making, everything foam with such fire and spirit, that in the fine condition I was in, being stirred up as fiercely as I was, I got the start of him and went off into the melting swoon, and squeezing him whilst in the convulsive grasp of it, drew from him such a plenteous bedewal as completely soaked all those parts and drowned in a deluge all my raging conflagration of desire.

When this was over, I was concerned how to make my retreat, for, though being extremely pleased with the difference between this warm broadside poured into me so briskly, and the tiresome pawing and toying to which I owed the unappeased flames that had driven me into this step, now I was cooler, I began to apprehend the danger of contracting an acquaintance with this agreeable stranger, who on his side spoke of passing the evening with me and continuing our intimacies with an air of determination that made me afraid of its being no easy thing to get away from him. In the mean time I was careful to conceal my uneasiness and readily pretended to consent to stay with him, telling him I should only step to my lodgings to leave a necessary message and then instantly return. This he very glibly swallowed on the notion of my being one of those unhappy street-errants who devote themselves to the pleasure of the first ruffian that will stoop to pick them up, and of course, that I would scarcely cheat myself of my hire by not returning to make the most of the job. Thus we parted, not before, however, he had ordered a supper which I had not the barbarity to disappoint him of my company to. When I finally got home and told Mrs. Cole of my adventure, she showed me so strongly the nature and folly, particularly the risks to my health, in being so open-legged and

free, that I made resolutions never to venture
so rashly again, and I passed a good many days
in continual uneasiness lest I should have met
with other reasons besides the pleasure of the
encounter to remember it by; but my fears
wronged my handsome sailor, for which I gladly
make him reparation.

I had now lived with Mr. Norbert nearly a
quarter of a year, in which time I circulated
my time very pleasantly between my amuse-
ments at Mrs. Cole's and a proper attendance
on that gentleman, who paid me profusely
for the unlimited complaisance with which I
passively humoured every caprice of pleasure
and which had won him so completely, that
finding, as he said, everything in me alone which
he had sought for in a number of women, I
had made him lose his taste for inconstancy and
new faces. But what was at least as agreeable,
as well as more flattering, was the love I had
inspired him with, which bred a deference to
me that was of great service to his health; for
having by degrees and with much patience
brought him to some husbandry of it so as to
insure the duration of his pleasures by moder-
ating their use and correcting his excess in them
which he was so addicted to and which had
shattered his constitution and destroyed his
powers in the very way he was most desirous
of living; he had grown more temperate and
more healthy, and his gratitude to me he was
about to show in a way very favourable for my
fortune, when once again caprice dashed the

cup from my lips.

His sister, Lady L., for whom he had great affection, desiring him to accompany her to Bath for her health, he could not refuse her such a favour, and accordingly thought he was only going to be gone from me for a week at the longest, however, he took his leave of me with an ominous heaviness of heart, and left me a sum far above the state of his fortune and very inconsistent with the intended shortness of his journey; but it ended in the longest leave that can be, and is never taken but once, for arriving at Bath, he was not there two days before he fell into a debauch of drinking with some friends that threw him into a high fever and carried him off in four days time, never once coming out of delirium. Had he been in his senses to make a will perhaps he might have made favourable mention of me in it. Thus I lost him, and as no condition of life is more subject to revolutions than that of a woman of pleasure, I soon recovered my cheerfulness and now beheld myself once more struck off the list of kept mistresses and returned into the bosom of the community, from which I had been for some time absent.

Mrs. Cole still continued her friendship and offered me her assistance and advice towards another choice, but I was now in ease and affluence enough to look about me at leisure, and as to any constitutional calls of pleasure, their pressure was greatly lessened by the knowledge of the ease with which they were to

be satisfied at Mrs. Cole's house, where Louisa
and Emily still continued in the old way; and
my great favourite, Harriet, used often to come
and see me and entertain me with her head and
heart full of the happiness she enjoyed with
her dear baronet, whom she loved with tenderness and constancy even though he was her
keeper and still further made her independent
by a handsome provision for her and hers. I
was then in this vacancy from any regular employ of my person in my way of business, when
one day Mrs. Cole acquainted me that there
was one Mr. Barville, who used her house, just
come back to town, and whom she was rather
perplexed about providing a suitable companion
for as he was under the tyranny of a cruel taste,
which was that of an ardent desire not only
of being unmercifully whipped himself, but of
whipping others in such fashion, that though
he paid extravagantly those who had the
courage and complaisance to submit to his
humour, there were few, particular as he was
in the choice of his subjects, who would exchange turns with him at so terrible an expense
to their skin. What still increased the oddity
of this strange fancy was that the gentleman
was young, whereas it generally attacks those
that are through age obliged to have recourse
to such drastic tactics for quickening the circulation of their sluggish juices and effecting a
conflux of the spirts of pleasure towards those
flagging, shrivelly parts that rise to life only
by virtue of the titillating ardours created by

the beating of the opposite sex.

Mrs. Cole could not ask me to submit to this treatment in any expectation of my offering my services; for in my easy circumstances it could only have been the temptation of a great novelty that would tempt me to tackle such a job, for I had never felt the least impulse or curiosity to know more of taste that promised so much more pain than pleasure to those who stood in no need of such violent goads; what then should move me to subscribe myself voluntarily to a party of pain, foreknowing it as such? To tell the plain truth it was just a sudden caprice, a gust of fancy for trying a new experiment, mixed with the vanity of proving my personal courage to Mrs. Cole that determined me at all risks to offer myself and relieve her from any further search. Accordingly I at once pleased and surprised her with an unreserved tender of my person to her friend's absolute disposal on this occasion. My good temporal mother was, however, so kind as to use all the arguments she could imagine to dissuade me, but as I persisted in my resolution and thereby acquitted my offer of any suspicion of its not having been sincerely made, she acquiesced thankfully and assured me that barring the pain I should be put to she had no scruple to engage me to this party, which, she assured me I would be liberally paid for, and which the secrecy of the transaction kept it safe from the ridicule that usually vulgarly attended those of its kind. For her part she considered pleasure of any kind the universal

port of destination, and every wind that blew
there a good one. provided it blew nobody any
harm, and that she pitied rather than blamed
those unhappy persons who are under a subjection to those arbitrary tastes that unac-
countably rule their appetites for pleasure and
which they cannot shake off.

I stood in no need of encouragement or
justification for this event, and now my word
was given I was determined to fulfill my engagement. Accordingly the night was set and I was
given all the necessary instructions of how to
act and conduct myself. The dining room was
duly prepared and lighted up, and the young
gentleman shown there waiting for my introduction to him by Mrs. Cole, who brought me
in and presented me to him in a loose dishabille
fitted for the part I was to go through. As soon
as Mr. Barville saw me, he got up with a visible
air of pleasure and surprise, and saluting me,
asked Mrs, Cole if so fine and delicate a girl
would voluntarily submit to such sufferings and
rigours as were demanded by him. She
answered him in the affirmative, and reading in
his eyes that she could not leave us too soon
alone together, she went out, after advising him
to use moderation with so tender a novice.
While she was employing his attention, mine
had been taken up with examining the figure
and person of this unfortunate young gentleman, who was condemned to have his pleasure
lashed into him as boys have their learning.

He was exceedingly fair and smooth complexioned, and appeared to me no more than twenty at most, though he was three years older; but then he owed this to a plumpness which spread through a short, squatty stature and a round plump, fresh-coloured face which gave him the look of a Bacchus, had not an air of austerity very unsuitable so that character spoiled the resemblance. His dress was very neat and plain, and far inferior to the ample fortune he was in possession of, but this was a taste of his and not avarice. As soon as Mrs. Cole had gone, he seated me near him, and now his face changed to an expression of the most pleasing sweetness and good humour the more remarkable for its sudden change from the other extreme, which I found afterwards when I knew more of his character was due to a dislike. and state of conflict with himself for being enslaved to a taste which rendered him incapable of receiving any pleasure till he submitted to the extraordinary means of procuring it by means of pain, and the constancy of this repining consciousness stamped at length that cast of sourness and severity on his features, which was in fact very foreign to the natural sweetness of his temper. After many apologies and much encouragement to go through my part without quitting, he stood up near the fire whilst I went to fetch the instruments of discipline from a closet; these were several rods made of two or three strong twigs of birch tied together, which he took and examined with as much pleasure as I did with foreboding.

Next he took from the side of the room a long broad bench made easy to lie at length on by a cushion, and everything being now ready, he took off his coat and waistcoat and at his desire I unbuttoned his breeches, and rolling up his shirt rather above his waist, he tucked it in securely, whilst I naturally directing my eyes to that master-movement in whose favour all this trouble was being taken, discovered it to be almost shrunk into his body, scarcely showing its tip above the sprout of hairy curls that covered those parts. He then gave me his garters to tie him down to the legs of the bench with, a circumstance no more necessary I suppose than that it carried out the humour of the thing, since he prescribed it for himself with the rest of the ceremony. I led him to the bed and according to my cue pretended to force him to lie down, which after some show of reluctance for form's sake, he submitted to, extending himself flat upon his belly on the bench with a pillow under his face, and as he thus tamely lay, I tied him slightly hand and foot to the legs of the bench, after which I drew his breeches down to his knees and he now lay in all the fairest display of that part of the back-view in which a pair of chubby, smooth-cheeked posteriors rose cushioning upwards from two stout, fleshy thighs to meet the scourge.

Seizing one of the rods, I stood over him, and according to his direction gave him, in one breath, ten lashes with such good-will as to make his buttocks quiver under them, whilst he

himself seemed no more concerned, or to mind
them no more than a lobster would a flea bite.
In the mean time I viewed closely the effect,
every lash had skimmed the surface of those
white cliffs which they had deeply reddened and
cut into on the side furthest from me, so that
the blood ran or stood in large drops on, and
from some of the cuts I even picked out splinters
from the rod that had stuck to the skin. Nor
was this to be wondered at considering the
greenness of the twigs and the severity of the
infliction while the surface of the skin was held
so as to yield no play. I was so moved at the
sight that I from my heart repented the under-
taking and would willingly have given up,
thinking he had had full enough, but he begged
and beseeched me to proceed. I gave him ten
more lashes, and then resting surveyed the increase of bloody appearances. At length steeled
to the sight by his stoutness in suffering, I
continued the discipline by intervals till I observed him wreathing and twisting his body in
a way that I could plainly perceive was not from
the effect of pain, but of some new and powerful
sensation. Curious to dive into the meaning
of which I approached in one of my pauses of
intermission, he kept working and grinding his
belly against the cushion under him and softly
putting my hand under his thigh, I felt the
posture of his thing which was surprising, for
that machine of his which I had taken for in-
competent of erection, or at least only to a
diminutive size, was now by virtue of all that

smart and havoc of his skin behind, grown not only to a prodigious stiffness of erection but to a size that startled even me, for its thickness was greater than I had ever seen and the head of it alone filled my hand to its utmost capacity. As he heaved and wriggled to and fro in the agitation of his strange pleasure it came into view and had something the appearance of a round fillet of veal, and like its owner, squab and short in proportion to its breadth; when he felt it in my hand, he begged I would go on briskly with my jerking or he would never arrive at the last stage of pleasure. After awhile resuming the rod and exercise of it, and fairly wearing out three bundles of them, I saw him lie still after an increase of struggles and a deep sigh or two, and he then desired me to desist which I instantly did, and proceeding to untie him, I could not but be amazed at his passive fortitude on viewing the skin of his butchered, mangled posteriors, lately so white, smooth and polished, and now a confused net work of weals, livid flesh, gashes and gore, insomuch that when he stood up he could scarcely walk. I plainly perceived on the cushion the marks of a plenteous effusion, but already his sluggard member had run up to its old nesting place and effaced itself again, as if ashamed to show its head, which nothing could raise but stripes inflicted on its opposite neighbours, who were thus constantly obliged to suffer for its caprices.

My gentleman had now put on his clothes

and recomposed himself, when giving me a kiss and placing me by him, he sat himself down as gingerly as possible on his rear-side which was too sore for him to bear resting much of his weight on. He then thanked me for the extreme pleasure I had procured him, and seeing perhaps some marks of terror in my countenance and apprehension of retaliation on my own skin, he assured me, he was ready to give up with me any further engagement I might deem myself under to him, but that if I gave my consent to proceed, he would consider the difference of my sex in its greater delicacy and incapacity to undergo pain. Reheartened at which, and piqued in honour, as I thought, not to flinch so near the trial, especially as I knew Mrs. Cole was an eye-witness from her peep hole to the whole of our transactions, I was now less afraid of my skin than of his not furnishing me with an opportunity of carrying out my resolution. My courage was still more in my head than in my heart, and as cowards rush into the danger they fear in order to be in the sooner rid of the pain of that sensation, I was entirely pleased with his hastening matters into execution.

He had little to do but to unloose the strings of my petticoats and lift them, together with my shift, navel high. Then looking me over with great seeming delight, he laid me at length on my belly upon the bench, and when expecting to be tied as he was, I held out my hands with some fear, he told me he would by no means terrify me unnecessarily with such a confinement, for though he meant to put my courage to a trial, the standing of it was to be completely voluntary on my side and therefore I might be at full liberty to get up whenever I found the pain too much for me. You cannot imagine how much I thought myself bound by being thus allowed to remain loose, and how much spirit this confidence in me gave me. All my back parts being naked half-way up were now fully at his mercy, and first, he stood at a convenient distance, delighting himself with a gloating survey of the attitude I lay in, and of all my secret parts thus exposed to him in fair display. Then springing eagerly towards me he covered all those naked parts with a fond profusion of kisses and taking hold of the rod rather wantoned with me in gentle inflictions on those soft tender, trembling masses of my flesh behind, till by degrees he began to tingle them with smarter lashes, so as to provoke a red colour in them, when I knew as well by the flagrant glow I felt there as by his telling me of it. When he had thus amused himself with admiring and toying with them, he went on to strike harder and still harder, so that I needed all my patience not to cry out or complain. At last he twigged me so smartly as to fetch blood in more than one lash, at sight of which he flung down the rods, and sucking the wounds eased a good deal of my pain. But now raising me on my knees and making me kneel with them straddling wide apart, that tender part of me, naturally the seat of pleasure and not of pain,

came in for a share of suffering; for now eyeing
it wishfully he directed the rod so that the
sharp ends of the twigs lighted there so sensibly
that I could not help wincing and writhing my
limbs with the smart, throwing my body into
a variety of postures and points of view fit to
feast the luxury of the eye. Still I bore everything without crying out, when presently giving
me another pause, he rushed, as it were, on that
part whose lips had felt his cruelty, and by way
of reparation, glued his own to them, then he
opened, shut, squeezed them, plucked softly the
overgrowing moss in a wild passionate rapture
that expressed great pleasure, till betaking
himself to the rod again, encouraged by my
passiveness and infuriated with this strange
taste of delight, he made my poor posteriors
pay for the ungovernableness of it; for now
showing them no quarter, he cut me so that I
nearly fainted away when he stopped. I did
not utter one groan or angry expostulation, but
in my heart I resolved never to expose myself
again to the like severities, the smart of which
made me pout a little, and not with the greatest
air of satisfaction receive the after caresses of
the author of my pain.

As soon as my clothes were huddled on in
a little decency, a supper was brought in by the
discreet Mrs. Cole herself, which might have
piqued the sensuality of a cardinal and was accompanied with a choice of the richest wines,
all of which she set before us and went out
again without having by a word or smile given

us the least interruption or confusion in those moments of secrecy that we were not yet ready to admit a third person to. I sat down gently then, hardly in a charitable mood with my butcher, for such I could not but help considering him and was rather piqued at the gay, satisfied air of his countenance, which I thought myself insulted by. But when I had had a glass of wine and eaten, all the while observing a profound silence, I felt somewhat cheered and restored in spirits, and as the smart began to go away my good humour returned which he did not fail to notice and do everything to increase. Hardly was supper over before a change so incredible was wrought in me, such violent, yet pleasingly irksome sensations took possession of me, that I scarce knew how to contain myself; the smart of the lashes was now converted into such a prickly heat, such fiery tinglings, as made me sigh, squeeze my thighs together, and shift and wriggle about in my seat with a furious restlessness, whilst these itching ardours in those parts on which the storm of discipline had principally fallen, caused legions of burning, subtle stimulating spirits to my pleasure-center where their titillating raged so furiously that I was even stinging mad with them. No wonder that in such a condition and devoured by flames that licked up all modesty and reserve, my eyes, now charged full of the most intense desire, showed my companion very intelligible signals of distress, my companion, who now grew every instant

more necessary to my urgent need and wish for
the immediate satisfaction of my desire.

Mr. Barville, no stranger by experience to
these situations, soon knew of the pass I was
in, and removing the table out of the way, he
began a prelude that promised me relief, but
not as soon as I could wish, for as he unbuttoned
and tried to provoke and rouse his unactive,
torpid machine, he blushingly owned that no
good was to be expected of it unless I took it in
hand to re-excite its languid loitering powers
by refreshing the smart of the recent raw cuts;
for it could no more than a boy's top keep up
without lashing. Seeing that I should work as
much for my own profit as his, I hurried to
comply with his desire and abridging the ceremony, by his leaning on the back of a chair, I
scarcely made him feel the lash before I saw
the object of my desires give signs of life, and
presently, as if by a magic touch, it started up
into a noble size indeed. Hastening then to
give me the benefit of it, he threw me down on
the bench, but such was the soreness of those
parts behind on my resting hard enough upon
them to compass the admission of the stu-
pendous head of his machine, that I could not
bear it. I got up then, and tried by leaning
forwards and turning the crupper on my assailant to let him at the back avenue; but here
it was likewise impossible to stand his bearing
so fiercely against me in his agitations and endeavours to enter that way, whilst his belly
battered directly against the recent sore. What

should we do now? Both intolerably heated,
both in a fury; but pleasure is ever inventive
for its own ends; he stripped me in a trice stark
naked and placing a cushion on the carpet before
the fire, tipped me gently, over on it, topsy-
turvy, and holding me only by the waist brought
my legs around his waist, so that my head was
kept from the floor only by my hands; thus I
stood on my head and hands supported by him
in such a manner that my thighs clung around
and my center of pleasure fairly beared the
object of its rage, which now stood in fine condition to give me satisfaction for my injuries.
But this was not the easiest posture, and, our
imaginations wound up to their height could
suffer no delay, he first with the utmost eagerness, just lipped-lodged that broad acorn
fashioned head of his instrument, and still be-
friended by the fury of his desire, he soon
stuffed in the rest, when with a series of thrusts,
fiercely urged, he absolutely overpowered and
absorbed all sense of pain and uneasiness,
whether from my wounds behind, my unac-
customed position, or the over-size of his
stretcher, in a predominant delight; and all my
spirits of life and sensation, rushing impetuous-
ly to the cockpit where the prize of pleasure was
hotly in dispute, I soon received the dear relief
of nature from my over violent strains and
provocations, syncronizing with which my
gallant spouted into me such a potent overflow
of balsamic injection as softened all those irritating stings of this new species of titillation,

which I had been so intolerably maddened with,
and restored my senses to some fair degree of
composure.

I had now achieved this rare adventure much
more to my satisfaction than I had thought
from the nature of it, it would turn out; nor
was it lessened by my spark's lavish praises of
my constancy and complaisance, which he gave
weight to by a present that greatly surpassed
my utmost expectation. I was not, however, at
any time, enticed to renew with him, or resort
again to the violent expedient of lashing nature
into more haste than good speed, which, by the
way, I conceive acts somewhat in the manner
of a dose of Spanish fly, with more pain perhaps
but less danger; it might be necessary to him
but was not to me, whose appetite needed the
bridle more than the spurs. Mrs. Cole now
looked on me as a girl after her own heart,
afraid of nothing, and on good account, willing
to fight all the weapons of pleasure. In consequence then of these impressions, he endeavoured to promote either my profit or
pleasure, and she therefore procured for me a
new gallant of a very singular turn of mind.

This was a grave, staid, solemn, elderly
gentleman, whose peculiar humour was a delight
in combing fine tresses of hair, and as I was
perfectly suited to his taste, he used to come
constantly at my toilet hours, when I let down
my hair and abandoned it to him to do what he
pleased with, and accordingly he would keep me
an hour or more playing with it, drawing the

comb through it, winding the curls round his fingers, even kissing it as he smoothed it, and all this led to no other use of my person, or any other liberties whatever, any more than if a distinction of sexes had not existed. Another peculiarity of taste he had was to present me with a dozen pair of white kid gloves at a time; these he would divert himself with by drawing on me, and then biting off the finger ends; all of which fooleries of a sickly appetite the old gentleman paid for with substantial favours. This lasted till a violent cough, seized and laid him up, delivering me from a most innocent and insipid trifler, for I never heard more of him after his illness.

You may be sure a side job of this sort interfered with no other pursuits or plan of life I led, in truth, with a modesty and reserve that was less the work of virtue than of exhausted novelty, a glut of pleasure, and easy circumstances that made me indifferent to any engagements in which pleasure and profit were not eminently united, and such I could afford to wait for at the hands of time and fortune, as I was satisfied I could never mend my pennyworths, having been served with the best and pampered with dainties; besides, in the sacrifice of a few momentary impulses, I found a secret satisfaction in respecting myself, as well as preserving the life and freshness of my complexion. Louisa and Emily did not carry indeed their reserve so far as I did; but still they were far from cheap or abandoned, though two of their adventures seemed to contradict this general character, which, for their singularity, I shall tell you, beginning first with Emily's.

Louisa and she went one night to a ball, the first in the habit of a shepherdess and Emily in that of a shepherd. I saw them in their dresses before they went, and nothing could represent a prettier boy than Emily, being so fair and well-limbed. They had kept together for some time, when Louisa, meeting an old acquaintance of hers, very cordially gave her companion the drop, and left her under her protection of her boy's habit, which was not much, and of her discretion, which was, it seems, still less. Emily, finding herself deserted, sauntered thoughtlessly about awhile, and as much for coolness and air as anything else, at length pulled off her mask and went to the sideboard, where eyed and marked out by a gentleman in a very handsome domino, she was accosted by and fell into chat with him. The domino, after a little discourse, in which Emily doubtless distinguished her good nature and easiness more than her wit, began to make violent love to her, and drawing her insensibly to some benches at the lower end of the masquerade room, got her to sit by him, where he squeezed her hands, pinched her cheeks, praised and played with her fine hair, admired her complexion, and all in a style of courtship dashed with a certain oddity, that not comprehending the meaning of, poor Emily attributed to his falling in with the humour of her dis-

guise; and being naturally not the cruelest of
her profession, began to incline the parley on
those essentials. But here was really the point
of the joke, he took her really for what she
appeared to be, a mock-faced boy; and she, forgetting her dress, and of course ranging quite
wide of his ideas, took all those addresses to be
paid to herself as a woman, when in fact she
owed them to his not thinking her one. However, this double error was pushed to such length
on both sides, that Emily, warmed by the wine
he had plyed her with and the caresses he had
lavished upon her, suffered herself to be persuaded to go to a bagnio with him, and thus,
losing sight of Mrs. Cole's cautions, with a blind
confidence put herself into his hands to be
carried wherever he pleased. For his part equally blinded by his wishes, whilst her egregious
simplicity favoured his deception more than
the most exquisite art could have done, he
supposed, no doubt, that he had lighted on some
soft simpleton, fit for his purpose, or some
kept minion broke to his hand, who understood
him perfectly well, and entered into his designs.
But, be that as it may, he led her to a coach,
went into it with her, and brought her to a very
handsome apartment, with a bed in it. When
they were alone together, and her inamorato
began to proceed to those extremities which
instantly disclosed her sex, she said that nothing
could describe the mixture of pique, confusion
and disappointment that appeared on his countenance, joined to the mournful exclamation, "By

heavens, a woman!" This at once opened her
eyes, which had been shut in downright stupidity. However, as if he meant to retrieve his
disappointment, he still continued to toy and
fondle her, but with so staring an alteration
from extreme warmth to a chill and forced
civility, that even Emily herself could not but
take notice of it, and now began to wish she
had paid more attention to Mrs. Cole's premonitions against ever engaging with a stranger.
Now an excess of timidity followed an excess
of confidence, and she thought herself so much
at his mercy that she stood passive throughout
the whole progress of his prelude; for now,
whether the impressions of so great a beauty
had made him forgive her sex, or whether her
appearance or figure in that costume still
humoured his first illusion, he recovered by
degrees a good part of his first warmth, and
keeping Emily with her breeches still unbuttoned, stripped them down to her knees, and
gently impelling her to lean over, with her face
on the bed, placed her so that the double way
between her posteriors presented a fair choice
to him, and he was so set on a mis-placement
as to give the girl no small alarm for fear of
losing a maidenhead she had not dreamed of.
However, her complaints and resistance checked
and brought him to himself, and turning his
steed's head, he drove him at length into the
right road, and his imagination having probably
made the most of those resemblances that
flattered his taste, he got to his journey's end

with much ado; after which he led her out
himself, and after walking with her a short
distance, got her a cab, and making her a
present nothing inferior to what she could have
expected, he left her after giving directions to
the cabman to drive her home. This experience
she related to Mrs. Cole and I the next morning.
Mrs. Cole remarked that her indiscretion being
caused by a habitual credulity, there were little
hopes of anything curing her of it except repeated severe experience. For myself, I could
not conceive how it was possible for mankind
to run to such a taste, not only odious, but
absurd, and from my experience of things, impossible to gratify because it was not natural
to force such great disproportions. Mrs. Cole
only smiled at my ignorance and said nothing,
and it was some months later that I was further
enlightened by a worse demonstration and one
still more unnatural which I will now relate so
as not to return to so disagreeable a subject.

I had hired a carriage to go to Hampton to
visit Harriet, who had taken lodgings there;
Mrs. Cole had promised to go, but some important business intervening to detain her, I
was obliged to go alone and had hardly gone
a third of the way before the axle broke and
I was lucky to get out safe and sound into a
public house of tolerable good appearance. Here
the people told me that the stage would come
by in a couple of hours at farthest, upon which,
determining to wait for it, sooner than lose
the jaunt I had got so far on, I was shown to

a very clean room up one pair of stairs which
I took possession of for the time I had to stay.
Here whilst I was amusing myself with looking
out of the window, a single horse chaise stopped
at the door, out of which lightly leaped two
young gentlemen, who came in as if to eat and
refresh a little, for they gave their horse to be
held in readiness till they came out. Presently
I heard the door of the next room open when
they were shown in, and after they were served
I could hear that they shut and fastened the
door on the inside. A spirit of curiosity
prompted me to see what they were and examine
their persons and behaviour. The partition of
our rooms was one of those movable ones that
when taken down, serve occasionally to open
them into one for the conveniency of a large
company; and now my closest search could not
show me the shadow of a peep hole, a circumstance which probably had not escaped the
notice of the parties on the other side; but at
length I observed a paper patch of the same
colour as the wainscoat, which I took to conceal
some flaw, I was obliged to stand on a chair
to reach it, which I did as quietly as possible,
and with the point of a pin pierced it and opened
sufficient espial room. Applying my eye closely,
I could see the room perfectly, and the two
young sparks romping and pulling one another
about. The eldest might have been nineteen, a
tall comely young man, and the youngest not
above seventeen, fair, ruddy and well made,
and a pretty stripling in truth, who I fancy was

a country boy by his dress.

After a look of inspection which the eldest cast about the room, but probably in too much hurry and heat to notice the very small opening I had made, he said something to his companion that presently changed the face of things. For now the elder began to embrace, to press and kiss the younger, to put his hand into his bosom and give him such manifest signs of an amourous intention as made me think the other to be a girl in disguise, a mistake I was soon aware of as they proceeded to accomplish their project of preposterous pleasure and soon went to such unnatural lengths as to sicken and disgust me.

I had the patience to see to an end the criminal scene they enacted simply that I might gather more facts against them in my design to have instant justice done them; and accordingly when they had re-adjusted themselves and were preparing to go out, burning as I was with rage and indignation, I jumped down from the chair in order to raise the house upon them, but with such an unlucky impetuosity that I caught my foot and fell on my face with such violence that I lay senseless some time before any one came to my relief, so that they had more than the necessary time to make a safe retreat, which they effected, as I learned, with a haste nobody could account for until I had acquainted those of the house with the whole transaction I had been witness of.

When I got home again and told Mrs. Cole of this experience she very sensibly observed

that there was no doubt of due vengeance one
time or another overtaking these miscreants
though they had escaped for the present, but
that if I had been the instrument of their
punishment, I would have been put to a great
deal more trouble than I imagined, for of the
thing itself, the less said of it the better, but
she protested against this form of passion,
whether she might be suspected of partiality or
not, for this practice took away not only our
own living, but something from all womankind
which nature intended them to have. She also
told me that whatever effect this infamous
passion had had in other ages and countries, it
was a blessing that in our country at least there
was a plague spot visibly imprinted on all that
are tainted with it, for that among numbers of
that kind whom she had known, or at least were
under the scandalous suspicion of it, she could
name an exception whose character was not the
most worthless and despicable; for stripped of
all the manly virtues of their own sex, and
filled up with only the worst vices and follies
of ours, they were hardly less execrable than
ridiculous in their monstrous inconsistency of
loathing and condemning women, and at the
same time aping all their manners, airs, lisps
and little modes of affectation, which become
them at least better than they do these unsexed,
male misses.

But washing my hands of them, I will con-
tinue my story, and relate a sally of Louisa's,
since I had some share in it myself, and, it will

add too, one more example to thousands in confirmation of the maxim, that when women once get out of hand there are no lengths of licentiousness that they are not capable of going to. One morning that both Mrs. Cole and Emily had gone out for the day and only Louisa and I were left in charge of the house, a poor boy came to sell us some flowers in a small basket, by selling which he helped out his mother to make a maintenance for them both; nor was he fit for any other way of livelihood, since he was not only a perfect idiot, but stammered so that there was no understanding even those sounds his half dozen animal ideas at most prompted him to utter. He was perfectly well made, stout, clean limbed, tall for his age, as strong as a horse, and withal, not bad looking; so that he was not such a figure to be snuffed at either if your nicety could, in favour of such essentials, have overlooked an unwashed face, tangled hair and clothes in the most ragged plight.

We had often seen this boy and bought his flowers out of compassion; but while he stood presenting us with his basket, a sudden whim of wayward fancy seized Louisa and without consulting me, she called him in, and picking out two nosegays, gave him a half crown to change, as if she really expected him to be able to change it; the boy scratching his head, made signs to explain his disability to do so in place of words which he could not articulate. Louisa, at this said: "Well, my lad, come up stairs

with me and I will get you your due," winking
at the same time to me, and beckoning me to
accompany them, which I did after securing the
street door.

As we went up, Louisa whispered to me that
she had conceived a longing to be satisfied, and
hoped the general rule held good with regard
to this idiot and that nature had made him
amends in her best bodily gifts for her denial
of intellectual ones; begging at the same time
my assistance in procuring this satisfaction. A
want of complaisance was never my vice, and I
was so far from opposing this strange frolic,
that now, bit with the same maggot, and my
curiosity conspiring with hers, I entered plump
into it.

As soon as we entered Louisa's bed-chamber,
I undertook the lead and began the attack. As
it was not very material to be modest with a
mere idiot, I presently made very free with him,
though at my first motion of meddling, his
surprise and confusion made him receive my
advances but awkwardly, insomuch that he
bashfully shyed, till encouraging him with my
eyes, plucking him playfully by the hair, sleek-
ing his cheeks, and forwarding my point by a
number of little wantonesses I soon turned him
familiar and gave nature her sweetest alarm.
Now aroused and beginning to feel himself, we
could, amidst all the innocent laughter and grin
I had provoked him into, perceive the fire light-
ing in his eyes and diffusing over his cheeks,
and the emotion of animal pleasure glared dis-

tinctly in the simpleton's countenance; yet
struck with the novelty of everything he did not
know which way to look or move, but tame,
passive, simpering, with his mouth half open,
in stupid rapture, stood and tractably suffered
me to do what I pleased with him. I had now
through more than one rent felt of his thighs,
and my fingers too had now got within reach
of the sensitive plant, which, instead of shrink-
ing from my touch, joyed to meet it, and swelled
and grew under it, pleasingly informing me
that matters were so ripe for the discovery we
meditated that they were too mighty for the
confinement they were trying to break. A
waistband that I unbuttoned and a rag of a
shirt that I removed, revealed the whole of the
idiot's standard of distinction, erect, in full
pride and display. But such a one! It was
positively of so tremendous a size, that prepared as we were to see something extraordinary, it still surpassed our expectation and
astonished even me, who had not been used to
trading in trifles. In fine, its enormous head
seemed in hue and size not unlike a sheep's
heart; and you might have rolled dice along the
broad back of the body of it; the length of it
too was prodigious, and the rich appendage of
the treasure bag beneath, large in proportion,
helped to fill the eye and complete the proof that
his being an idiot was not quite in vain, since it
was manifest that he inherited, and largely too,
the prerogative of majesty which gives rise to
the saying: "That a fool's bauble is a lady's

playfellow." Nature, in short, had done so
much for him in these parts, that she perhaps
held herself acquitted in doing so little for his
head. For my part, who had sincerely no intention to push the joke further than simply
satisfying my curiosity with the sight of his
machine, I was content in spite of the temptation
that stared me in the face, with having raised
a May-pole for another to hang a garland on,
for by this time, easily reading Louisa's desires
in her wistful eyes, I acted the commodious part
and made her, who sought no better sport,
significant terms of encouragement to go
through with her adventure; intimating too that
I would stay and see fair play, for I had in
view to humour a new curiosity, and that was
to observe what appearances nature would put
on an idiot in the course of her darling occu-
pation.

Louisa, whose appetite was up, and who, like
the industrious bee was not above gathering the
sweets of so rare a flower, though she found
it planted on a dung hill, was but too readily
disposed to take the benefit of my work. Urged
strongly by her own desires, and emboldened
by me, she presently determined to risk a trial
of parts with the idiot, who was by this time
nobly inflamed for her purpose, by all the irri-
tation we had used to put the principles of
pleasure effectively into motion, and to wind up
the springs of its organs to their supreme pitch;
it now accordingly stood stiff and straining
ready to burst with the blood and spirits that

swelled it to a bulk. Louisa, then taking hold of the fine handle that so invitingly offered itself, led the docile youth by that master tool of his towards the bed, which he joyfully gave in to under the incitation of instinct, and delivered up to her the goad of desire. Stopped by the bed, she took the fall she loved, and leaned gently backward upon it still holding fast to his tool and taking care to give her clothes a convenient toss up, so that her thighs uncovered, and elevated, laid open all the outward prospect of the treasury of love; the rose lipped aperture presenting the cock pit so fair that it was not in nature for even an idiot to miss it. Nor did he, for Louisa, fully bent on grappling with it, and impatient of dalliance or delay, directed the point of his battering-ram, and bounded up with a rage of so voracious an appetite, to meet and favour the thrust of insertion, that the fierce activity on both sides effected it with such a sudden pain of distension, that Louisa cried out violently that she was hurt beyond bearing. But it was too late, the storm was up, and forced her to give way to it, for now the man-machine, strongly worked upon by sensual passion, felt so manfully its advantage and superiority, felt withal the sting of pleasure so intolerable, that maddening with it, his joys began to assume a furiousness which made me tremble for the too tender Louisa. He seemed at this juncture greater than himself; his countenance, before so void of meaning, or expression, now grew with the importance of

the act he was upon. In short, it was not now
that he was to be played the fool with. I, myself, was awed into a sort of respect for him by
the comely looks his actions dressed him in. His
eyes shot sparks of fire; his face glowed with
ardours that gave another life to it; his whole
frame agitated with a raging, ungovernable
impetuosity; all sensibly betraying the formidable fierceness with which the sexual instinct
acted upon him. Butting and goring all before
him, and mad and wild like an overdriven steer,
he plowed up the tender furrow, insensible to
Louisa's complaints; nothing could stop, nothing
could keep out a fury like his; which having
once got its head in, its blind rage made way
for the rest, piercing, rending and breaking
open all obstructions. The torn, split, wounded
girl cried, struggled, and invoked me to her
rescue, and endeavoured to get from under the
young savage, or shake him off, but in vain.
Her breath might as soon have stilled a storm
in winter, as all her strength have quelled his
rough assault, or put him out of his course.
And indeed, all her efforts and struggles were
managed with such disorder, that they served
rather to entangle and fold her the faster in
the twine of his boisterous arms, so that she
was tied to the stake and obliged to fight the
match out if she died for it. For his part.
instinct-ridden as he was, the expression of his
animal passion, partaking something of feroci-
ty, was rather mauling than kissing, intermixed
with eager ravenous love-bites on her cheeks

and neck, the prints of which did not wear out
for some days after.

Poor Louisa, however, bore up better than
could have been expected, and though she
suffered, yet, ever true to the good old cause,
she suffered with pleasure and enjoyed her pain.
And soon by dint of an enraged enforcement,
the brute machine, driven like a whirlwind,
wedged its way into her to its utmost extremity
and left her, in point of penetration, nothing
to fear or to desire; and now: "Gored with
the dearest morsel of the earth," Louisa lay
satisfied to her heart's content with every fibre
in those parts stretched almost to breaking on
a rack of joy, whilst the instrument of all this
over-fullness searched her senses with sweet
excess, till the pleasure gained upon her and
stung her so, that catching at length the rage
from her furious rider and sharing the riot of
his wild rapture, she went wholly out of her
mind into the favorite part of her body, the
hole of which was so fervently filled and employed; there alone she existed, lost in those delirious transports, those ecstacies of the senses,
which her winking eyes, the brightened vermillion of her lips and cheeks, and sighs of
pleasure deeply fetched, so plainly expressed.
In short, she was now a mere machine and had
her motions as little at her own command as
the idiot himself, who thus forced into her,
made her feel with a vengeance the tempestu-
ous mettle he fought with. Their active loins
quivered with the violence of their conflict, till

the surge of pleasure, foaming and raging to
its height, drew down the pearly shower that
allayed this hurricane. The idiot first shed
those tears of joy that attend its last moments
with an agony of delight, and almost gave a
roar of rapture as the gush escaped him;
Louisa kept him faithful company, going off
in unison with the old symptoms of a delicious
delirium, a tremulous, convulsive shudder, and
the passionate dying "Oh!" And now on his
getting off, she lay pleasure drenched, and
gorged with its essential sweets, but quite spent
and gasping for breath, without other sensation
of life than in those exquisite vibrations that
trembled yet on the strings of delight, which
had been so ravishingly touched and which
nature had been too intensely stirred with for
the senses to be quickly at peace from. As for
the idiot, whose enormous engine had thus been
successfully played off, his shift of countenance
and gesture had something droll, or rather
tragi-comic in it; there was now an air of sad
repining foolishness added to his natural one
of no meaning, and as he stood with his label
of manhood, now lank, unstiffened, and flapping
against his thighs, down which it reached half
way and terrible even in its fall, whilst under
the dejection of spirit and flesh, which naturally
followed, his eyes, by turns cast down towards
his struck standard, or piteously lifted to
Louisa, seemed to require at her hands what
he had parted from to her and now ruefully
missed. But the vigour of nature soon re-

turning dissipated the blast of faintness which the common law of enjoyment had subjected him to! and now his basket became his main concern, which I brought him whilst Louisa restored his dress to its usual condition and afterwards pleased him perhaps more by taking all his flowers off his hands and paying him at his rate for them, than if she had embarrassed him by a present that he would have been puzzled to account for, and might have put others on tracing the source of.

Whether she ever returned to the attack I know not, and to tell the truth, I believe not. She had had her freak out, and had pretty plentifully drowned her curiosity in a glut of pleasure, which, as it happened, had no other consequence than that the lad, who retained only a confused memory of the transaction, would, when he saw her, recognize her only to forget her in favour of the next woman, tempted, on the report of his parts, to take him in. Louisa did not long outstay this adventure at Mrs. Cole's, to whom we took care not to boast of our exploit till all fear of consequences were clearly over, for an opportunity presenting itself for proving her passion for a young fellow, she packed up her toilet at half a day's warning and went with him abroad, since which I entirely lost sight of her, and it never fell in my way to hear what became of her.

A few days after she left us, two very nice young gentlemen, who were Mrs. Cole's especial favourites, easily obtained her consent for

Emily's and my attendance to a party of pleasure at a little house belonging to one of them, situated not far up the river Thames, on the Surrey side. Everything being arranged, and it being a fine summer day, we set out after dinner and got to our rendezvous about four in the afternoon, where, landing at the foot of a neat pavillion, Emily and I were handed into it by our 'squires, and there drank tea with a cheerfulness and gaiety that the beauty of the view, the pleasantness of the weather, and the tender politeness of our sprightly gallants, naturally led us into. After tea, taking a turn in the garden, my particular, who was the master of the house, and had in no sense schemed this party of pleasure for a dry one, proposed to us, with that frankness which his familiarity at Mrs. Cole's entitled him to, as the weather was excessively hot, to bathe together under a commodious shelter that he had prepared for that purpose in a creek of the river, which a side door of the pavillion immediately communicated with and where we might be sure of having our diversion out safe from interruption and with the utmost privacy.

Emily, who never refused anything, and I, who ever delighted in bathing, or to those pleasures it was easy to guess it preceeded, took care not to wrong our training at Mrs. Cole's, and agreed to it, upon which, without loss of time, we returned to the pavillion, one door of which opened into a tent and formed a pleasing

defense against the sun, or the weather and
was as private as we could wish. The lining of
it represented forest foliage from the top down
to the sides, which were figured with fluted
pilasters, with the spaces between filled with
flower vases, the whole having a gay effect upon
the eye wherever you turned it. It reached
sufficiently into the water, yet contained convenient benches round it, on the dry ground,
either to keep our clothes, or, in short, for more
uses than resting upon. There was a side-table
loaded with sweet-meats, jellies, and other
eatables and bottles of wine and cordials, by
way of occasional relief from any rawness or
chill of the water; in fact my gallant, who
understood hospitality perfectly, had left no
requisite towards convenience or luxury un-
provided.

As soon as we had looked around this inviting spot and every preliminary of privacy
was settled, strip was the word and the young
gentleman soon dispatched the undressing of
his partner and reduced us to the naked confession of all those secrets of our persons which
dress generally hides, and of which the discovery of, generally speaking, is not one's advantage. Our hands, indeed, mechanically
carried towards the most interesting part of
us, screened, at first, everything from the tufted
cliff downwards, till we took them away at their
desire and employed them in helping off with
their clothes, in the process of which there
passed all the little wantonesses and frolic that

you might imagine. As for my spark, he was undressed all to his shirt, the fore part of which, as he leaned languishing on me he smilingly told me to observe, as it bellied out or rose and fell according to the unruly starts of the motion behind it; but it was soon fixed, for now taking off his shirt, and naked as Cupid, he showed it to me at so upright a stand as prepared me indeed for his application to me for instant ease, but, though the sight of its fine size was enough to fire me, the cooling air as I stood in this state of nature, joined with the desire I had of bathing first, enabled me to put him off, and tranquilize him with the remark that a little suspense would only set a keener edge on our pleasure. Leading the way, and showing our friends an example of constancy, which they were giving signs of losing respect to, we went hand in hand into the stream till it was up to our necks, and the grateful coolness of the water gave my senses a delicious refreshment from the sultriness of the season, and made me more alive to voluptuous impressions.

I wantoned with the water, or sportively played with my companion, leaving Emily to deal with hers at discretion. Mine, at length, not content with making me take the plunge over head and ears, kept splashing me, and provoking me with all the little playful tricks he could devise, and which I strove not to remain in his debt for. We gave a loose to mirth, and nothing would do him but giving his hand the regale of going over every part of me, neck, breasts, belly, thighs, and all the et cetera so dear to the imagination, under the pretext of washing them as we stood in the water, now no higher than the pit of our stomachs, and which did not hinder him from feeling and toying with the leak that distinguishes our sex, and is so wonderfully watertight; for his fingers, in vain dilating and opening it, only let out more flame than water into it. At the same time he made me feel of his own engine, which was so well wound up as to stand working in water, and he accordingly threw one arm round my neck and was endeavouring to get the better of the harsh constriction due to the surrounding fluid, and had in fact won his way so far as to make me sensible of the pleasing stretch of its lips from his in-driving machine, when independent of my not liking that awkward mode of enjoyment, I could not help interrupting him in order for us to become joint spectators of a plan of joy in hot operation between Emily and her partner, who, impatient of the fooleries and dalliance of the bath, had led his nymph to one of the benches on the green bank, where he was very cordially proceeding to teach her the difference betwixt jest and earnest.

There setting her on his knee, and gliding one hand over the surface of that smooth polished snow white skin of hers, which now doubly shown with a dew-bright lustre, and presented to the touch something like what one

would imagine of animated ivory, especially on
those ruby nippled globes, which the touch is
so fond of and delights to make love to, with
the other he was lusciously exposing her sweet
secret of nature, in order to make room for a
stately piece of machinery that stood upreared
between her thighs, as she continued sitting on
his lap, and which pressed her hard for admission, which the tender Emily, in a fit of
humour deliciously protracted, affected to decline, and elude the very pleasure she sighed for,
but in a style of waywardness so prettily put
on and managed as to render it ten times more
poignant; then her eyes expressed at once a
mock denial and extreme desire, whilst her
sweetness was zested with a coyness so
pleasingly provoking, her moods of keeping
him off were so delightful, that they redoubled
the impetuous rage with which he covered her
with kisses, kisses which she seemed to shy from
or scuffle for, the cunning wanton contrived
such sly returns of, as were doubtless the
sweeter for the gust she gave them, of being
stolen or ravished. Thus, Emily, who knew no
art but that which nature itself, in favour of
her principal end, pleasure, had inspired her
with, the art of yielding, coyed it indeed, but
coyed it to the purpose, for with all her straining, her wrestling, and striving to break from
the clasp of his arms, she was so far wiser than
to mean it, that in her struggles it was visible
she aimed at nothing more than multiplying
points of touch with him, and drawing yet

closer the folds that held them everywhere
entwined, like two tendrils of a vine intercurl-
ing together, the same effect as when Louisa
strove in good earnest to disengage from the
idiot, was now produced by different motives.
Meanwhile, their emersion out of the water had
caused a glow over their bodies; both equally
white and smooth skinned, so that as their
limbs were thus amorously interwoven in sweet
confusion, it was scarce possible to distinguish
who they respectively belonged to, but for the
brawnier, bolder muscles of the stronger sex.
In a little time, however, the champion was
fairly inside her and had tied the true lover's
knot, when now, adieu all the little refinements
of a finessed reluctance! adieu the friendly
feint! She was presently driven forcibly out
of the power of using any art, and indeed, what
art must not give way when nature conspiring
with her assailant, invaded the heart of her
capitol, which carried by storm, lay at the
mercy of the proud conqueror who had made
the entry triumphantly and completely, soon,
however, to become a tributary, for the engagement growing hotter and hotter at close
quarters, she presently brought him to the pass
of paying down the dear debt to nature, which
she had no sooner collected in, but like a duellist
who had laid his antagonist at his feet when he
has himself received a mortal wound, Emily
had scarce time to plume herself upon her
victory, for shot with the same discharge, she,
with a loud expiring sigh, the closing of her

eyes, the stretch-out of her limbs, and a relaxation of her whole frame, gave manifest signs that all was as it should be.

I, for my part, who had not with the calmest patience stood in the water all this time to view this warm action, leaned tenderly on my gallant, and at the close of it, seemed to ask him with my eyes, what he thought of it; but he, more eager to satisfy me by his actions than by words or looks, as we shoaled the water towards the shore, showed me the staff of love so intensely set up, that had not even charity, beginning at home, in this case, urged me to our mutual relief, it would have been cruel indeed to have suffered the youth to burst with straining when the remedy was so obvious and near at hand. Accordingly we took to a bench, whilst Emily and her spark, who belonged it seems to the sea, stood at the side-board drinking to our good voyage; for, as then he observed, we were well under weigh, with a fair wind up channel and full freighted; nor indeed were we long before we finished our trip to Cythera, and unloaded in the old haven, but as the circumstances did not admit of much variation, I shall spare you the description. You may be pleased to know, that what with a competent number of repetitions, all in the same strain, there was not a moment lost to joy all the time we stayed there, till late in the night we were escorted home by our 'squires who delivered us safe to Mrs. Cole with generous thanks to our company.

This was Emily's last adventure in my
company, for scarce a week after she was found
by accident by her parents, who were in good
circumstances and who had been punished for
their partiality to their son by the loss of him
caused by a circumstance of their over-in-
dulgence to him, upon which their love turned
to their lost and inhumanly abandoned child,
whom if they had not neglected enquiry about,
they might long before have recovered. They
were now so overjoyed at finding her, that, I
presume, it made them much less strict in
examining to the bottom of things; for they
took for granted everything that the grave and
decent appearing Mrs. Cole was pleased to tell
them, and soon afterwards sent her a handsome
acknowledgement. But it was not easy to
replace in our community the loss of so sweet
a member of it, for not to mention her beauty,
she was one of those mild, pliant characters,
that if one does not entirely esteem, one can
scarce help loving, which is not a bad combination either. Owing all her weakness to good
nature, and an indolent facility that kept her
too much at the mercy of first impressions, she
had just sense enough to know that she wanted
leading strings, and thought herself so much
obligated to any one who would take the pains
to think for her and guide her, that with that
very management she was capable of being
made a most agreeable and virtuous wife; for
vice had never been her choice, or her fate,
if it had not been for chance. This, her conduct

afterwards verified, for meeting with a match
with a neighbour's son of her own rank, who
took her as the widow of one lost at sea, for so
it seems one of her gallants, whose name she
had made free with, really was, she naturally
took to all the duties of her domestic life with
as much constancy as if she had never swerved
from a state of undebauched innocence from
her youth.

These desertions had now so far thinned Mrs.
Cole's flock that she was left with only me, but
though she was earnestly entreated and encouraged to recruit her corps, her growing in-
firmities, and above all, the tortures of a stubborn
hip gout, determined her to break up her
business and retire with a decent pittance into
the country, where I promised to go down and
live with her as soon as I had seen a little more
life and improved my small matters into a
competency that would make me independent,
for I was now, thanks to Mrs. Cole, wise enough
to keep that essential in view. Thus I was to
lose my kind preceptress, who never racked her
pupils with extortions, nor even put their hard
earnings, as she called them, under the contribution of poundage. She was a severe enemy to
the seduction of innocence, and confined her
acquisitions solely to those unfortunate young
women, who having lost it, were but the juster
objects of compassion, among these, indeed,
she picked out such as suited her views, and
taking them under her protection, rescued them
from the danger of the public sinks of ruin and

misery, to place, or form them, well or ill, in
the manner you have seen. Having settled her
affairs, she set out on her journey after taking
the most tender leave of me, and giving me
some excellent instructions with an anxiety
perfectly maternal.

I had, on my separation from Mrs. Cole,
taken a pleasant, convenient house at Marle-
bone, easy to manage for its smallness, which
I furnished neatly and modestly. There, with a
reserve of eight hundred pounds, the fruit of
my deference to Mrs. Cole's advice exclusive of
some clothes, jewels and plate, I saw myself in
purse for a long time, to wait without impatience for what the chapter of accidents might
produce in my favour. Here under the character of a young gentlewoman whose husband
had gone to sea, I had laid out such lines of
life and conduct, as leaving me at liberty to
pursue my desires, bound me nevertheless
strictly within the rules of decency and discretion, a course in which you cannot escape
observing a true pupil of Mrs. Cole's. I was
scarce in my new abode, when going out one
morning pretty early to enjoy the freshness
of it with my maid, we were alarmed with the
noise of violent coughing while we were walking
among the trees; on looking in the direction of
the noise we saw a well dressed elderly gentleman, who attacked with a sudden fit of choking
was so overcome as to be forced to give way
to it and sit down at the foot of a tree, where
he seemed suffocating with the severity of it,

being perfectly black in the face; frightened by
which we flew to his relief, loosened his cravat
and clapped him on the back, but whether to
any purpose, or whether the cough had had its
course, I know not, but the fit immediately
stopped; and now recovered to his speech and
legs, he returned me thanks with as much
emphasis as if I had saved his life. Thus naturally engaging in conversation, he acquainted
me where he lived, which was quite a distance
from where I met him and where he had strayed
on a morning walk.

He was, as I afterwards learned in the course
of the intimacy which this little accident gave
birth to, an old bachelor of sixty, but of fresh
vigorous complexion, insomuch that he scarce
looked five and forty, having never racked his
constitution by permitting his desires to over-
tax his ability. As to his birth and condition,
his parents, honest mechanics, had by the best
traces he could get of them, left him an infant
orphan on the parish, so that it was from a
charity school that by honesty and industry he
made his way into a merchant's counting house,
from whence, being sent to a house in Cadiz,
he there, by his talents and activity, acquired
not only a fortune, but an immense one, with
which he returned to his native country, where
he could not, however, fish out so much as one
single relation out of the obscurity he was born
in. Having a taste for retirement he passed his
days in all the ease of opulence without the
least parade of it; and rather studied the con-

cealment than the show of a fortune. But as I intend to devote a letter entirely to all the particulars of my acquaintance with this ever, to me, memorial friend, I shall in this touch on no more than may serve to obviate your surprise that one of my blood and relish of life should count a gallant of three score such a catch.

The progression of our acquaintance, certainly innocent at first, insensibly changed as might be expected from one of my condition of life, and as age had not subdued his tenderness for our sex, neither had it robbed him of the power of pleasure, since whatever he lacked in youth he supplemented with the advantages of experience, the sweetness of his manners and above all in touching the heart by his understanding. From him it was I first learned, and not without infinite pleasure, that I had another portion of me worth bestowing some regard on; from him I received my first instructions how to cultivate it, which I have since pushed to the little degree of improvement you see it at; he it was who first taught me to be sensible that the pleasures of the mind were superior to those of the body, at the same time that they were so far from incompatible with each other that the one served to exalt and perfect the taste of the other to a degree that the senses alone can never arrive at. Himself a rational pleasurist, much too wise to be ashamed of the pleasures of humanity, loved me indeed, but loved me with dignity far from the sourness of forwardness by which age is unpleasantly characterized, and from that childish, silly dotage that so often disgraces it, and which he himself used to turn into ridicule.

With this gentleman, who took me home soon after our acquaintance commenced, I lived near eight months, in which time my constant complaisance and docility, my attention to deserve his confidence and love, and a conduct in general devoid of the least artifice and founded on my sincere regard and esteem for him, won and attached him so firmly to me, that, after having generously trusted me with a genteel, independent settlement, continued to heap marks of affection on me, and he appointed me by an authentic will, his sole heir and executrix; a disposition which he did not outlive two months, being taken from me by a violent cold that he contracted as he unadvisedly ran to the open window on an alarm of fire some streets distant, and stood there naked breasted and exposed to the fatal damp night air.

After acquitting myself of my duty towards my deceased benefactor and paying him a tribute of unfeigned sorrow, which a little time changed into a most tender, grateful memory of him which I shall ever retain, I grew somewhat comforted by the prospect that now opened to me, if not of happiness, at least of affluence and independence. I saw myself then in the full bloom and pride of youth, for I was not yet nineteen, and my only regret, a mighty and just one, since it had my only truly beloved Charles for its object. Given him up, I had completely, having never once heard from him since our separation, which, as I found afterwards, had been my misfortune and not his neglect, for he wrote me several letters which had all miscarried; but forgotten him I never had, and amidst all my personal infidelities, not one had made a pin's point impression on a heart impenetrable to the true love passion but for him.

As soon as I was mistress of this unexpected fortune, I felt more than ever how dear he was to me, from its insufficiency to make me happy, whilst he was not to share it with me. My earliest care, consequently, was to endeavour at getting some account of him; but all my researches produced me no more than that his father had been dead for some time; and that Charles had reached his port of destination in the South Seas, where, finding the estate he was sent to recover, dwindled to a trifle by the loss of two ships, in which the bulk of his uncle's fortune lay, he had come away with the small remainder, and might, according to the best advice, in a few months return to England, from whence he had, at the time of this inquiry, been absent two years and seven months. A little eternity in love! You cannot conceive with what joy I embraced the hopes thus given me of seeing the delight of my heart again. But, as it would be some months yet, in order to divert my impatience for his return, after settling my affairs with much ease and security. I set out on a journey for Lancashire, with an

equipage suitable to my fortune, and with a
design purely to revisit my place of nativity,
for which I could not help retaining a great
tenderness; and might naturally not be sorry
to show myself there, to the advantage I was
now in pass to do, after the report Esther Davis
had spread of my being spirited away to the
plantations, for on no other supposition could
she account for my disappearance since her
leaving me so abruptly at the inn. Another
intention I had was to look for my relatives,
though I had none besides distant ones, and
prove a benefactress to them. Then Mrs. Cole's
place of retirement, laying in my way, I
promised myself the pleasure of visiting her on
this expedition.

I had taken nobody with me but a discreet,
decent woman to pass as my companion, and
we had hardly arrived at an inn about twenty
miles from London, where I was to sup and pass
the night, when such a storm of wind and rain
came on, as made me congratulate myself on
having got under shelter before it began. This
having continued a good half hour, when be-
thinking me of some directions to be given the
coachman, I sent for him, and not caring that
his shoes should soil the clean parlour in which
the cloth was laid, I stepped into the hall kitchen
where he was and where, whilst I was talking
to him, I observed two horsemen driven in by
the rain, and both wringing wet, one of whom
was asking if they could not be assisted with
a change, while their clothes were dried. But

heavens! what can express what I felt at the sound of a voice, ever present in my heart, and that it now rebounded at, and when directing my eyes toward the person it came from, they confirmed its information, in spite of so long an absence and a costume one would have taken for a disguise—but what could escape the alertness of a sense truly guided by love? A transport of joy like mine was above all consideration or schemes of surprise; and I, that instant, with the rapidity of the emotions that I felt the spur of, shot into his arms, crying out as I threw mine around his neck: "My life! My soul! My Charles!" And without further power of speech, swooned away under the pressing agitations of joy and surprise. Recovered out of my trance, I found myself in my charmer's arms in the parlour, surrounded by a crowd which this event gathered around us, and which immediately on a signal from the discreet landlady, who took him for my husband, cleared the room and left us alone to the raptures of this reunion; my joy at which had like to prove its power superior to that of my grief at our separation.

The first object that my eyes opened on was their supreme idol, and my supreme desire, Charles, on one knee, holding me fast by the hand and gazing on me with a transport of fondness. Observing my recovery, he attempted to speak, and giving vent to his impatience to hear my voice again to satisfy him that it was I; but the suddenness of the surprise continuing

to stun him, choked his utterance and he could
only stammer out a few broken, half-formed,
faltering accents, which my ears greedily drinking in, spelled and put together so as to make
out their sense: "After so long, so cruel an
absence! My dearest Fanny! Can it, can it
be you?" Stifling me at the same time with
kisses that stopped my mouth and prevented
the answer that he longed for, and increased
the delicious disorder in which all my senses
were rapturously lost. However, amidst this
crowd of blissful ideas there obtruded one cruel
doubt, that poisoned nearly all the transcendent
happiness; and what was it but my dread of its
being too excessive to be real. I trembled with
the fear of its being no more than a dream,
and of my waking out of it into the horrors of
finding it one. Under this apprehension, imagining I could not make too much of the
present prodigious joy before it would vanish
and leave me in the desert again, I clung to him
and clasped him as if to hinder him from
escaping me again. "Where have you been?
How could you leave me? Say you are still
mine; that you love me," and kissing him as if
I would consolidate lips with him, "I forgive
you, forgive my hard fortune in favour of this
restoration." All these interjections breaking
from me, in that wildness of expression that
justly passes for eloquence in love, drew from
him all the returns my fond heart could wish
or require. Our caresses, our questions, our
answers, for some time observed no order; all

crossing or interrupting one another in sweet confusion, whilst we exchanged hearts with our eyes and renewed the ratifications of a love unabated by time or absence; not a breath, not a motion, not a gesture on either side, but what was strongly impressed with it. Our hands locked in each other's returned the most passionate squeezes, so that their fiery thrill went to the heart again.

Thus absorbed and concentrated in this unutterable delight, I had not attended to the sweet author of its being, thoroughly wet and in danger of catching cold, when in good time the landlady, whom the appearance of my equipage, which, by the way, Charles knew nothing of, had gained me an interest in for me and mine, interrupted us by bringing in a decent shift of linen clothes, which now, somewhat recovered into a calmer composure by the coming in of a third person, I pressed him to take the benefit of, with a tender concern, and anxiety that made me tremble for his health. The landlady leaving us again, he proceeded to shift, in the act of which, though he proceeded with all his modesty which became these first solemn instants of our remeeting, after so long an absence, I could not refrain certain snatches of my eyes, lured by the dazzling discoveries of his naked skin, and which I could not observe the unfaded life and complexion of without emotions of tenderness and joy, that had his health too purely for their object to partake of a loose or mistimed desire.

He was soon dressed in these temporary clothes which neither fitted nor became him, yet they looked extremely well on him, in virtue of that magic charm which love put into everything that he touched; and where indeed was that dress that a figure like his would not give grace to? For now as I eyed him more in detail, I could not but observe the even favourable alteration which the time of his absence had produced in his person. There was still the requisite lineaments, still the same vivid vermillion and bloom reigning in his face, but now the roses were more fully blown, the tan of his travels and a beard somewhat more distinguishable, had, at the expense of no more delicacy than what he could well spare, given it an air of becoming manliness and maturity, that symmetrized nobly with that air of distinction with which nature had stamped it, in a rare mixture with the sweetness of it; his shoulders were grown more square, his shape more formed, more portly, but still free and airy.

In this interval I picked out of the broken, often interrupted account of himself, that he was at that instant actually on his way to London, in not the best of circumstances or condition, having been wrecked on the Irish coast and lost the little all he had brought with him from the South Seas; so that he had not got this far on his journey with his friend the captain without great shift and hardship, and having learned of his father's death and circumstances, he now had the world to begin again on a new account, a situation which he assured me in sincerity gave him no pain except that he had it not in his power to make me as happy as he wished. My fortune, you will observe, I had not mentioned, reserving it to feast myself with the surprise of it to him in calmer instants. My dress could give him no idea of the truth, not only was it mourning, but likewise in a style of plainness and simplicity that I had ever kept to with studied art. He pressed me tenderly to satisfy his ardent curiosity both with regard to my past and present state of life since his being away from me, but I found means to elude his questions by answers that promised him satisfaction at no great distance, won upon him to waive his impatience, in favour of the thorough confidence he had in my not delaying it except for reasons I should in good time acquaint him with.

Charles thus returned to my longing arms, tender, faithful, and in health, was a blessing; Charles reduced and broke down to his naked personal merit was such a circumstance, in favour of the sentiments I had for him, as exceeded my utmost desire; and accordingly I seemed so visibly charmed, so out of time and measure pleased at his mention of his ruined fortune, that he could account for it no way, but that the joy of seeing him again had swallowed up every other sense or concern. In the mean time my woman had taken all possible

care of Charles' traveling companion, and as
supper was coming in, he was introduced to
me. We four then supped together in the style
of joy, congratulation and pleasing disorder that
you may guess. For my part, though all these
agitations had left me not the least appetite
except for that uncloying feast, the sight of
my adored youth, but I endeavoured to force
myself to eat by way of example to him, who
I conjectured must want a meal after riding,
and indeed he ate like a traveler, but gazed at
and addressed me all the time like a lover.

After the cloth was taken away and the hour
of repose came on, Charles and I were without
further ceremony, in quality of man and wife,
shown up together to a very handsome apartment, and, all in course, the bed, they said, the
best in the inn. And here, decency forgive me
if once more I violate thy laws, and keeping the
curtains raised, sacrifice thee for the last time
to that confidence, without reserve, with which
I engaged to recount to you the most striking
circumstances of my youthful misdemeanors.
As soon then as we were in the room together,
left to ourselves, the sight of the bed starting
the remembrance of our first joys, and the
thought of my being instantly to share it with
the dear possessor of my virgin heart, moved
me so strongly, that it was well I leaned upon
him or I must have fainted again under the
overpowering sweet alarm. Charles saw my
confusion and forgot his own, which was scarce
less, in applying himself to lighten mine. But

now real passion had gained thorough possession of me with all its train of symptoms; a
sweet sensibility, a tender timidity, love-sick
yearnings tempered with diffidence and modesty,
all held me in a subjection of soul incomparably
dearer to me than the liberty of heart which
I had been long, too long, the mistress of, in
the course of those grosser gallantries, the
consciousness of which now made me sigh with
a virtuous confusion and regret. No real virgin
in view of the nuptial bed, could give more
bashful blushes to unblemished innocence than
I did to a sense of guilt; and indeed I loved
Charles too truly not to feel severely that I did
not deserve him.

As I kept hesitating, Charles with a fond
impatience, took the pains to undress me, and I
can remember amidst the flutter and discomposure of my senses, his exclamations of joy
and admiration, more especially at the feel of
my breasts, now set at liberty from my stays,
and which panting and rising in tumultuous
throbs, swelled upon his dear touch, and gave
it the welcome pleasure of finding them well
formed, and unfailing in firmness. I was soon
laid in bed and scarce languished an instant for
the darling partner of it before he was undressed and between the sheets with his arms
clasped around me, giving and taking with inexpressible fervour a kiss of welcome, that my
heart rising to my lips stamped with its warmest
impression, concurring to my bliss with that
delicate and voluptuous emotion which Charles

alone had the secret to execute, and which con-
stitutes the very life, the very essence of
pleasure. Meanwhile, two candles lighted on
a side table near us, and a joyous wood fire,
threw a light over the bed, and the sight of
my idolized youth was alone, from the ardour
with which I had wished it, without other
causes, a pleasure to die of.

But as action was now a necessity to desires
so much on edge as ours, Charles, after a short
prelude of dalliance, lifting up my night dress,
laid his broad manly chest close to my bosom,
both beating with the tenderest alarms; when
now, the sense of his glowing body in naked
touch with mine, took all power over my
thoughts out of my own disposal, and delivered
up every faculty of the soul to the greatest joy,
which affected me infinitely more because of
the person, than because of sex, now brought
my heart deliciously into play, my heart, which
eternally constant to Charles, had never taken
any part in my occasional sacrifices to the calls
of constitution, complaisance, or livelihood. But
ah! what became of me, when as the powers of
solid pleasure grew upon me, I could feel the
stiff stake that had been adorned with the
trophies of my despoiled virginity, bearing hard
and inflexible against one of my thighs, which
I had not yet opened from modesty, revived by
a passion too sincere to suffer any aiming at
the false merit of difficulty, or of my putting on
an impertinent mock coyness.

I have, I believe, somewhere before remarked,

that the feel of that favourite piece of manhood has, in the very feel of it, something inimitably pathetic. Nothing can be dearer to the touch, or can affect it with a more delicious sensation. Think then, as a lover thinks, what must be the consummate transport of that quickest of our senses, in their central seat, when after so long a deprival, it felt itself reinflamed under the pressure of that peculiar sceptre member which commands us all, but especially my darling, elect from the whole world. And now, at its mightiest point of stiffness, it felt to me something so subduing, so active, so solid and agreeable, that I know not what name to give its singular impression; but the sentiment of consciousness of its belonging to my beloved youth, gave me so pleasing an agitation, and worked so strongly on my soul, that it sent all its sensitive spirits to that organ of bliss in me dedicated to its reception. There concentrating to a point, like rays in a burning-glass, they glowed, they burnt with the intensest heat; the springs of pleasure were, in short, wound up to such a pitch, I panted now with so exquisitely keen an appetite for the eminent enjoyment, that I was even sick with desire and unequal to support the combination of two distinct ideas that delightfully distracted me; for all the thought I was capable of, was that I was now in touch with the instrument of pleasure, and the great seal of love; and I lay overwhelmed, absorbed, lost in an abyss of joy, and dying with immoderate delight.

Charles roused me out of this ecstatic distraction with a complaint softly murmured
amidst a crowd of kisses, at, my position, which
was not favourable to his desire and urgent
insistence for admission, his insistence alone
was so engrossing a pleasure, that it made me
inconsistently suffer a much dearer one to keep
him out; but how sweet to correct such a
mistake. My thighs, now obedient to the in-
timations of love and nature, gladly opened,
and with a ready submission, resigned up the
soft gateway to the entrance of pleasure. I
feel the delicious velvet tip! He enters me
might and main, with oh!—my pen drops from
my hand in the ecstacy now present from my
faithful memory! Description too deserts me,
and delivers over a task above its strength to
the imagination; but it must be an imagination
exalted by such flame as mine that can do justice
to that sweetest, most delightful of all sensations, that welcomed and accompanied the stiff
insinuation all the way up, till it was at the
end of its penetration, sending up through my
eyes, sparks of the love-fire that ran all over
me and blazed in every vein and pore of me,
a system incarnate of joy all over.

I had now totally taken in love's true arrow
from the point up to the feather, in that part,
where making no new wound, the lips of the
original one of nature, which had owed its first
breathing to his dear instrument, clung, as if
sensible of gratitude, in eager suction round
it, whilst all its inwards embraced it tenderly,

with a warmth of gust, a compressive energy,
that gave it in its way the heartiest welcome in
nature, every fibre there gathering tight around
it, and straining ambitiously to come in for its
share of the blissful touch. As we gave then a
few moments pause to the delectation of the
senses, in dwelling with the highest relish on
this intimate point of reunion, and chewing the
cud of enjoyment, the impatience natural to
pleasure soon drove us into action. Then began
the driving tumult on his side and the responsive
heaves on mine, which kept me up to him, whilst
as our joys grew too great for utterance, our
mouths, voluptuously joining, became one, how
delicious! how poignantly luscious! And now,
now I felt to the very heart of me the prodigious keen edge with which love, presiding
over this act points to pleasure; love, that may
be styled the Attic salt of enjoyment, and indeed
without it, the joy, great as it is, is still a vulgar
one, whether in a king or a beggar, for it is
undoubtedly love alone that refines, ennobles
and exalts it. Thus, happy in heart, happy in
senses, it was beyond all power, even of thought,
to form a conception of a greater delight that
what I was now consummating the fruition of.

Charles, whose whole frame was convulsed
with the agitation of his rapture, whilst the
tenderest fires trembled in his eyes, assured me
of a perfect concord of joy, and penetrated me
so profoundly, touched me so vitally, took me
so much out of my own possession, whilst he
seemed himself so much in mine, that in a

delicious enthusiasm, I imagined such a trans-
fusion of heart and spirit, as that coalescing,
and making one body and soul with him, I was
him, and he me. But all this pleasure tending
towards its own dissolution, lived too fast not
to bring on upon the spur its delicious moment
of mortality; for presently the approach of the
tender agony showed itself by the usual signals,
that were quickly followed by my dear lover's
emanation of himself, that spurted out and shot
feeling indeed up my ravished indraught, where
the sweetly soothing balmy titillation opened all
the sluices of joy on my side, which ecstatically
in flow, helped to allay the purient glow and
drowned our pleasures for a while. Soon, however, to be afloat again, for Charles, true to
nature's laws, in one breath, expiring and
ejaculating, languished not long in the dis-
solving trance, but recovering spirit again, soon
gave me to feel that the springs of pleasure were
by love, and perhaps by a long vacation, wound
up too high to be let down by a single explosion;
his stiffness still stood my friend. Resuming
then the action afresh, without dislodging, or
giving me the pain of parting from my sweet
tenant, we played over again the same opera
with the same harmony and concert; our
ardours, like our love, knew no intermission,
and my lover, lavish of his stores and pleasure-
milked, overflowed me once more from the
fullness of his oval reservoirs with genital
emulsion; whilst on my side a convulsive gasp,
in the instant of my giving down the liquid

contribution, rendered me sweetly subservient at once to the increase of joy, and to its effusions, moving me so as to make me exert all those springs of compressive suction with which the sensitive mechanism of that part thirstily draws and drains the nipple of love, with such instinctive eagerness and attachment as infants do at the breast when by the motion of their little mouths and cheeks they extract the milky stream prepared for their nourishment. But still there was no end to his vigour; this double discharge had so far from extinguished his desires for that time, that it had not even calmed them, and at his age, desires are powers. He was proceeding then amazingly to push to a third triumph, still without withdrawing, if a tenderness, natural to true love, had not inspired me with self-denial enough to spare and not over-strain him; and accordingly, entreating him to give himself and me quarter, I obtained, at length, a short suspension of arms, but not before he had exultingly satisfied me that he drew out standing. The remainder of the night, with what we borrowed from the day, we employed with unwearied fervor in celebrating thus the festival of our reunion, and arose pretty late in the morning, gay, brisk and alert, though rest had been a stranger to us; but the pleasures of love had been to us what the joy of victory is to an army—repose, refreshment, everything.

My journey into the country now being entirely out of the question, and orders having been given for turning the horses' heads towards London, we left the inn as soon as we had breakfasted, not without a liberal distribution of the tokens of my grateful sense of the happiness I had met with in it. Charles and I were in my coach; the captain and my companion in a chaise hired purposely for them to leave us the conveniency of a tete a tete. Here, on the road, as the tumult of my senses were tolerably composed, I commanded enough head to break properly to him the course of life that the consequences of separation from him had driven me into, and while he tenderly deplored it with me, he was not so shocked at, as on reflecting how he had left me circumstanced he could not be entirely unprepared for it. But when I informed him of the state of my fortune, and with that sincerity which from me to him was so natural to me, begged him to accept it on his own terms, I must appear to you perhaps too partial to my passion if I attempt to do justice to his delicacy. I shall content myself then with assuring you that after his flatly refusing the unreserved, unconditional donation that I long persecuted him in vain to accept, it was at length, in obedience to his serious commands, for I stood out unaffectedly, till he exerted the sovereign authority which love had given him over me, that I yielded my consent to waive the remonstrance I did not fail of making strongly to him against his defrauding himself, and incurring the suspicion, however unjust, of having for a fortune, bartered his

honor for infamy and prostitution in making
one his wife who thought herself too much
honoured in being his mistress. The plea of
love then overruling all objections, Charles
entirely won with the merit of my sentiments
for him, which he could not but read the sincerity of in a heart ever open to him, obliged me to
receive his hand, by which means I was able,
among other innumerable blessings to bestow
a legal parentage on those fine children you
have seen by this happiest of matches.

Thus, at length, I got snug into port, where,
in the bosom of virtue, I gathered the only in-
corrupt sweets, where, looking back on the
course of vice I had run, and comparing its
infamous blandishments with the infinitely
superior joys of innocence, I could not help
pitying, even in point of taste, those who, im-
mersed in gross sensuality, are insensible to
the delicate charms of virtue, than which, even
pleasure has not a greater enemy. Thus temper-
ance makes men lords over those pleasures that
intemperance enslaves them to; the one, parent
of health, vigour, fertility, cheerfulness, and
every other desirable good of life; the other, of
diseases, debility, barrenness, self-loathing, with
only every evil incident to human nature.

You laugh, perhaps, at this tail-piece of
morality, extracted from me by the force of
truth, resulting from compared experiences;
you think it, no doubt, out of place; possibly
too, you may look on it as the paltry finesse of
one who seeks to mask a devotee to vice under

a rag of a veil, impudently smuggled from the
shrine of Virtue; just as if one was to fancy
one's self completely disguised at a masquerade, with no other change of dress than turning one's shoes into slippers; or, as if a writer
should think to shield a treasonable libel, by
concluding it with a formal prayer for the king.
But, independent of my flattering myself that
you have a juster opinion of my sense and
sincerity, give me leave to represent to you, that
such a supposition is even more injurious to
Virtue than to me, since consistently with
candour and good nature, it can have no foundation but in the falsest of fears, that its pleasures cannot stand in comparison with those of
Vice; but let truth dare to hold it up in its
most alluring light, then mark, how spurious,
how low of taste, how comparatively inferior
its joys are to those which Virtue gives sanction
to, and whose sentiments are not above making
even a sauce for the senses, but a sauce of the
highest relish, whilst Vices are the harpies that
infect and foul the feast. The paths of Vice
are sometimes strewed with roses, but then they
are forever infamous for many a canker-worm;
those of Virtue are strewed with roses purely,
and those eternally unfading roses. If you do
me justice then, you will esteem me perfectly
consistent in the incense I burn to Virtue. If
I have painted Vice in all its gayest colours, if
I have decked it with flowers, it has been solely
in order to make the worthier, the solemner
sacrifice of it to Virtue.

You know Mr. C. O., you know his estate, his worth, and good sense; can you, will you pronounce it ill meant, at least of him, when anxious for his son's morals, with a view to form him to virtue, and inspire him with a fixed, a rational contempt for vice, he condescended to be his master of ceremonies, and led him by the hand through the most noted bawdy-houses in town, where he took care he should be familiarized with all those scenes of debauchery, so fit to nauseate a good taste? The experiment, you will cry, is dangerous. True, on a fool, but are fools worth so much attention?

I shall see you soon, and in the mean time think candidly of me, and believe me ever, madam, yours, etc.

THE END